Sasha's Truth

QUEENY

Eh List Publications
P.O Box:
Etobicoke, Ontario

Edited By: Terry Brand

Cover Design by: Shaw 'S Twizz' Samuels

First Printing, 2014

ISBN 10: 0991882008
ISBN-13: 978-0991882007 (Eh List Publications)

DEDICATION

To all the Sasha's roaming the streets. This is your story

PROLOGUE

The elevator door opened. A short, middle-age, brunette woman holding a stack of papers stood behind two, white men who were holding brief-cases. Sasha clutched her Guess city bag and took a deep breath before she joined them. The two men took no shame undressing her from the wide collared, black, trench coat she was wearing. Sasha fluttered. If only they could see the black, wool dress she wore underneath. It crowned her curvy body perfectly. Her dress went just above her knees and allowed everyone in the elevator to catch a glimpse of her thighs between her dress and her black, leather, knee-high boots. The Victoria Secret push-up bra she was wearing made her 34C's look plump and perky, and there was nothing Sasha could wear that could hide the fact that she had a generous amount of ass. She wore an eighteen inch, bone-straight, black weave with bangs that brought out her brown eyes.

Sasha glanced at the two men in the corner of her eyes. They both grinned like two, high school boys who got their first glimpse inside of the girls change room. As aroused as they were by Sasha's sight, it was evident they were all wondering what she was doing at Harper and Associates.

Sasha was indeed no lawyer, but she was in desperate need of one. She fired her first lawyer, John Greenburg, after an expensive, conniving consultation. Greenburg was only in it for the money and had no intentions of helping Sasha win her case.

Sasha licked her red full lips. She kept her eyes on the numbers on the left corner of the elevator until it reached the eleventh floor. She took another deep breath and strutted out the elevator confidently towards the front desk.

"Hi. I have a one o'clock with Nicole Cooper."

A young, red-haired woman with a face full of freckles sat behind the receptionist desk.

"Sasha Brown?"

Sasha nodded.

The receptionist reached for the phone. "Ms Cooper, Sasha Brown is here to see you...Ok I will bring her in."

The receptionist walked around her desk and motioned Sasha to follow. They walked down a long corridor filled with color abstract paintings. Nicole's office was at the end of the hall. The receptionist knocked the polished, black, walnut, double door and opened it. She peeped her head inside.

"Ms Cooper?"

A woman responded in a soft voice. "Yes, come in."

Sasha walked into the office and nodded in approval at the decor. The walls were rusty red and lined with African themed paintings, sculptures and plants as tall as Sasha. The windows were floor to ceiling and gave a beautiful view of downtown Toronto. If they had been on a higher floor, Sasha would have been able to see the city's skyscraper and the gorgeous sunset on Lake Ontario.

A dark skinned woman with long, brown dreadlocks sat behind the desk. She stood up, showing off the stylish, brown pantsuit she was wearing. She extended her hand to Sasha and smiled. "It's a pleasure to meet you, Ms Brown."

As Sasha leaned over the desk to shake Cooper's hand, she caught a whiff of her perfume. It had a strong, citrus scent and it made Sasha's nose tingle.

"The pleasure is all mine. Thank you for taking the time to see me."

Sasha sat in the low, leather arm chair across from Cooper. She had no idea what she was going to say to her. Sasha wondered what Cooper would think of her after she heard how Sasha had ended up in her office. She considered lying but that would only make her situation worse.

Nicole smiled at Sasha as she organized the papers on her desk. She spoke with sincerity. "How could I refuse? I'm sorry that you're going through all of this."

Sasha looked outside the window with doleful eyes. "What I went through was traumatizing. I wouldn't wish that upon any one, not even my worst enemy."

Nicole nodded her head in agreement as she logged onto her laptop. "Well, I commend you for sticking up for yourself. Self-defense can be a sensitive issue in courts. Women have no faith in the justice system. They would rather brush it under a rug and leave it unjustified."

Sasha smiled. The lawyer seemed genuine. She sighed with relief trying to warm up to the idea of having Cooper represent her. She was a black, successful woman in Toronto. The women Sasha was used to seeing were drug addicts, prostitutes or hood chicks trying to cop a cheque from welfare. Cooper may have still been involved with the law, but she was on the right side.

"Thank you, and please just call me Sasha."

"Ok, Sasha. You may also call me Nicole. Ms Cooper makes me feel older than I am. Now let's get down to business. First things first. If I am going to represent you, I need you tell me everything. Don't hide anything, even if you feel like it may hurt the case. I need you to tell me the truth about what happened."

Cooper leaned back in her chair and looked at Sasha sternly. Sasha sunk in her seat and looked outside the window.

"What do you want to know?" asked Sasha.

"Everything. I want details. How do you know Michael? What were you doing at a senior accountants condo so late at night? Was it a one-night stand or did you have a secret, sexual relationship? Are you a prostitute? How long have you been prostituting? Do you have a pimp?"

Cooper watched as Sasha coiled in her seat once more. Sasha looked around the room. She noticed Coopers law degree hanging on the wall beside her. Cooper graduated with honours in 2004 from University Of Toronto.

"I was a dancer for three years," said Nicole. "I used the money I made to pay my way through school. I took a paralegal course at Humber and worked as a paralegal for two years before I went to Law School."

Cooper was beautiful. She was fresh-faced. Her skin looked soft and flawless and her dreads sat neatly on her shoulders. Sasha never would have guessed she was once a stripper. Sasha found herself staring at Cooper and quickly looked away at the figurine of an African man and woman dancing on the desk.

Cooper smiled. "I'm not here to judge you. I'm here to protect you. The only way I can do that is by you trusting me."

The thought of the dead accountant made Sasha squirm. Two months had passed since their encounter. Sasha remembered it like it was yesterday. She could still smell the hard liquor on his breath when he spoke to her. She could see the craze in his grey eyes. Sasha was only eighteen years old and had already experienced the worst things a woman could experience in her lifetime. This time she couldn't run from it. Sasha cleared her throat and fought back her tears.

CHAPTER 1

Sasha Brown was the daughter of Theresa Brown and Robert Da'Silva. Theresa came from a good home. She was the only child of Jamaican, Dr Marcus Brown and his Trinidadian housewife, Annie Brown. Marcus was attending Medical School at Ryerson University and living in a bachelor apartment when Annie got pregnant with Theresa in 1973. Thankfully, Marcus was a hard working man. He tried to make certain his two favourite women in the world were always taken care of. Marcus quit his part-time job at a carwash and started working full-time at night as an industrial janitor. He moved out of his bachelor and moved into a one bedroom apartment with his baby mother-to-be. They lived in their apartment for two years before Marcus was able to buy a four bedroom house in the suburbs.

Theresa had a wonderful childhood and two parents who loved and adored her. She got good grades in school and always kept herself out of trouble. Theresa's dream was to follow in her father's footsteps and become a doctor. When she got accepted to medical school, it was the happiest day of her life. It took Theresa an hour and a half to get to school every day using public transportation. It wasn't long before it became an irritation. Determined like Marcus once was, Theresa got a part-time job at a cafe close to school and started saving up to buy herself a car.

Theresa was twenty one years old and attending her first year in medical school at University of Toronto when she met Da'Silva. One evening, in April 1995, Theresa was working at the Cafe. It was raining outside and business was slow. Theresa stood behind the counter in her green and white uniform with her eyes glued to her textbook. She was studying for a biology test she had the next morning.

A black, well-built man, standing about six feet two inches tall, walked into the cafe. He was wearing a black, silk, button-down shirt, a pair of black, dress pants and shiny, black shoes. He wore a thick, gold chain around his neck and a gold watch on his wrist. He was handsome. The most handsome man Theresa had ever seen. The man caught Theresa staring and she blushed.

"Welcome to Red Cafe," she squealed. "What can I get you?"

The man stood in awe as he checked Theresa out from head to toe and smiled.

"When is your next break?"

Theresa grinned, looking at the clock on the wall. "It's actually in about ten minutes. Why?"

He leaned over the counter. "Because I want to have my mocha with you."

Theresa was flattered, but she was no sucker. She was an exotic beauty thanks to her mother's splash of Indian. Guys, young and old were always trying to hit on her. She knew game when she saw it. "Well, I appreciate your compliment—"

"Da'Silva," he cut her off, extending his hand to her.

"Well, I appreciate your compliment, but I don't sit with the customers." Theresa grabbed a pen and pad. She became a server again. "Now can I take your order?"

"You're just going to leave me hanging like that?" he laughed as he read her name tag. He had perfect, straight, white teeth and he looked younger when he smiled. "Theresa, can I get a large mocha?"

Theresa rolled her eyes as she prepared his mocha. Da'Silva watched her with a boyish grin. Her reddish brown complexion, coarse hair and pretty face reminded him of Pocahontas, and he found her attitude intriguing. Da'Silva wanted Theresa—not like the chicks that he fucked along the way. He wanted her as his woman. Theresa was young, pure, beautiful and smart. She was perfect in his eyes. Da'Silva took his mocha to go. He came back to the cafe almost every day for two weeks until Theresa gave in and went on a date with him.

Theresa and Da'Silva fell in love with each other instantly. After seeing each other for three months, Da'Silva moved Theresa out of her parents house and into his condo downtown. Theresa's parents never liked him because he was eight years older than her and they suspected he was a drug dealer. They tried to warn Theresa about getting caught up with someone like him, but she was too love-struck to listen. Most women would have ran for their life and never looked back when they saw a gun. Not Theresa. It turned her on. Being the bad boy's girlfriend made Theresa feel important.

Da'Silva showered Theresa with expensive gifts and took her to fancy restaurants. Theresa went to the salon to do her hair and nails every Saturday whether it needed to be done or not. On Sunday's, she hosted dinner parties and mingled with her new friends while their men spoke business. People respected Da'Silva and adored her innocence and she loved it. Silva introduced her to a whole new world.

Da'Silva was an occasional cocaine user. He only got high when he was partying amongst friends. When Theresa saw Da'Silva sniff coke for the first time, she was scared and horrified at what she saw but not enough to make her leave him. The anger soon turned into curiosity, and it wasn't long before Theresa started sniffing coke too. Theresa became a full blown addict within months. She dropped out of school, and detached herself from her friends. When her parents tried to help her she pushed them away. Theresa eventually found herself new friends. Friends that wouldn't judge her about getting high.

When Theresa was twenty three years old, she got pregnant. Da'Silva was excited about becoming a father. He hated himself for allowing Theresa to become an addict and forced her to stop using drugs the same day he found out. It was an unpleasant process for the both of them but Theresa was able to kick her habit and Sasha Brown was born a healthy baby at North York General Hospital on August 13th, 1988. She came into the world an exotic beauty just like her mother. She had thick, curly, black hair, brown eyes and a rich, caramel complexion.

Da'Silva loved Sasha with all his heart and wanted the best for her. He started making plans to move them out of his condo and into a house somewhere in the suburbs. He wanted them to live away from the inner-city. His goal was to retire from running the streets so they could be a normal family.

Da'Silva was well known in the streets, especially in

the east end. He had many allies and connects. His coke was coming from Staten Island, thanks to an Italian guy he grew up with as a child. Nobody could beat his quality and nobody could beat his prices. Da'Silva had Scarborough and Downtown on lock with his product. For that reason, he also had a lot of envious enemies. Greedy mother fuckers who craved the power.

Early one morning, when Sasha was one, Da'Silva and Theresa were fucking while she was asleep in her room. Four men wearing black clothes and black masks kicked down the door of their condo.

"Climb out the pussy, Da'Silva," yelled one of the masked men as they burst into their bedroom.

Silva scrambled to his feet, trying to pull up his boxers. Before he could reach for his gun on the nightstand, one of the guys pointed his gun to his head.

"You won't be needing that," he said as he picked up Da'Silva's gun and tossed it to one of his partners.

When Theresa heard Sasha crying, she got out of the bed and fled towards the door, but she ran right into one of the robbers. He pointed his gun to her head.

"Boss, tell your bitch to stop crying or I'm going to blow her fucking brains out," he threatened.

Da'Silva looked at Theresa calmly and nodded for her to stop crying. Theresa took a deep breath as she glimpsed at Sasha's bedroom door. The robber who captured her took her by the arm and dragged her into Sasha's room. Theresa hurried to the crib, picked up Sasha and held her tightly. She kissed her on the forehead and rocked her in her arms.

"Everything is ok, baby," said Theresa softly, trying to calm Sasha down while glaring at the man holding them captive.

He grabbed Theresa by the arm, and they rejoined

everyone in the living room. Da'Silva was on his knees with two men standing behind him, pointing their guns to his head. The fourth guy was trashing their bedroom.

"Where is the money, Da'Silva? We know it's here. If you don't tell me, I'm going to kill you, your wife and your precious, little baby," the man warned as he took a knife to their mattress.

When he was convinced there was no money in their bedroom, he started looking in the kitchen. He pulled out all the drawers and flung them on the floor. He emptied the fridge and the trash can and checked the dishwasher and oven, but he didn't find anything. He fumed with frustration, walked over to Da'Silva and hit him on the head with the back of his gun.

"Where is it?" he screamed.

"Please, just tell him," Theresa pleaded.

When Da'Silva wouldn't budge, the man grabbed Sasha out of Theresa's hands and sat her on the couch. He took Theresa by the hair and dragged her to stand in front of Da'Silva.

"If you don't tell him where the money is right now, she is going die. If she dies, that's on your hands!"

"Please don't let them kill me," Theresa begged. She was sure she was going to die. "Just tell them where the money is so they can leave."

"They won't hurt you," Da'Silva assured her. He was unmoved by their actions. "They will kill me regardless, but they won't hurt you. I promise."

The man tugged Theresa by the hair and pointed the gun in her face. "Do you know where the money is?"

"No," she lied.

He hit her with his gun and she fell to the floor. He pointed the gun at the back of her head. "You are lying!"

"I'm not lying! I don't know where it is. I swear," she

bawled with her hands in the air. "Please don't kill me. I don't know where it is."

"No women, no children. Leave the bitch alone," ordered one of the men holding Da'Silva at gunpoint.

"Fuck that! She dies first, then the baby. Then he will see how serious we are bout this paper. This ain't no motherfucking joke. There is at least fifty thousand dollars cash in here and I'm not leaving till I get it."

Even after the threats, Da'Silva called their bluff and refused to give them anything. He would rather die than hand over his money to a bunch of cowards who couldn't show their faces. After fifteen minutes of torture, they shot Da'Silva twice in the chest and once in the head and fled with nothing but a bunch of jewellery and a stack of cash they found in his pants pockets.

When the police came, they never found any drugs or the money in the condo. Theresa had a clean record and was never with Da'Silva when he did business so the police were unable to connect her to any illegal activity. The crime, however, was still viewed as gang and drug related and Theresa's name wasn't on the lease, so she was forced to move out by the end of the month. In that time, Theresa applied for welfare and housing. She stayed with Sasha in a shelter for two months before she received a placement. It was a two bedroom apartment on the sixteenth floor in the Jane and Finch area.

Losing Da'Silva and her home and being unemployed with a daughter took a toll on Theresa. Theresa started sniffing coke again, and the money Da'Silva had left for them soon vanished. Welfare and child benefits were a relief. She had enough money to take care of her home and keep up with her coke habit. Theresa never wanted to admit she had a drug problem. Even when they spent days hungry or without hydro, she waved it off.

It soon became hard for Theresa to hide her addiction. She lost a tremendous amount of weight and her glow was gone. She stopped doing her hair and her clothes were sloppy, wrinkled, dirty and torn.

Theresa had a strong personality before she met Da'Silva. Their relationship weakened her. It stripped Theresa of her strength and spoiled her out of her dreams. She lost her self-respect and she had no willpower or motivation.

Theresa tried to reach out to her parents. She asked them for her forgiveness, but they shut her out. They tried many times to warn her about Da'Silva and the drugs. She turned her back to them until they were no longer a part of her life. They wanted nothing to do with Theresa or her drug baby. The reality hit her hard. She was alone with nobody to help her.

As time passed, Theresa did not heal. Sasha turned three, and Theresa grew more ill. She was still wounded by Da'Silva's death and was struggling to keep up with her bills. The coke was no longer enough to get Theresa into her zone. She started using crack by the time Sasha turned four.

Theresa's living situation went from bad to worst. Their home became a pig sty. Dirty dishes were piled up in the sink with mold. The floor was rarely swept or vacuumed, and the garbage was barely taken out, leaving the house smelling like a dump. There was hardly ever any food to eat and Sasha was forced to spend many nights drinking water to fill her stomach so she could sleep.

Sasha had a friend named Jennifer who lived in the building. Jennifer's parents never befriended Theresa because of her addiction, but Sasha and Jennifer took a liking so they allowed Sasha to come play with Jennifer every once and a while. When Sasha was at Jennifer's house she ate until her belly hung out. When she left, Jennifer's parents sent her home with leftover food and clothes that were too small for Jennifer's older sister, Michelle. Jennifer and her family moved out of their building a year later, and Sasha was devastated. The only person she had left to show any amount of care for her was Theresa's no good friend Deedee.

Deedee was a middle-aged, black woman from Nova Scotia. She lived three apartments down from Theresa and Sasha. Deedee was a crack head too, and when Theresa moved into the building, they instantly became partners in crime.

In 1992, Sasha was supposed to start junior kindergarten. Theresa was so caught up in her drugs, she completely forgot, and Sasha missed her first year of school. Sasha sat at the window every morning and watched all children leaving for school, wondering why she wasn't allowed to go with them. The following year, Deedee made certain that Sasha was enrolled.

"They gon' take away Sasha and lock your ass up for not taking care of her, cuz," she told Theresa after a week of pushing. They were sitting on Theresa's couch getting high. "If your ol' man could see you now."

Theresa glared at Deedee with shameful eyes. She did not respond.

"All those nice things you told me about him," Deedee continued as she took a hit off the pipe. "Ahhh yes! Here we go." She exhaled and closed her eyes, allowing the crack to take control.

Theresa snatched the pipe out of Deedee's hand and looked at Sasha who sat on the floor with a toy, pretending she wasn't listening to their conversation.

Deedee was right. If Da'Silva was alive, Theresa could never be so careless never mind be on drugs.

Theresa went into the school with Sasha the following morning to register her. When the school secretary asked why Sasha was being registered so late into September, Theresa made up a lie about moving and changing her mind at the last minute. The gullible secretary bought the story and Sasha started the following Monday.

Sasha was excited and relieved that she would be attending school. She hated being at home. The more Sasha went to school, the more she disliked when Theresa and Deedee got high. There was nothing Sasha wanted more than for her mother to be normal like the other parents she saw at school.

Sasha's first school year was a challenge. She worked extra hard to catch up to the curriculum. Sasha didn't want her classmates or teachers to think she was stupid because she was far from it. Being behind wasn't her fault. Sasha was anxious to learn but her access to resources outside of school was scarce. Sasha never got help from Theresa or Deedee. They always brushed her off to get high instead.

Sasha's first A was a major success and proof of her hard work. She couldn't wait to go home and show Theresa. When she finished school, she didn't stop to chat with her friends. She ran home, pushed her key through the door and burst into the house.

"Mama! Look!"

Sasha ran into the living room and scrambled to open her Minnie Mouse backpack. Theresa was sitting in the couch with Deedee. They were both coming down from their highs.

"What did I tell you about running in the damn house!" Theresa kissed her teeth and rolled her eyes.

"This is not a soccer field, this is your home. Stop treating it like a playground."

"I'm sorry, mommy," said Sasha looking at the floor. She pulled the test out of her bag. "But I got an A in math!"

"You see that?" Deedee chirped as she patted Theresa on the thigh. "Sasha got her first A!"

Deedee pulled Sasha to her and hugged her. She smelt like stale cigarettes and rum.

"Mommy? Can I have a pizza slice for dinner tonight because I got a good grade?" asked Sasha excitedly.

"Little girl, don't you hear me and Deedee talking about going to the grocery store to get you something to eat? I can't stick a pizza slice up my pussy!" Theresa stood up. She was still wearing the same wrinkled up, jogging pants and t-shirt from the day before. "And I sure in hell ain't selling no pussy just so you can eat a greasy slice of pizza, eh."

"Don't worry, Wild Flower." Deedee gave Sasha a faint smile and patted her on the shoulder. "I will bring you back a slice of pizza."

"Thanks, Deedee," said Sasha excitedly as she looked at Theresa with dreary eyes.

"With what money?" Theresa continued. "I just bought the last ten piece and we were suppose to go half's on it. If you have any money, you need to pass it this way."

"My dude is working at the pizza shop today. He knows I will pay him back by tomorrow for it." Deedee replied annoyingly. The truth was that Deedee had the money but was saving it to buy her own piece.

"All that stealing and tricking you do, you better be able to pay his $2.50 tomorrow."

Within the hour Deedee took off and Sasha never got

the pizza she was promised. Little did she know, it wouldn't be the last time her heart was filled with broken promises. Sasha came home dozens of times after that with good grades she made at school. Theresa never acknowledged any of them. That school year, Sasha learned to read and write, but she also learned no A was ever going to make her mom proud of her.

CHAPTER 2

Sasha obsessed herself with school. It was her home away from home, where she wasn't surrounded by drugs. The summer of 1995 arrived too fast. When the last day of school arrived, all the kids ran out the school doors rushing to start their summer vacations. Sasha walked home with her best friend Genesis in tears.

Genesis was in the same class as Sasha and also lived in the same building. Theresa was friends with her mother, Rebecca. Rebecca was also a cokehead, but her addiction didn't have the best of her like it had done to Theresa. Rebecca was a social user. She only got high on the weekends or when she was out partying with friends. She was still able to maintain her home and provide Genesis with the affection that she needed. Rebecca and Theresa shared the common tale of a hustlers wife. Like Da'Silva, Rebecca's husband was a drug dealer. He was drawn down by the cops and had two kilos of coke in the car. He went to prison and was killed a year into his sentence by a fellow inmate.

"Sasha, why are you crying? It's that last day of school,

you should be happy," said Genesis as she bounced her basketball.

"I am going to have to stay home every day with my mom. Sometimes I feel like she doesn't like me," Sasha confessed to her friend.

Genesis stopped bouncing her ball and looked at Sasha like she was crazy. "Of course she loves you, Sasha! She is your mom!"

Sasha knew what she was talking about. Theresa was starting to resent her. Theresa hated how much Sasha looked like her. Sasha took Theresa's coarse, Indian hair and exotic features, making Sasha look identical to Theresa when she was child. Sasha was a constant reminder of who Theresa used to be and what Theresa used to have. Theresa didn't like thinking about her past life because it always came down to Da'Silva, and she wasn't ready to let him go.

Genesis threw the ball in the air as if she was taking a shot. "Maybe your mom will let you play with me now that we are friends."

From that day on, Sasha and Genesis spent every day playing together. Sasha spent most of her summer at Genesis's house and she cherished every second there. She didn't have to sit in her clutter of a home and watch Theresa get high. Theresa saw it as away to get high without having to watch over Sasha. They both thought they were winning out of situation but really, they were creating a serious wedge in their relationship.

When the end of summer arrived, Theresa never went back to school shopping for Sasha. Instead, she found Sasha's old Minnie Mouse backpack that was torn and didn't zip properly, and she scraped up a few old pens in the house to throw inside. After her first day of school, Sasha came home with a list of all the materials she needed. Theresa contributed only what she could find in the house.

"They have rooms full of unused pens and paper in schools, but they want us to spend our money to go and buy it." Theresa puffed on her cigarette. "I'm not buying none of that shit. Sasha could get them at school and bring them home."

Deedee shook her head in disgust. "Why do you want to teach Sasha to be like us? I don't want to see Wild Flower out there stealing, cuz."

"Because that's what she is going to be," Theresa argued back. She frowned at Sasha as if it were obvious. "She's a drug baby. Her father was a drug dealer. I'm fucking high right now!" Theresa closed her eyes for a moment to enjoy her buzz. "The truth is she is either going to marry a drug dealer, have a baby for one, or she is going to start doing drugs. That's what's going to happen. It's a cycle. Her father crumbled, I crumbled…"

Theresa let her memories batter her like an excited sadist. She closed her eyes and let the crack hug and comfort her. She thought she was making a rational point about Sasha. She was almost certain Sasha would also crumble. Regardless of how she felt, Da'Silva's death and her downfall was an excuse to treat Sasha like shit.

Sasha refused to be anything like her mother. Theresa never bathed and her hair was always messy. Her clothes were dirty and smelly. Theresa looked anorexic because she never ate and she was always high. Theresa was no role-model for Sasha. Sasha lived her life through her friends, taking a little bit of what she could from their lives, whether it was cooked food, or the feeling of being part of a cozy, family-oriented home.

Sasha got used to Theresa's rants and raves. Theresa called her names like "drug baby" or "crack kid" and

Sasha tried to ignore her. She never once got mad or spoke back to Theresa because she knew it was the drugs making her talk like that. Sasha continued to bury herself with schoolwork to keep her mind off her problems at home. When she wasn't at school, she continued going to Genesis's house until it was time for Genesis to get ready for bed.

By the time Sasha was nine, she had full knowledge of crack and cocaine. She knew which apartments were crack houses and which guys in the neighbourhood were dealers. When Theresa was too lazy to buy it herself, she would send Sasha for her. The dealers felt sorry for her having to buy drugs for Theresa, but it didn't stop them from taking the money and sending Sasha on her way. The more Sasha learned about drugs, the more irritated she became with Theresa. She was tired of watching Theresa get high everyday and decided it was time for a change.

One night, Theresa and Deedee took off and left Sasha alone in the house. Sasha cleaned the apartment from head to toe. She asked her neighbours for plastic bags and threw out all the garbage. Sasha swept every room and used a piece of cardboard from an old pizza box to pick up all the debris. She did all the dishes and she wiped down all the counters. The only thing that Sasha was unable to do was clean the bathroom because she ran out of cleaning products.

Theresa came home to a spotless apartment. She put her purse down on the kitchen counter and looked around reluctantly. She was unmoved by Sasha's efforts.

"Who did you have up in my house?"

"No one. I did it by myself," Sasha answered proudly.

"Do I look like a damn fool to you?" Theresa marched

into her room and checked her drawers. "Where is my pipe? You smoking dope now?"

Sasha fidgeted around. She began playing with her fingers.

"I am going to ask you one more time eh, and you are going to tell me the truth, Sasha Brown. Who was in my fucking house, and where the hell is my god damn pipe?" Theresa pranced from foot to foot and scratched on her arms.

"I'm not lying to you," said Sasha as she took a step back. "I didn't feel like playing and I was bored."

"So where is my pipe? It was in my drawer, in the bedroom." Theresa raised her voice. "Who went into my stuff?"

"I....I did. I threw it out so that you couldn't smoke it anymore." A tear ran down Sasha's face. There was no acclaim for her good deed. "I was just trying to help."

Theresa slapped Sasha across the face. "What I tell you about touching my stuff? I tell you every fucking day not to touch my shit and you wait for me to leave!" She held Sasha by her arm and slapped her on her leg. "Did you think cleaning the house would make it better?"

"No! I just want you to stop smoking crack and be normal," Sasha mumbled.

"Do not touch my shit!" Theresa yelled as she continued beating on Sasha. She couldn't hear Sasha's plea for her to stop doing drugs. All she could hear was that her pipe was gone.

"Is it true?" asked Genesis while walking to school one day. "I heard my mom and Deedee talking. They said you threw out your moms pipe and she beat you. That's why you got all those bruises."

"Yes, it's true, but you can't tell anyone," Sasha

warned. "I don't want those people to come and take me away."

A few kids got taken away from their parents in Sasha's building for neglect. Their parents were drug dealers and addicts too. Sasha dreamed of a better life than the one she had but she refused to have it without her mother.

Genesis patted Sasha on the back and started bouncing her basketball. She bounced it between her legs as they walked. "I cross my heart and hope to die with a needle in my eye. My mom beats me too sometimes. Not as hard as your mom beats you though."

"She gets really mad at me, and I don't know why," Sasha told her, shrugging her shoulders. She looked at the ground. "But I know it's the crack that makes her do it."

Sasha took Theresa's beatings without telling a soul. Only Genesis knew and she promised on their friendship she would never tell anyone. Sasha learned how to cover the bruises discretely with her clothes and kept a smile on her face every day while she was at school. Nobody knew what she was going through.

Despite the fact Sasha was often bruised, she still began developing beautifully. She got curvier and she started to develop breasts. Sasha grew tremendously in height, giving her long beautiful legs, fit to be a runway model. Boys were slowly starting to pay her attention and older men found themselves staring at her, recognizing the beauty in the making.

When Sasha was twelve years old, she came home from school to something that would change her life forever. Sasha got a ride with a friend, and she got home thirty minutes earlier. When she walked into the house, Theresa was on her knees, giving head to a fat, mid-aged white guy in the living room. He looked at Sasha and grinned.

Theresa scurried to her feet and tried to fix her shirt. "Sasha, you are home early."

Sasha closed the door behind her and quickly took off her shoes. "I got a ride from one of my friends at school."

"Is that your daughter, Veronica?" asked the man as he stared at Sasha with hungry, dark eyes. He ran his hands through his grey hair.

Theresa smiled nervously. "Yes, this is Sasha. Sasha, I'd like you to meet my friend Bill."

Sasha rolled her eyes as she tried to keep herself from laughing. She shook her head at her mother for lying about her name and proceeded to her room.

"Wait," he hollered desperately.

Sasha stopped but never looked back.

"How old are you?" he asked.

Sasha sighed. All she wanted to do was go into her room and bury her head into a book. Sasha took babies steps in the direction to her room, hoping they would take the hint.

"You don't hear the man talking to you?" Theresa snapped.

"I'm twelve," she replied dryly.

"A ball." The man's voice was stern. His eyes were locked on Sasha.

"What the fuck are you talking about, Bill?" asked Theresa confusingly.

"I'll give you a ball right now, if you let me fuck her."

Bill pulled a pearl rock wrapped up in siren wrap out of his pocket. He counted out some money and threw it on the table. "And I will still give you six hundred dollars cash."

Sasha's eyes widen with freight as she looked at Theresa. Theresa looked at Sasha nervously and then at Bill. She was feigning. Her plan was to suck him off for just enough money to buy a small piece and some food, but this seemed like a better deal to her. It was the worst thing she could ever put Sasha through, but the drugs had her weak. She figured if she used the money to buy groceries and new clothes for Sasha, it would justify the trade.

Theresa started fidgeting and looked at the crack hungrily. "Are you being serious with me? Don't fuck around eh."

"It's right there on the table." He pointed at the dirty table with a victorious grin.

Sasha took a step towards her room when she realized Theresa was actually contemplating the idea.

"He is not going to hurt you," Theresa choked on her words. "He is doing the both of us a big favor. Sometimes we have to make sacrifices so that we can live better."

"And such a beautiful sacrifice you are," Bill chuckled devilishly. He rubbed his hands together as he proceeded towards Sasha.

He grabbed Sasha's hand and forced her to touch his erect penis. Sasha looked away in disgust. Her stomach turned. Tears ran down her face as she looked at Theresa for help. Theresa looked away cowardly. The betrayal and embarrassment drenched her face like clothes in the wash.

Bill stroked his penis with Sasha's hands. His eyes rolled to the back of his head. "Have you ever felt a hard dick before, Sasha?"

Sasha shook her head. She stood there trembling and crying. She looked at Theresa and Theresa was staring at

CHAPTER 3

Theresa never saw Bill again. Everyone questioned her about where she got the crack and the cash from. Theresa admitted getting it from a trick who was trucker. Theresa was known for turning tricks so nobody grew suspicious of her story.

Sasha knew Theresa's drug problem was bad, but she couldn't understand what she did to be treated so horribly. What kind of mother would do that to her only daughter? She often locked herself in her bedroom when she was home, reading and listening to music to avoid any fights with Theresa. It didn't stop the fights from happening, in fact, the fights between Theresa and Sasha escalated.

Sasha had enough of Theresa's disrespect and started cursing back at her. She told Theresa how much she hated her and that she was a bad mother. Majority of the time, Theresa would be left embarrassed and in tears. She turned to her pipe for comfort—another excuse to get high.

There were days when Sasha longed for her mother

and, she would try desperately to talk to Theresa about her bad habits. Theresa brushed her off with false promises to seek help. When Sasha realized talking to her wasn't going to work, she started throwing Theresa's crack and pipe out again. She took every beating for it like a champ. If it kept Theresa sober for a couple of hours, it was worth it. Sasha wanted Theresa to get better. She had hope for the first while, but when Theresa refused to make an effort, Sasha started to resent her. She realized she couldn't get love because it didn't exist in her home so she started seeking it elsewhere.

Sasha was pretty and she loved the attention she got for it. All the girls wanted to be her friends and all the boys wanted to kiss her. Sasha only hung out with pretty girls, and they only spoke to boys that they could use to do their homework or buy stuff for them. It wasn't long before Sasha started heading to the mall to steal clothes and make-up. She spent two hours every morning in the bathroom getting ready for school.

"Where are you going dressed like that?" asked Theresa one morning when Sasha walked out of the bathroom.

"Obviously to school," Sasha replied rolling her eyes. She was wearing a pair of jean shorts that barely covered her ass and a black, spaghetti strapped tank top that read "spank me" in gold writing.

"No you aren't!" Theresa got up. "You aren't going to school dressed like you are ready to hit the club with your friends. You are only thirteen. You have no business dressing like a hooker. And where did you get this shit anyway? I don't remember buying them for you."

"I stole them," answered Sasha emotionlessly as she put her books in her bag.

"You did what?"

"I said I stole them. Holy fuck!"

Sasha wanted to leave but Theresa was blocking the door.

"You are stealing now?" A look of disappointment slid across Theresa's face. She folded her arms. "Are you having sex, Sasha?"

"Oh my god! I'm not having sex. I stole the clothes because I wanted them. It's not like you're going to get them for me," Sasha retorted as she stomped her feat impatiently.

"I wouldn't steal never mind spend a dollar on that mess you have on," said Theresa in disgust. "Next time you out there stealing shit, why don't you steal some food for the house instead of that shit you call clothes. You look like a cheap whore!"

"You know I'm worth at least six hundred."

Theresa swallowed, unsure of what to say. Sasha kissed her teeth, pulled Theresa away from the door and slammed it behind her. Theresa's blood was boiling. She took Sasha's unworn clothes that she just had stolen and sold it in the apartment lobby for little to nothing. Theresa initially wanted to teach Sasha a lesson but after seeing how much money she made selling the clothes, Theresa bought herself crack and went back home to get high. That wasn't the last time Theresa stole from Sasha. Sasha soon had to hide her clothes at Genesis's before Theresa got a hold of them. Theresa started giving Sasha orders and Sasha would steal what she could just to keep the peace.

Sasha was excited to start high school in 2002. Genesis chose a different school to go to for their basketball team. Sasha wasn't as mad as she should have been about losing her best friend to a different high school. Genesis was into basketball and she was into boys. They were bound to drift apart.

Sasha's stolen attire kept her looking fly, and her bitchy, flirtatious attitude gave her the popularity she wanted. Everyone knew Sasha's name and wanted to be associated with her. Sasha never went to school to learn, she went to school to be the center of the attention and the talk of the day.

Sasha was taking the bus home from school when a group of boys wearing grey pants and burgundy sweaters came on. They spoke loudly about a fight that had just went down at the mall. A tall, light skin boy out of the bunch caught eyes with Sasha and smiled at her. She looked away. He was cute. He had green, dreamy eyes and thick, curly hair. He walked through the isle to where Sasha was sitting and sat down beside her confidently.

"How you are doing, sexy? My name is Desmond, but my friends call me Dessy."

She shook his hand and smiled shyly. "I'm Sasha."

"How old are you?"

"I'm seventeen," she lied.

"You're lying. You aren't seventeen, girl," Dessy laughed as he called his friends over. "Hey J-rock, come here. Does this girl look seventeen to you?"

Another skinny, dark skin boy with braids came up to where Sasha was sitting and looked at her long and hard.

"Damn she's sexy," he said as he checked her out. "But she doesn't look seventeen."

Dessy nodded and directed his attention back to Sasha. "You don't have to lie to me. I am only sixteen."

Sasha blushed. "Ok, I'm fourteen."

"Where are you from?"

"Jane and Finch."

"I live ten minutes from you. I am in Sherham," said

Dessy in excitement. "We are going to my place to go hang out and smoke some weed. You should get one of your girls and come through." Dessy pulled a cell phone out of his pocket. "What's your number?"

"I don't have a cell phone," she told him embarrassingly.

Dessy pulled a pen and a bus transfer out of his pocket. He scribbled his cell phone number on it and gave it to Sasha. "I work part-time at Walmart, but you can call me anytime if you want to hang out. If I don't pick up, I'm at work."

Sasha started skipping school to hang out with Dessy. She started smoking weed with him and his friends on a regular basis. Theresa didn't care that Sasha smoked weed. When Sasha started coming with red, squinted eyes, smelling drenched of weed, Theresa waved her off and said, "And this is where it starts. Just like me and your father."

Theresa allowed Dessy to come to the house, as long as they stayed out of her way and he gave her some free weed. Dessy and Sasha became very close and a couple months into their relationship, he bought Sasha a prepaid phone so she didn't have to sit in the living room and talk to him with Theresa listening. Theresa was furious when she found out Dessy bought her a cell phone.

"If you weren't fucking before, I know you are now," Theresa snapped one night as she passed her cigarette to Deedee.

"Why do I have to be fucking? Because Dessy bought me a cell phone?" argued Sasha as she continued doing the dishes.

"Yes," said Theresa screaming. "Because he bought you a fucking cell phone. Listen to me, Sasha Brown. You want to be a slut I don't give a fuck, but you make sure two things: one, if he getting some ass, get some cash, and two, you are *not* bringing any babies into my house."

Deedee shook her head in disbelief. "Leave the damn girl alone, cuz. Burn the bridge when it comes. Sasha hasn't been fucking yet, trust me. And you should be happy. These days, girls her age are fucking and having babies before they become a senior never mind graduating high school."

Theresa cut her eye at Deedee. "Nobody is talking to you! And how the fuck would you know?"

"Because Wild Flower don't got the glow yet." Deedee waved her hand around. "You know that glow dem girls get when they pop their cherry."

Theresa frowned, unwilling to admit the truth about Sasha's virginity. Sasha's face saddened as she recalled the day Bill raped her.

"Don't let your mother get to you. Don't be in a rush to have sex. The headache and heartache that comes with it is not worth the weight," Deedee laughed unaware of the reality.

CHAPTER 4

After grade nine, Sasha started skipping classes, smoking weed and drinking more. Dessy became a star player on his school's football team and his popularity grew. He gained a handful of female fans who wanted to be his girlfriend. Everyone knew that Dessy was with Sasha but that didn't stop the girls from sliding their numbers into his locker, or trying to catch a feel of his body in the hallways. Some girls were bold enough to step to Sasha, but she knocked them down like bowling pins, one by one. Sasha had no problem fighting girls, but she knew if she wanted to keep her man she was going to have to give up her goodies.

On Sasha's fifteenth birthday, Dessy bought her a silver necklace, a silver, S pendant and an iPod. After they went shopping, they went to a nice restaurant and Sasha stuffed her belly with a well-done New York sirloin steak, mash potatoes and a Caesar salad. They continued the celebration at his house because his mom was working a night shift. She wasn't due back until at least eleven in the morning.

"What's wrong, Sash?" he asked as he threw his shoes into the closet and took her by the hand.

Sasha shook her head. She wrapped her arms around Dessy's neck and kissed him passionately. Dessy was stunned. He kissed her back, lifted Sasha up and wrapped her legs around his waist. Sasha moaned in excitement as she began sucking his neck gently.

Dessy carried her into his room and sat her on his bed. He picked up the scattered clothes on the floor and threw them in the closet. He turned on his computer, turned on some music and stepped out the room to grab his weed.

Sasha watched him nervously. The butterflies in her stomach were going crazy. She thought about how excited Bill was to fuck her and she cringed. She closed her eyes and took a deep breath. She refused to let Bill wreck her moment. Sasha stripped herself down to her bra and panties and stretched on the bed, legs closed, arms above her head.

Dessy returned the room and stood at the door in awe. "You have to be the most beautiful girl I have ever seen in my life."

He walked to the edge of the bed where Sasha awaited him on her knees. He took off his shirt, exposing his perfect eight-pack. Sasha ran her hands down his body before she started kissing him on his smooth but rippled stomach. A bulge quickly grew in Dessy's pants. He unzipped his pants and pulled out his dick.

Sasha looked at it with wide eyes. Dessy's package was far more appealing than Bill's but it was also a lot bigger and longer.

Dessy smirked at Sasha's reaction. "So, you're not going to get it wet for me first?"

"What do you mean?" asked Sasha in confusion.

"You know," Dessy grinned even harder. "Get it hard.

Give him a little kiss."

Sasha raised an eyebrow. "But it is hard."

"Just try it. If you don't like it, you can stop."

Sasha gulped as she eyed Dessy's seven inches of meat. She took his erection into her hands and stroked it slowly. Dessy placed his hands on the back of Sasha's head and pulled her gently towards him. Sasha closed her eyes as she took Dessy in her mouth. The salty taste of pre-cum made her gag as she sucked him slowly. Dessy moaned in pleasure and tilted his head back on his pillow. It didn't take Sasha long to get the hang of it. She slobbered all over him, making his toes curl and his eyes roll back. When the pleasure became too much, Dessy motioned for Sasha to stop and he lay her on her back, on the bed. He grabbed a condom out the back of his wallet and slipped it on.

Dessy kissed Sasha on her lips, down to her neck and then to her breasts. Sasha moaned excitedly. She was overwhelmed by the electric flow running through her body. Sasha wanted him badly. Dessy kissed slowly down to her naval and slid his right hand under Sasha's panties. Sasha melted in the bed at the feel of Dessy's touch. He rubbed her love pearl until she was sopping wet.

Dessy lay himself on top of Sasha and entered her slowly. Sasha tried not to think about the pain she was in when Bill fucked her. This was a different pain—it was a beautiful agony that was spell bounding. Sasha closed her eyes and exhaled slowly as Dessy penetrated her slow and deep. With every thrust, Sasha felt an electric pull building up inside of her. When it became too much, Sasha dug her nails into Dessy's back and her body trembled as she screamed in ecstasy. The look on Sasha's face when she had her first orgasm was enough to make Dessy release into his condom. Dessy was embarrassed for busting a quick nut, but Sasha thought it was perfect. Sasha felt like her virginity was taken all over again. Now Sasha felt like a real woman.

Sex kept Sasha's relationship with Dessy alive until she heard stories about him with other girls. Sasha didn't want to believe the rumours. She was sure that if she kept fucking Dessy on the regular, he wouldn't need to be with other girls. One day while sitting in her fourth period English class, Sasha got a picture message on her cell phone of him and some girl kissing in his bed. Sasha sent the picture to Dessy`s phone hoping for an explanation, but he never responded to the text, worse, he never spoke to Sasha again.

Sasha got over Dessy easily by replacing him with someone new. However, almost every week it was someone different and Sasha had sex with all of them. Sasha was becoming promiscuous and she didn't care. Sex was her new high. She was addicted to the hungry eyes of boys. She loved the feeling of being wanted and being in control. It was considered a privilege to fuck Sasha Brown and only the popular boys who were willing to buy her stuff had a chance.

Word got back to Theresa about Sasha's promiscuity. Theresa used every chance she got to slander Sasha's name. Sasha brushed Theresa off every time. When she felt like entertaining Theresa`s bullshit, she called Theresa a crack whore or an unfit parent just to see her cry. Theresa continued putting her hands on Sasha, and Sasha started fighting back with full force until they were both covered in scratches and bruises. When Sasha went to school, no one ever questioned the scratches. Sasha was known for fighting girlfriends of the guys she slept with or girls that simply didn`t like her and envied her popularity.

Sasha and Theresa became two strangers living in the same house. They rarely spoke to each other and when they did, it turned into an argument. Sasha came and left when she pleased and Theresa never confronted her about it. They figured the best solution was to stay out of each other's way.

Things got worse when Genesis and her mom moved out of the city. Sasha and Genesis grew apart over their first high school year, but Sasha still found herself at her house when she wasn`t on the prowl. It was still her safe house, and Genesis was like the sister she never had. It was nothing for Sasha to visit Genesis, but it wasn't the same. Her safe house was gone and since Sasha didn`t have a permanent boyfriend, she was forced to stay home even more.

In November 2004, when Sasha was sixteen, a man moved into their building by the name of Suave. Suave was a tall, good looking, light skin man from Hamilton. He had a bad leg from a work injury and walked with a cane. Suave was also a crack head.

One Saturday night, Sasha stumbled into the house drunk from drinking with a bunch of guys from their school. Theresa and an old, skinny, black guy were sitting on the couch watching reruns of *Family Guy*. Sasha was revolted. His beige ,button up shirt was wrinkled and wasn't buttoned properly, and his jeans were dirty and ripped.

"Sasha, I want you to meet my boyfriend, Suave," said Theresa excitedly as she patted Suave on the leg. "Suave lives in apartment 305. He just moved in here a month ago."

"Nice to meet you," said Sasha dryly as she kicked off

her boots.

"Pleasure is all mine," he said in admiration. "You told me she was sixteen. She don't look nothing her age. She will put a man in jail with that body."

"Well lucky for them I don't lie about my age." Sasha hung her jacket in the closet. "I'm going to bed now. It was nice meeting you, Smoothie."

"I bet you don't," Suave smirked. "And it`s Suave. You have yourself a good night, young lady."

Suave started sleeping at the house on the regular. Sasha hated when he was at the house and tried her best not to be home when he was there. Suave always got on her nerves with his slick comments about her blooming body and pretty face. Sometimes he would purposely brush himself on Sasha and apologize as if it were a mistake.

One night, Theresa went out to Bingo with Deedee, she left Suave alone in the house with Sasha. Sasha was suppose to go to Brampton to visit Genesis but Genesis wasn't feeling well. Her throat was congested and she had a headache. Suave had been drinking Appleton and getting high all day and when he saw Sasha walk out the bathroom after taking a long, hot shower, he wasted no time to pursue her.

Sasha was laying on her stomach on her bed listening to music and reading a book when Suave opened her room door.

"Don't you know how to knock?" asked Sasha dryly, not taking her eyes off her book.

Suave entered the room and closed the door behind him. Sasha's stomach turned and her heart grew heavy as she sat up on her bed.

"What the fuck are you doing in my room?" she asked

him suspiciously.

"I see the way you look at me, Sasha," Suave slurred. "I know you want me."

"Are you high out of your mind?"

"You walk around the house in those short shorts yours always wearing. You know what that does to an old man like me. And those little tank tops with the strip straps..." Suave used his fingers to show how thin the straps were. "You have those perky titties bouncing in my face like you want me to give you some."

"Give me some what? Trust me, Suave. I don't want you. See yourself out of my bedroom," Sasha rolled her eyes and directed her attention back to her book.

Suave grabbed Sasha by the wrist and pulled her to her feet. She slapped him in the face with her other hand but he managed to get a hold of it and he threw her on her bed. Sasha kicked and screamed for her life as he raped her but the music was too loud for anyone to hear her. Suave was smaller than Sasha but still stronger. When he was finished, he threatened to tell Theresa of Sasha's feeling for him. It was a lie, but they both knew Theresa was gullible and would believe him.

Suave knew Sasha never liked him, but he still used it as an excuse to force himself on her whenever Theresa left them alone together. Sasha had to go to the doctors to get birth control and an STD test because Suave was fucking her without a condom. Thankfully, Sasha's tests all came back negative and she was STD free.

CHAPTER 5

Sasha hated her life and contemplated ending it but never had the courage to do it. She didn't tell anyone about her situation with Suave—not even Genesis, Sasha's confidante in fear that it would get back to her mother. Genesis thought Sasha was dealing with the stress of her mother on drugs. She could sense the sadness in her voice when they spoke on the phone.

Sasha stopped fighting Suave off of her when he came to her room. Fighting Suave made him short of breath, but it exhausted Sasha before she could tire him out. When he crept into her room at night, Sasha pretended she was sleeping. Suave undressed her, fucked her and then saw himself out without saying a word.

Suave kept threatening to tell Theresa about their doings even though they both knew that he wouldn't. Suave loved Sasha's pussy too much to be the one to squeal. He genuinely cared for Theresa, but he had a soft spot for young girls and the drugs and alcohol did not help.

"And this place better be fucking clean," said Theresa one evening as she put on her shoes to leave. She was on her way out with Deedee. "I didn't say anything to you when they kicked your whoring ass out of school. All I ask is that you keep the fucking place clean, and not even that you can do."

Sasha sighed. "Mom, you and Suave make all the mess. I'm tired of cleaning up after you."

"Clean the fucking house!" Theresa grabbed her bag. "I don't care who's mess it is. I want it clean by the time I get back."

Sasha knew what awaited her in the night. When she finished doing the dishes, she dried off her hands, grabbed a glass of juice and stomped to her room.

"That's exactly what I am talking about," said Suave as he slouched into the couch, watching Sasha. "You in those short shorts, shaking your behind when you walk."

"Whatever, you sick fuck," she snapped as she slammed the door behind her.

Sasha smoked a joint and fell asleep but was awaken two hours later by a very drunk and high Suave. His wrinkled shirt was unbuttoned to the top of his stomach. His erection was poking out of his torn jeans. His breath smelt like cigarettes and whisky. Suave moved his hand along Sasha's thigh, pushing himself onto her.

"I didn't mean to wake you up," he whispered in her ear. "You look so sexy when you sleep. I just need to..."

Suave closed his eyes. He dug his hands into Sasha's shorts and palmed her warm pussy. Sasha tried to wiggle away but Suave kept himself mounted on her so she couldn't move. He stuck his finger up her pussy and grinded himself onto her. He groaned as he took off his pants. He had no boxers on. Sasha gave Suave as much trouble as she could before he was finally able to tear off her shorts and flip her on to her stomach.

He plunged himself inside of her and Sasha groaned as she squeezed her sheets. He talked dirty in her ear, but Sasha wasn't paying attention. She wanted him to hurry up so she could go back to sleep.

Sasha and Suave were so caught up in their own worlds, they didn't hear the front door open. Before they even realized that someone was in the house, Theresa busted through the door with a knife in her hand.

"I knew it! I knew you were fucking Suave, you whore!"

Theresa charged at Sasha but Suave was able to jump between them and keep Theresa from chopping Sasha into pieces. Sasha screamed and curled herself on the floor in the corner of her room, shaking and crying.

"Mom, it's not what it looks like!"

"Really? Because it looks to me like you were fucking my man!" Theresa tried to charge at Sasha again but Suave had a good grip on her. "I know I'm a bad mother. I know I don't win the award for the greatest parent, but this, Sasha?"

"He raped me!" Sasha pleaded. "At least once or twice a week. He comes in here, and he—"

"How dare you!" Theresa's blood boiled at Sasha's audacity. "How dare you accuse Suave of raping you. Suave wouldn't even hurt a fly. You know that."

"Ask him!" Sasha pushed, directing her attention to Suave. She pointed her finger at Theresa. "Tell her. Tell her, Suave!"

"Come on now, baby. You know I wouldn't do something like that," denied Suave as he tried to take Theresa by the hand.

Theresa pulled her hand away and took a step back looking at Suave and Sasha as if they were both crazy. "Is it true, Suave?"

"What difference would it make?" asked Sasha. "You aren't going to believe me anyway. Just say it, mom. You don't believe me."

"She don't need to believe anyone because you are lying!" Suave pointed at Sasha.

Sasha screamed as she lunged at Suave and punched him in his face. Suave stumbled back. Sasha picked up a black heel laying on her bedroom and attacked him again. She hit Suave in the face with the back of the heel. Theresa grabbed it out of her hand and tried to pull Sasha away, but Sasha broke free of her hold and charged for Suave again, punching and scratching him everywhere and anywhere she could. Theresa grabbed Sasha by the shoulders and yanked her off Suave. She wrapped her arms around her so this time she couldn't break free.

"You are the fucking liar!" Sasha bellowed out. "I hate you! I fucking hate you!"

"You are a city slut!" Suave lashed back. "Every Tom, Dick and Harry has been up in that pussy. I should have been a stronger man, but you kept teasing with all those skimpy clothes, and eyeing me down like you wanted it."

"I kept teasing you?" Sasha broke free of Theresa's hold and turned to face her. "Mom, please tell me you don't believe him."

Theresa shrugged. "Sasha, don't act like you haven't been sleeping around. I always thought you two were fucking, but I never thought you would steep so low. If Toronto wasn't enough you just had to fuck my man too."

"So what happens now?" asked Sasha. She was no longer crying. Her head was hurting tremendously. She squeezed her eyes shut and exhaled slowly.

"What happens now is Suave can get the fuck out of

my house," Theresa pointed to the door as she looked at the floor in disappointment.

"But baby, I love you," Suave whined as he grabbed his shirt off the door.

"Don't baby me!" Theresa followed him out the room. "That doesn't defeat the purpose that you were in here fucking my daughter! I will bring you all your shit tomorrow or whenever I have time. Right now you need to get the fuck up out of here. Go on now! Get!"

Theresa followed Suave into the living room cursing and screaming in his ear. They went back and forth for a few minutes before Sasha heard the front door open and slam shut. Sasha sighed in relief and sat on her bed. Tears started streaming down her face. She sobbed and gasped for air, trying to stop crying. She was tired of crying over Theresa. Sasha couldn't believe Theresa would actually think that she found Suave attractive much less sleep with him.

Sasha slammed her room door as she burst into tears. Sasha pushed everything off her dresser and ripped her clothes out of her closet. She kicked the clothes on the floor around and threw her pillows around the room, pretending that they were Suave.

Sasha was at her peak with Theresa. She wanted to wipe her hands clean of her. Sasha didn't care to mend their relationship or help Theresa fight her addiction. She just wanted to be free from it all.

When Sasha was convinced that Theresa was asleep, she packed her clothes into a duffle bag and two back packs. *I am not staying here* she thought as she grabbed some underwear out of her drawer. *I deserve better than this. I am better than this.* She called Genesis after she was done packing. Surprisingly, Genesis answered the phone.

"Hey girl, it's Sasha," Sasha whispered.

"Yeah, I know who it is. I got caller ID. Why are you calling at me at 3:45 in the morning?" Genesis groaned over the phone as she stretched.

"I need you to do me a favor. Suave raped me, and I need to get out of here."

"What! What happened?"

"I can't talk right now. I just need to know if I can come to your house."

"You know I have no problem with you being here, but my mom is going to act up and start asking questions."

"You are right. I'm going to make some phone calls. I will call you later."

"Where are you going?"

"I'll burn that bridge once I'm out this damn house."

Sasha hung up with Genesis and called a couple of her friends from school, but they never answered. Sasha groaned in frustration. She had nobody else in her corner. She wanted to call Deedee, but there was nothing Deedee could do. Even if Deedee confronted Theresa, it wouldn't be long before Theresa got caught up into another perverted junky who wanted to get into her panties.

Sasha took a deep breath and thought long about her final option. It was the last person she wanted to call. She hadn't talked to Dessy since she sent him the picture of him and the girl kissing in his bed. Despite the fact that he cheated on her and made her look like a fool, Dessy was a good boyfriend to her. He genuinely cared for Sasha. She could never understand what it was that made him cheat. Maybe it was the glamour of being a star, high school, football player. After ten minutes of contemplating, Sasha decided to call him. If he didn't answer, she would go to a shelter until she can figure out her next move.

Dessy was wide awake playing on his Playstation 3 when Sasha called. Sasha cried to him as she told him what had happened in details. Dessy paused his game and gave Sasha's full attention.

"So what do you want to? You want to come stay and with me?" he asked emotionlessly.

"Even if it's just for the night. I will be gone before your mom gets home from work. I promise."

"You know I have a girlfriend right?"

"And whose fault is that?" Sasha smirked. "If you weren't busy sticking your thing in everything, we would probably still be together."

"I might have made a mistake, but it didn't take you long to move on," Dessy shot back.

There was silence on the phone. Sasha didn't want to upset him. She desperately needed his help. She rubbed the phone with her hand and closed her eyes. "Listen, I'm sorry if I hurt you by moving on, but you hurt me too and I have bigger problems on my hands. Are you going to help me or not?"

"I have a cousin downtown. If I tell him you're situation, he would be more than happy to let you stay with him until you get on your feet."

"I will clean. I can't cook, but I can learn. I will do *anything* he wants if he lets me stay there. Anything is better than being here in this fucking shithole."

"That motherfucker never sleeps. I know he is up right now. I am going to call him and tell him your situation. He will set you up. Fuck with him. He will have you making money and living that bad bitch life style you love so much. You will be fine."

"What's his name?"

"Breezy."

Breezy agreed to let Sasha stay with him and sent a

driver to pick her up. Sasha thanked Dessy, unaware of what she was about to leave her home for.

CHAPTER 6

Sasha threw on a jacket and a pair of sneakers. She grabbed her bags and crept out of her bedroom. The television in the living room was still on, but Theresa was in her room sleeping. Sasha walked passed Theresa's room, peeping inside the cracked door. Sasha wanted to cry again as she gazed at her mother. She had no idea when she would see or speak to her again. Sasha sighed and tip toed towards the front door. She left her keys on the kitchen counter on the way out.

A taxi was waiting for Sasha as promised. Sasha had no idea where she was going. The Indian driver threw her stuff in the trunk and assured Sasha her ride was paid for and he had the address to where she was going.

Sasha's heart was racing the whole ride. She didn't know who Breezy was or what he was into. What if he was dangerous? Sasha fiddled with her hands as they drove down a ramp off the highway into the streets of downtown. It was after four in the morning and the streets were crowded with cars and drunk people on their way home from the bars and clubs. They pulled into a set of high rise condos. Sasha's jaws dropped as she gazed at the main entrance. There was a huge fountain in the middle of the driveway. A stoned pathway lined by tall columns led to the glass double doors. A tall, chocolate man with dark, seductive eyes and luscious lips was standing outside. He looked at the taxi and grinned. Sasha fluttered as he eyeballed her before directing his attention to the driver. He leaned into the passenger window and smiled.

"How's it going, Gill? Sorry to have you up so late."

"No problem, my brother," said the driver in a thick, Indian accent. "You are very nice to me. You help me, I help you, no problem."

Breezy pulled a stack of cash out his pocket. He counted out $160 and gave it to the driver. "I hope this compensates you for your time. Thanks again."

The driver took the cash and stuffed it into the glove compartment.

Sasha jumped out the taxi and waited quietly at the door while Breezy grabbed her bags. Her heart was pounding out of her chest as if it were trying to break free. Sasha followed Breezy into the lobby. A young, black, male concierge sat half asleep behind a desk. They took the elevator to the sixteenth floor in silence.

Sasha let out a sigh of relief when they entered Breezy's condo. There was a cross smell of weed and incense. Sasha couldn't help but notice how fashionably clean it was. Breezy's shoes were lined up neatly at the door and the hardwood floors were so clean they were glistening. There were no dishes in the sink, or pots on the stove. Even the windows looked like they had been recently wiped.

Breezy gave Sasha a towel and rag so she could take a shower. When she was done, she greeted Breezy in the living room where he awaited with a small bottle of Hennessy and a rolled blunt.

Breezy gazed at Sasha with curious eyes. "You smoke?"

"Who doesn't?"

Breezy grinned as he handed her the blunt. He watched as she sucked on it hungrily. "Desmond told me what happened to you. I'm sorry you had to go through that."

"I just don't understand how a mother could put her daughter through the shit my mother put me through." Sasha sunk into the couch, staring at the floor. She took another draw off the blunt and then passed it back to Breezy. "I had to leave. That was my last straw. I'd rather fend for myself than live in that hell hole."

"So, what do you plan on doing?"

Sasha shrugged. "To tell you the truth, I don't know."

Sasha hadn't given it much thought as to what she was going to do after she left the house. She had to make money and go back to school, but she had no idea where to start. Everything happened so fast. The only thing on Sasha's mind at the time was leaving. Almost two hours had passed since she left. She wondered if Theresa realized she was gone yet.

"Listen, Desmond really cares about you or he wouldn't have sent you here. I won't front, I'm a nigga, but I wear my heart on my sleeve. I can't stand seeing a young girl like yourself walking homeless on the streets for some crazy fool to snatch you up." Breezy took Sasha's hand into his. "But nothing in life comes for free."

Sasha nodded her head. "I know, and I promise that I will find a job and be out of your way."

"We don't have time for you to find a job," Breezy

smirked. He sat himself up, ready to talk business. "We need to get you on the payroll ASAP. Tomorrow I am going to take you to my girl, Cherry. We're going to set you up. We're going to get your hair done, get you new clothes, all of that."

Sasha raised her eyebrow as she looked at Breezy suspiciously. "I mean, I appreciate your generosity, but I can do my own hair and I got like three or four bags of nice, brand new clothes in the room. On a regular day, I would have jumped on the offer, but I don't have anything to offer in return."

"Like I said nothing in life comes for free. I'm going to put it like this without being rude." Breezy leaned into Sasha with a faint grin across his face. "You look like a girl who likes to fuck. Correct me if I'm wrong."

Sasha was caught off guard by Breezy's bluntness. She looked at the floor, unsure of what to say.

Breezy chuckled at Sasha's reaction. "Relax. I'm asking you a straight up question. The way you been looking at me with them pretty eyes of yours, if I wanted to fuck you, that would have happened a long time ago."

"I do like having sex. But who doesn't?"

"Well, what do you have to show for all that dick you take?"

Sasha sat up straight and gave Breezy her full attention realizing that he was being earnest. "I get boys to buy me clothes, jewellery and other stuff."

Breezy nodded his head in approval. "Clothes and jewellery don't pay the bills. You are in the real world now. You left the nest the moment you jumped into the taxi and came here."

"Yeah I know."

"You think it's a joke, eh? The good thing is that you already know how to get these nigga's to come out of pocket. Now all we need to do is teach you how to make cash and make it quick."

"Do you mean prostitution?" Sasha thought about the day she walked into her mother giving head to Bill. "Hell fucking no!" Sasha slid her hand out of Breezy's. "My mom sold me to a trick for six hundred dollars and crack. She always told me I was going to end up just like her. I'm not about to let her win."

"The fuck you talking about letting her win?" said Breezy almost screaming at Sasha. He stood to his feet. "You are a sixteen-year-old runaway. What the fuck did you think was going to happen? Someone was going to come and be your night and shining armor?"

Sasha's eyes filled with water. She squeezed them shut and exhaled slowly. Breezy wiped the tears off Sasha's face with his hand. He crunched down beside her and took her hands into his again.

"I'm just trying to break it down to you raw. It's a cold world out there. I don't need to tell you that because you already know. Only the strongest survive. You need to take that negative and turn it into a positive." He pulled a Ziploc bag of weed out of his pocket. "Can you roll a blunt?"

Breezy took out a big bud and placed it on a magazine on the coffee table. Sasha grinded the weed with her hands. Her face was tight with anxiety.

"Don't let your mother ruin what could be the start of a new life for you," Breezy continued. He took a gulp of the Hennessey from the bottle and sat back down. "You're mother is a fiend and only fiends do dumb shit like that. What I am offering you is an opportunity to be a part of a team. I'm running a business here, eh. I am twenty five years old and look how I am living. Don't you want to live like this?"

Sasha nodded her head shyly as she rolled the blunt.

"Guys are willing to pay for that pussy and there is nothing wrong with that. There is no reason why you should feel ashamed of surviving." Breezy looked at Sasha for a long moment with a crooked, boyish grin. "Just think, you won't have to worry about anything. Clothes will be taken care of. Your hair will be taken care, and you will have somewhere nice to live. You will have money in your pocket. Anything you want, you can have. You want weed?" Breezy threw the bag of weed at Sasha. "Keep that, I can buy more of that shit tomorrow."

Sasha glanced out the window. The sun was pushing its way through the horizons over Lake Ontario. Breezy pulled Sasha towards him and she sat on his lap. He gave Sasha a penetrating gaze that made her shiver. He gripped her ass firmly and kissed her on her neck. Sasha moaned softly as she stood up facing him. She smirked as she put the blunt on the coffee table and got on her knees. Breezy tilted his head back in awe as Sasha took him into her mouth.

It wasn't long before Breezy pulled a condom out of his jeans pocket. Sasha jumped on top of Breezy and bounced on him vigorously with no shame. Breezy looked at Sasha with bright, unblinking eyes. With every thrust, Sasha was giving herself to him and she didn't even realize it. When they were finished, Sasha curled into the couch with a radiant smile and closed her eyes. Breezy had her right where he wanted her—young, desperate, blind and ready to do anything he said.

CHAPTER 7

Sasha was awaken by the loud vibration of her cell phone on the coffee table. She had fourteen missed calls from Theresa and Genesis. It was 9:37 A.M. Sasha looked around for Breezy. His bedroom door was closed. Sasha sat up and noticed the green blanket that covered her to her waist. She smiled as she picked up her phone to call Genesis.

"Oh my god! Sasha, you had me worried sick about you," said Genesis sounding rejoiced. "I thought some crazy man snatched you off the streets or something."

"I'm ok," Sasha whispered. "I'm with Dessy's family. His cousin is going to set me straight."

"Dessy's cousin? That doesn't sound right to me."

Sasha tried to assure Genesis that Breezy was a genuinely nice guy, but Genesis knew it was too good to be true. Nothing in life comes that easy.

"Just be careful. I'm not trying to turn on the news and see your picture," Genesis joked. Her tone quickly changed. "You're mom is worried sick about you."

"Fuck her!" Sasha hissed. "She is the reason why I am

here in the first place. She chose that nasty crack head over me. I'm done with my mom, Suave, the drugs, and that fucking excuse for a home. I'd rather be out here fending for myself."

Sasha's blood was boiling. She shut her eyes and took a deep breath. Sasha couldn't understand why Theresa never believed her.

"Well, you just keep in touch with me so I don't have to worry, eh," said Genesis, unmoved by Sasha's decision.

As Sasha was saying bye to Genesis, Breezy walked out into the kitchen and grabbed orange juice out the fridge. He drank the juice from the container.

"Rise and shine," he said as he strolled into the living room. "It's time to make this money. We got a long day ahead of us."

Sasha was now excited and couldn't wait to go on the road with Breezy. The hurt in her heart was her ammo, and it gave her the adrenalin she needed. Sasha wanted to show Breezy that she was strong and able bring in the cash.

Breezy opened up the blinds to let some sunlight into the condo. Sasha was amazed at the view of the city. She never had a chance to look at it when she got there because she was so distraught. High-rise commercial and residential buildings created an eye-catching skyscraper right along the lake. Breezy turned the TV to the news, plopped himself on the couch beside Sasha and put his legs up on the coffee table. He picked up the bag of weed that was left on the coffee table.

"I am going to send you over to my girl, Cherry. She is going make you look like a million bucks."

Sasha folded her arms. "What are you trying to say? I am pretty. There isn't much to change."

"Trust me, you definitely look sexy, but customers

aren't paying for a bad bitch. They are paying for high class girls with good pussy. If you want clients that pay big money you have to look like a million bucks. Cherry is going to make sure of that."

Sasha frowned. "Who is this Cherry girl anyway?"

"She is family," he answered sternly.

Cherry was one of the first girls Breezy put to work when he got into the pimping. She was the most profitable girl he had. Breezy got Cherry pregnant a year after she started working for him. After Cherry had the baby, Breezy moved her and his son into a townhouse in Mississauga.

Sasha was nervous. She didn't think prostituting would require so much work. Sasha thought Breezy would just send her guys to fuck and they would pay her. Breezy relaxed Sasha's nerves with a blunt and a quickie before they got ready to hit the road.

Cherry's townhouse was two minutes from the 403 highway. It was newly built and looked like it had three floors from the outside. There was a balcony on the top floor large with a four-seat patio set with Heineken umbrellas. The two-door garage was opened and there was a black, 2010 Audi A6 parked inside. Sasha frowned. It was the same type of car as Breezy's.

A curvy, light skin women with a curly, brown fro greeted them at the door. She had on a pair of jeans that sucked onto her body and a fitted tee that read "I love bad boys" across the chest. She wore gold bangles, a gold chain and a pair of large, gold hoops.

"Hello Breezy," she said softly.

She looked at Breezy the way a wife would look at her husband. She cleared her throat and caught a glimpse of Cherry's left hand. There was no sign of a ring. Sasha smirked as she looked away, trying to keep herself from staring.

"Beautiful!" he complimented as he pulled Cherry to hug him He kissed her on the cheek. "Where's our son?"

"He's at my mom's house for the day. You know I don't like him in the house when I am working," she said as she looked at Sasha.

Sasha felt awkward being inside the house of Breezy's baby mother. She stepped forward nervously and reached her hand out to shake Cherry's. "Hi, I'm Sasha."

"And I am Cherry. That's a firm grip you have, and you are fucking gorgeous. Breezy, where did you find her?"

"This is actually Dessy's friend. She was in a tough situation at home with her mom's boyfriend. You know how that story goes," said Breezy.

Cherry hugged Sasha like a concerned friend. "Don't worry. We are your family now. We are going to see you straight and with a body, face and hair like that, we won't have to do much tweaking." Cherry ran her hands through Sasha's hair.

"Well, I am going to leave ya'll ladies to it. I got some things to do on the road," said Breezy as he grabbed his keys out of his pocket.

Sasha grabbed Breezy's arm. "Wait! You're not staying with me?"

"Don't worry. Cherry is good people and the mother of my child. I trust her with my life which means you can too." Breezy hugged Sasha tightly. "Plus Cherry is older and very experienced. She might be able to answer certain questions better than I can."

Sasha sighed nervously. She didn't have much choice. Sasha reminded herself that it was all temporary. After she had enough money, she was going to get her own place and her life together. She might as well take what she could because there was nothing else better out there for her.

"What time are you coming back for me?" she asked.

"When you are ready," he replied as he headed to the door. Cherry followed behind him.

Sasha couldn't hear what they were saying but she did see Breezy give Cherry a stack of cash. Cherry stuffed the money in her back pocket. She kissed him on the cheek and he left.

"Are you hungry? Can I fix you something to eat?" asked Cherry as she walked into the kitchen.

"No I'm fine, thanks."

"How about a blunt? I know you're not going to say no to that."

Cherry grabbed a bag of Doritos out of the cupboard. She went into the living room and motioned Sasha to join her.

"You're right. I'm not going to say no to that," Sasha laughed.

Cherry pulled a small baggy out of her bra and handed it over to Sasha. She looked at Sasha with curious eyes. "How old are you?"

"I'm sixteen and a half."

"Sixteen? Girl, you could pass for nineteen or twenty." Cherry took a handful of chips and stuffed it into her mouth. "What happened at your moms house? Her boyfriend was touching you?"

Sasha sparked the blunt and inhaled slowly. She sunk into the couch. "More than touching me. He was having sex with me. The night I ended up at Breezy's, my mom walked in on him fucking me and thought I was trying to take her man."

"Damn, why didn't you tell her that he was forcing

himself on you?"

"I did tell her! She thought I was lying. It doesn't matter. They are both crack heads. He could have told my mom anything and she would have believed him."

Cherry took the blunt and put her hand softly on Sasha's shoulder. "I'm sorry to hear that. I know what it's like to go through that shit. I share the same story only it was worse. It was my real father. He was an alcoholic and used to beat my mother in front of me. He was always yelling at me, but he didn't start putting his hands on me until I was twelve. Then, when I hit puberty, the beating turned into sly comments about my body. He would ask me if I was having sex, knowing I was still a virgin."

"At twelve years old he thought you were having sex?"

"You would be surprised. Babies having babies is the new trend," Cherry smirked as she passed the blunt back to Sasha. "When I was seventeen, I ran away from home. I was from friend to friend's house for a year until I met Breezy."

"Did your father ever touch you?"

"Touch me? That cock sucker used to stand at the edge of my bed and make me suck his dick. He would cum on my face and tell me that I was a bastard child and a whore," Cherry explained.

Sasha was stunned. She forgot that she wasn't the only one with a story. Her face saddened as she empathized with Cherry.

"I was young and scared just like you. Anything was better than being at home. I stayed with my girl Shawna in Shoreham and sold weed and coke with my nigga's to get by. Breezy was a friend of the guy she was fucking at the time. Breezy put me on and here I am today." Cherry smiled at her success. She looked around the house proudly. "I got myself a handsome little boy, I have a beautiful home, food in my fridge and name brand clothes in our closets. Everything worked out for the best. What doesn't kill you makes you stronger. You just have to learn how to turn your negatives into positives, girl.

"We are beautiful women. We are the ones that control this shit. Pussy runs men. If you know how to use your pussy as a tool, you can get anything you want out of a man."

Sasha sat quietly as Cherry coached her on the game, sucking everything up like a sponge. Cherry glorified prostitution and Sasha took the bait without any question.

Cherry took Sasha to the hair store and bought a pack of black, sixteen inch hair and then took her to the nail salon. Sasha wanted to get a funky design but Cherry demanded she get French tips. "Business men don't like ghetto girls," Cherry explained. Sasha also got a pedicure and her eyebrows done for the first time. After they left the nail salon, Cherry dragged Sasha into a lingerie store and bought her three outfits and a pair of seven inch stilettos. When they got back to the house, Cherry styled Sasha's hair into a high ponytail then made Sasha put on all the outfits to take pictures.

"What are the pictures for?" Sasha had asked when Cherry pulled out her camera. She sat up on the bed nervously wearing a black and red corset and a matching, red g-string.

"For your ads."

"My ads?"

"Yes, when I post your ad, I need pictures of you so that the guys can see what you look like."

Sasha cringed. She didn't like the idea of having her pictures on the internet for everyone and anyone to see.

Cherry sat beside Sasha and placed her hand again, softly on her shoulder.

"Don't worry. Nobody will know that it's you, your face will be cut off in all the pictures. All they are really interested in is your body."

Sasha was still not convinced. "So why can't I just put up my description?"

"Because pictures get more customers."

Cherry got up and continued snapping away at Sasha. When they were done, Cherry came up with the name Lisa as Sasha's "working" name.

"Why can't I use my real name?" Sasha continued naively with the questions.

Cherry sighed and rolled her eyes. "For the same reasons why we are cutting your face out of the pictures. Someone might recognize you and you are still a minor. If anyone finds out you are under eighteen, me and Breezy could go to jail. When you are eighteen, you can call yourself whatever you want, but right now, its Lisa."

"What if they ask me what my real name is?"

"Give them another fake name," said Cherry as if she were stating the obvious.

Breezy returned to Cherry's house minutes after ten. He was very pleased with Sasha's new look. Sasha modeled a couple of her new outfits for him. It took everything in Breezy not to pounce on her and fuck her right in front of Cherry. Instead he grinned and nodded his head in approval at each outfit she put on for him.

"So where are we going now?" asked Sasha excitedly as they headed onto the highway.

"We are going to go pick up one of the girls from a call and we are going to get something to eat. Then I am going to drop you guys back to the condo for the night. It's Sunday. Relax and take it easy. Clock-in is soon as that sun goes up."

Sasha frowned and folded her arms. "Which girl is this now?"

"She is another working girl. She is young like you. She actually just turned eighteen. She been fucking with me for about eight months now. Her name is Mel."

Sasha frowned. For a moment she forgot she wasn't the only one on Breezy's payroll. She wanted to be his main chick. It was hard enough for her to accept Cherry as his baby mother, now she had to accept another working girl. She couldn't help but wonder how many girls he had working for him. Even though she had just met him, she was jealous.

They drove thirty minutes to a house in Brampton. Breezy parked on the side of the street and within minutes a young, black girl came walking around the corner. She was short and dark skin with huge breasts and a round face. She jumped into the backseat of the car.

"It's all there," she stated as she handed Breezy a handful of cash and eyeballed Sasha.

Breezy counted the money, added it to his stack of cash and put it in his pocket. "Mel, I want you to meet Sasha. She is the newest addition to the team. You guys are going to be working together so make friends."

They drove back to Breezy's condo in silence. Sasha was unsure of what to say to Breezy or Mel. She didn't see the point of working with Mel. Mel wasn't going to be fucking her clients for her. There was nothing Mel could teach her that Cherry couldn't. Breezy took the girls upstairs. He used the bathroom and spoke to them briefly before he left for the night. Mel went straight into the shower and left Sasha alone in the living room. When Mel was done, she joined Sasha.

"So where are you from?" Mel asked as she sat beside her on the couch.

"I'm from Jane and Finch. You?"

"Scarborough. How did you end up here? Are you from a group home too?"

"No. I ran away from home. Breezy is my ex's cousin. He sent me to him."

Mel smirked as she sat on the couch beside Sasha. "You're ex-man sent you to Breezy? That's fucked up."

Sasha raised her eyebrow. "Why?"

Mel rolled her eyes and chuckled at Sasha's ignorance. "I come from a group home. It was like living in prison in there. All they did was boss me around and make me feel like shit. I couldn't take it. One day, Breezy spotted me down the street. We talked. He took me out to eat a few times, and here I am today."

"Was he your boyfriend?" asked Sasha, trying to fill in the gap between dinner and working.

Mel frowned. "Far from it. My advice to you is don't get too comfortable. Do what you have to do and get the fuck out of here."

Sasha was unable to take the hint. "What's that supposed to mean?"

"Exactly what I said. Do what you have to do and get the fuck of here. He is selfish, manipulative and doesn't give a fuck about anything but his money and his son. He don't even give a fuck about Cherry's stupid ass."

Sasha frowned. "Whatever, Mel. I'm here because I want to be. I know what I am getting myself into. Don't be mad because you made the wrong choice for yourself. I know what I am doing."

"Whatever yourself. Don't say I never warned you. I used to think the exact same way you did when I first started working for him."

CHAPTER 8

Breezy called Mel's phone at six in the morning to wake her and Sasha up. He wasn't joking when he was talking about the crack of dawn. Early birds catch the worm and Breezy always wanted to be the first.

Sasha forced herself to get up. She shared the bed with Mel, but she barely slept. Mel's advice about Breezy was stuck in her thoughts. Breezy seemed genuine and didn't sound like a snake to her. Plus, he never found Sasha, she found him. Sasha couldn't understand why Mel felt so hostile towards him. Breezy took her out of a fucked up situation and gave her a way of making money, just like he did for Sasha.

"No half dressing," Mel explained as she skimmed through her duffel bag for something to wear. "Breezy likes us looking our best at all times, even if we are going to the grocery store."

"There is nothing wrong with looking good," Sasha smirked. "I love dressing myself up. I don't know why he sent me to Cherry's. She didn't really do nothing for me that I couldn't do for myself."

"Because Cherry's stupid ass needs to feel important." Mel struggled to put on a pair of black leggings. She squatted down and yanked the leggings over her butt then wiggled it up to her waist. "You don't understand because it's your first day. You will see for yourself, Sasha. Trust me."

"I guess I will."

After they were done getting ready, they packed their bags of lingerie, lube, condoms, and toys and went downstairs to meet Breezy. The cold, winter breeze slapped Sasha on her face, making her eyes water, but she still strut herself like she was a million bucks.

Mel jumped into the passenger side, and Sasha jumped into the backseat, excited about her first day on the job. They stopped at the McDonalds drive-thru and bought breakfast before they hit the highway.

"Today you guys are going to be working in Mississauga by the airport. I booked two rooms beside each other. If one or both of you guys get a call, nobody loses out on money. You can hang out in one room between calls," explained Breezy.

He took a rolled blunt out of his cigarette pack and handed it to Mel. She rolled up her window and lit it.

"No outcalls today?" she asked. A few customers have been calling me for outcalls."

"What are outcalls?" Sasha asked shyly.

"A call is when you meet a customer," Mel explained trying not to laugh. "An incall is when they come to see you and outcall is when you go to see them."

Sasha looked at Breezy. "Do you come with us to the outcalls?"

"I drive you there, but I don't go inside. Tricks don't like girls who work with guys. I park down the street, and you call me when you are done. If time is up and I still don't hear from you, then that's a different story."

"Are we going to be doing duos?" Mel inquired.

Sasha felt her brain starting to hurt as she tried to consume all this new information. "What's that?"

"Threesomes," Mel laughed. "You never had a threesome before?"

Sasha blushed. "I have but not with another girl."

She had thoughts of being with a girl many times but she never saw herself actually carrying through with it. When her and her school friends used to roll out, they kissed a couple times in front of their guy friends. That was the farthest Sasha had gone with a girl.

"I'm bisexual. I don't mind fucking bitches," Mel chirped proudly. She took a pull off the blunt and passed it to Sasha. "A girl can get up in this any day."

"I am going to post some ads for duo's and see how it turns out," said Breezy, nodding his head in agreement. "That's a good look right there. The two of you fucking. Shit, my dick is getting hard just thinking about it."

Mel laughed as she grinned at Sasha with alluring eyes. Sasha squirmed in her seat. She looked out the window and took a deep breath. All the information she got in the last twenty four hours had her feeling overwhelmed. Who knew prostituting was so much work. In twenty-four hours, Sasha got a new name, a new look, learned new terminology and had thoughts of having sex with another girl. It was a lot to take in and she still had more learning to do.

When they got to the hotel, Breezy sat Sasha down and explained to her what was going to go down. Mel and Sasha were to stay at the hotel for two nights to do calls. Breezy would pop in periodically to check up on them and collect the money. He explained that it was safer to keep the money outside of the room in case the police came knocking or a client tried to rob them.

"How much money do I get out of it?" asked Sasha.

"How much money do you need right now?" Breezy replied back.

Sasha thought hard but she couldn't come up with an answer. As Breezy promised she had shelter, food, clothes and anything Sasha needed.

"I guess I don't really need any money," she finally admitted, feeling like she asked a stupid question.

Breezy pulled a wad of money out of his pocket and counted out one hundred dollars in twenties and tens. He gave fifty dollars to Mel and fifty dollars to Sasha. "This is to take care of yourselves while I'm gone. If you are hungry and want to buy some food, if you run out of condoms, whatever, that should do you guys straight." Breezy also handed Sasha a brand new cell phone. "Give me your old phone."

"I don't need a new phone. Why can't I use mine?" she protested.

Sasha's phone was the only connection she had to her old life. Even though she hated Theresa for doing her like that, she was still her mother. Seeing the countless amount of missed calls from Theresa was her only way of knowing that Theresa was thinking about her.

"Who are you trying to call anyway? Your mama?" Breezy questioned her. "Fuck your crack head mother. She's the reason why you are here in the first place. You asked for my help and I'm giving it to you. Now you need to stop asking so many questions. Say goodbye to your past and all the fucked up people in it and say hello to your future and all the money you are about to make."

Mel folded her arms and rolled her eyes as she watched Breezy lure Sasha into his fantasy world. A part of her wanted to tell Sasha she was wasting her time but she didn't want to face the consequences of having to deal with Breezy after.

Breezy looked at Sasha with intense eyes. "You can either go hard or I can take you back to your mother and her perverted boyfriend."

Sasha looked at the floor and sighed. Sasha had no intentions of going back home. She didn't want to give up her phone but she knew better than to call Breezy's bluff. She squeezed the phone tightly before handing it over. Breezy couldn't hide his victorious grin as he slipped the phone into his back pocket.

"If you're phone rings, let Mel answer it the first couple of times." he said before he left.

"So why did you run away from home?" asked Mel as she turned on the TV.

"Because my mom is a crack head, and her boyfriend is a pedophile," Sasha answered bluntly.

"Damn that's harsh. Both my parents are crack heads too. I got taken away by Children's Aid Society when I was twelve. I have been in and out of foster care and group homes ever since."

"Just when you thought you had it bad."

"Someone always has it worst than you, girl. Trust me," Mel chuckled.

They gossiped with each other like two old friends for an hour before Sasha's phone rang.

Mel took the phone and answered. "Please call back with your number showing...no I do not respond to private calls...then dial *82 before my number and your number will show." Mel hung up the phone and rolled her eyes.

"What was that all about?" asked Sasha.

"We do not take private calls. It could be the police. If they want to book an appointment they have to call with a number that we can see and call back."

Sasha frowned and folded her arms. "So many fucking rules!"

"Don't worry. You will get used to it. By the end of the night you will literally be a pro," said Mel as the phone rang in her hand. She gave Sasha a reassuring smile before answering the phone. "Hello...yes this is Lisa...I am eighteen years old. Yes, those are all my pictures...aww thank you...I am Jamaican and Trinidadian...it's a one hundred dollars for the half hour and one hundred and eighty dollars for the hour...yes I am available now. How long did you want to book an appointment for?...ok a half hour is fine...I am by the airport at the Monte Carlo...Ok call me back when you are here and I will tell you what room I am in."

Sasha's heart grew heavy and sunk slowly into her stomach. She was way out of her league. *Am I really doing this?* She thought as she fiddled with her hands. No one had ever given her a hundred dollars before. The most valuable gift she got from a guy was the necklace Dessy bought her for her birthday.

"So he is on his way here?" she asked.

"Yes, and you have to get ready." Mel pushed Sasha off the bed. "Go fix up your makeup and put on one of the outfits you packed."

Sasha sighed as she fumbled through her bag. She chose out a black, laced corset and a black G-string. She fixed her makeup and put on the black, seven inch stilettos that Cherry bought her.

"I can't lie, you're sexy as hell," Mel commented in awe. "These tricks are going to love you."

Sasha laughed nervously. She began playing with her hands again. She was having a hard time grasping the fact she was about to fuck someone she had never seen or spoke to before.

"So when he gets here, what am I suppose to do?" asked Sasha.

"Just go with the flow. Don't start anything until he gives you your money. After he gives you the money then you can send on the pussy."

"Cash before ass."

"Exactly."

Sasha's client called fifteen minutes later to inform her that he was in the hotel lobby. Mel told him what room to go to then grabbed her stuff to go.

"Don't worry you will be fine," she said as she closed the door behind her.

Sasha paced the room apprehensively. She looked in the mirror and almost didn't recognize the girl looking back at her. Lisa didn't look like a sixteen-year-old, young lady. She looked like a young vixen, or a stripper. Lisa was every man's fantasy. She was strong, beautiful and fearless. Sasha took a deep breath. Her heart was racing. She wasn't sure if she can handle it all and for a moment, she considered backing out. Sasha had fifty dollars in her pouch, and it was enough for a taxi and food. But where would she go? *Don't be a pussy* she thought to herself. Sasha thought long and hard about the money she was going to get and how fast she was going to get it. She had to stick to the plan or she would end up right back home or even worse, homeless.

When the door knock came, Sasha jumped as if she was about to be put out of her misery. She sprayed perfume on herself before she answered. A short, fat, Indian man wearing glasses awaited her.

"Lisa?" he asked in an Indian accent.

Sasha opened the door and invited him inside. She looked in the hall to see if anyone was watching before she closed the door.

"You look even more beautiful in person," he complimented.

"Thank you."

"I love black girls," he said hungrily as he proceeded towards Sasha.

"Before we begin—"

"Oh yes, my apologies," he said, cutting her off. He pulled a black, leather wallet out of his pocket and handed her five twenty dollar bills.

Sasha smiled as she put the money in her pouch on the dresser.

"Do you kiss?" he asked.

"No."

He pulled Sasha to him and hugged her tightly. His breath stunk of alcohol, and it reminded her of Suave. His odor was bad and it made Sasha's stomach turn. Sasha forced herself to kiss the man on his neck as she placed his hands on her butt. He grabbed it aggressively and moaned in her ear. Sasha was disgusted. She wanted to puke all over him. She cracked a weak smile as she began undressing him. His hands wondered her body hungrily. She thought of Suave and Bill, who had have gladly paid her for sex and her body lost all of its feeling. Suave and Bill could have easily had been the Indian man. Her client was just a nicer version of them. At least this time she was in control of the situation and was getting what she wanted out of it.

"So, what's your name?" she asked in a soft voice.

"My name is Gurpreet," he moaned as he closed his eyes.

His chest was hairy, and he was sweating profoundly. Sasha faked a smile as she ran her hands down his chest to his navel. He exhaled as Sasha played with his waist line. She took a condom out of her pouch and got on her knees. Sasha pulled Gurpreet's pants down. He wasn't holding much. Sasha smiled and put her hand to her mouth to keep herself from laughing. She stroked him until he was hard and put the condom on. She took a deep breath and took him into her mouth. Gurpreet exhaled and tilted his head back. He was having the time of his life, but Sasha's stomach was turning. She thought about the hundred he had just given her. Nobody said she had to like it, she just had to pretend. It was strictly business. She was getting paid to provide a service.

Sasha sucked and slurped on Gurpreet until his body tensed with excitement. She hopped on the bed and laid on her back. Gurpreet climbed on top of Sasha excitedly. He took his time as he inserted himself into her slowly. He took her by the waist and clumsily proceeded to fuck her. Within seconds, he was sweating profoundly and dripping all over Sasha's face and chest.

Sasha desperately needed a distraction from thinking about Gurpreet or she wouldn't be able to hide how turned off she was by his presence. She thought about the condo she called home and the Audi that she drove around in everyday. She thought about the hundred dollars in her pouch again and how much money she had the potential to make while the day was still young.

Sasha moaned in Gurpreet's ear and rubbed his sweaty back. He bawled as he pulled out of her and ejaculated on her ass. He looked at Sasha and smiled with approval as he stood to his feet. He went into the bathroom and grabbed two towels off the rack. He gave Sasha one and she quickly wiped herself off.

"You are very good," he commented as he wiped his sweaty face. "I will save your number and call you again."

"No problem."

Sasha was relieved when he left. When she checked the time on her cell phone she was sure that they went over thirty minutes but Gurpeet was only there for fifteen. Sasha laughed to herself as she threw her phone on the bed and went to take a shower.

Sasha could hear moaning coming from Mel's room. Sasha sat on the bed, grabbed her phone and texted Genesis to let her know she was ok and had changed her number. She never told Genesis that she started prostituting. Genesis knew that Sasha was fast but prostitution was a whole different story. If she told Genesis what was really going on, Genesis would try to talk her out of it. Genesis's opinion still mattered to Sasha, and she didn't want her friend to be disappointed in her. Nevertheless, there was nothing Genesis could say to talk Sasha into going home, especially after Sasha had finally grasped the power of pussy.

Sasha grabbed her pouch. She looked at the five twenty dollar bills inside and grinned. With money coming in like that she would be back on her feet in no time. One hundred dollars or more per client would add up quickly. Sasha thought about all the things she could do with her money. She could get her own place. She could put her mom in rehab. Sasha could live a luxurious life in her own condo with her own car.

"How did it go?" asked Mel as she sat at the table. Her hair was wet from taking a shower.

Sasha shrugged her shoulders. "It was ok I guess. Definitely not what I was expecting."

"What were you expecting? A bunch of thirsty niggas with money?"

Sasha didn't really know what to expect. All she knew was that she was going to be having sex for money. She never took into account who she would be having sex with.

Mel laughed hysterically. "If only it were that easy. Girl, expect the ugliest, horniest, cockiest, freakiest and most normal guys to walk through those doors."

"Well, that's true," Sasha agreed. "Good looking guys don't need to pay for pussy."

"A lot of good looking guys buy pussy. Don't ever let their handsome faces fool you. Those are the ones with boring girlfriends, too much time for girlfriends, hate the idea of girlfriends, or they are just selfish assholes who can't get enough."

Mel and Sasha laughed with each other as Mel shared some outrageous stories about the clients she had in the past. One of Mel's clients used to book a hotel in the Mississauga everyday to meet with different escorts. Other escorts used to call him the cock-ring guy because he always wore a pink cock-ring when he saw them. He was a nasty, perverted old man who liked his balls sucked while he jerked off. After he was done, he would tell the girl he was with that he had something important to do and rush her out of his room When they left, he would pick up his phone and call another girl to come.

Mel had another client named George. He was a rich Italian guy that lived in Woodbridge. He had a wife and two kids. Every two weeks, the wife and two kids would pack up to go see her mother in Owen Sound. George would invite Mel over for an hour of fun. Georges idea of fun was him dressing in women underwear and letting Mel treat him like a little bitch. Sometimes he would pay her extra to have her fuck him in his ass.

Sasha was grateful for Mel's stories. It shook away some of the nervousness she had about the industry. It made her wonder about the type of clients she would run into in the near future. Sasha couldn't help but feel excited again about making money. Now that she had see her first client and knew what to expect, the rest of them would be a breeze.

The rest of the day was slow. Sasha's and Mel's phones rang with inquires, but only two clients actually came to see them. They ordered some pizza and wings for lunch and caught up on some sleep they missed out on the night before. Breezy stopped by at the hotel later in the afternoon. He had on a different outfit from the one he was wearing when he dropped them off.

"So how was your first trick?" he questioned Sasha.

"It was so gross. He was this fat, Indian man with a heavy accent," she explained as she made up her face. "He had a small dick and his sweat kept dripping on me. I didn't think I was going to last."

"I hate when they sweat on me. I feel like telling them to stop to wipe their face. It's such a turn off," Mel agreed as she cringed.

"But the money made it worth it though, right?" asked Breezy in a serious tone. "These tricks know they don't stand a chance with you without money. They know you don't want to be there. So don't remind them. Let them have their thirty minutes in heaven. You *want* them to come back to you."

Sasha hugged the pillow tightly as she thought about Breezy's words long and hard. He was right. It was just something she had to get used to doing. She had to remember that it was all about the money.

Before Breezy could ask, Sasha reluctantly gave him the two hundred dollars she made. She wasn't keen on the idea of him holding all of her money, but after seeing Mel doing it, Sasha assumed he could be trusted. Breezy nodded his head in approval as he added it to Mel's and stuffed it into his pocket. He put a quarter bag of weed and a bottle of Hennessey on the nightstand.

"Don't finish this tonight. Save some for tomorrow because I'm not buying you guys another bottle, and I'm not coming back with any more kush," he instructed when he was leaving. "And don't have too much fun either. I see the way you're eyeballing Sasha, Mel."

"I think I would make a really good stripper," Sasha joked as she moved her waist seductively. Hours had passed and neither of their phones rang, even for an inquiry. Sasha was in one of her outfits dancing around the room to Rihanna's "Pon De Replay". She tripped over her foot and stumbled onto the bed.

"Guys don't like drunk strippers," Mel laughed. She sat up on the edge of the bed, urging Sasha to come to her. "But I do."

"Would you like to buy a dance, baby?" Sasha moaned playfully. She bit her bottom lip as she stood in front of Mel.

Sasha waved her hips from side to side and wined her waist slowly. Mel licked her lips as she stared at Sasha with kindle eyes. Sasha placed her hand on her mouth and giggled. She turned her back to Mel and bent over. Mel quickly palmed Sasha's ass. Her breathing was heavy.

If Sasha hadn't been drinking and smoking, she would have never danced for Mel, let alone allow Mel to touch her. The weed and alcohol had Sasha feeling vibrant, alive and vulnerable. She sat in Mel's lap and placed her hands on Mel's face. Her skin was soft and smooth. Mel wrapped her arms around Sasha and placed a faint kiss on her neck. Sasha's heart started beating quickly. Her breaths were staggered. She knew what would happen next if she didn't stop. It felt good. It felt right. It felt sexy. Sasha didn't want to stop. Mel's touches were driving her body crazy and she wanted more.

Mel lay Sasha on her back on the bed. She straddled herself on top of Sasha. She sucked and nibbled on Sasha's neck then trailed to her lips and kissed her passionately. Sasha allowed her hands to explore Mel's body curiously. She started at Mel's face, down her neck and across her chest to her breasts. Sasha squeezed her breasts gently. Mel tilted her head back and exhaled slowly. Sasha let out a soft moan as she trailed her hands down to her stomach, around her waist and to Mel's ass. She squeezed it and pulled Mel into her. They gave each other an inebriated stare before kissing each other aggressively on the lips.

At two o'clock in the morning, Sasha was awaken by her cell phone. She felt drained from smoking, drinking and fucking Mel. Mel was beside Sasha knocked out, snoring. Sasha hit the ignore button on her phone and put the phone back on the nightstand. Within seconds it started ringing again.

"We have to answer that," Mel groaned as she shuffled around under the sheets.

Sasha sighed and answered the phone. Another customer called asking to come in for a half an hour. He was already in the area. Sasha and Mel scrambled to tidy the room and air it out so it didn't smell like weed. The client came fifteen minutes after they finished cleaning. He was a young, Italian guy with beautiful, grey eyes. He was short and slim built and dressed in khakis and a white polo shirt. He canvassed Sasha nervously before entering the room.

"Don't be shy baby, I don't bite," Sasha teased as she leaned on to the table. She had a headache and her stomach felt uneasy. She even forgot to put on her heels.

Luckily for her he didn't mention anything to her about it.

"I'm sorry if I come across shy. This is my first time," he explained as he looked around the room. "My name is Frank. Me and my girlfriend just broke up a couple days ago. I am very horny. I need to have sex."

"I'm sorry to hear that," Sasha pouted as she played in Frank's hair. She pressed herself into Frank and allowed him to smell her sweet scent. "I'm sure, we can figure out ways to get her off your mind. But before we begin, can you pay me so we can get that out of the way?"

"No problem," said Frank reaching for his wallet. "One hundred dollars, right?"

He took out a fresh hundred dollar bill and handed it to Sasha. Sasha put the bill in her pouch and got to work. She gave Frank a back-massage as requested before throwing a condom on and riding him like a stallion. As Sasha was fucking, it finally hit her that she had sex with Mel. She could almost taste Mel's nectar in her thoughts as she pictured her having an orgasm. Frank thought the excitement was all about him as he watched Sasha with aroused eyes.

Frank was more than pleased with Sasha when she was finished. He promised to save her number and he gave her an extra thirty dollars. Sasha was pleased with herself for making her first tip and couldn't wait to tell Breezy about her accomplishment.

"You better keep that thirty dollars for yourself," Mel warned Sasha when Sasha told her about it.

"Outside of Breezy's cut, it's all mine anyway," Sasha argued. "If money keeps coming in like that, I'm going to have my shit together in no time."

"On top of what? How much is Breezy's cut?" Mel pushed.

"He doesn't get that much," Sasha snapped.

Sasha hadn't discussed how Breezy's cut would be. It never really crossed her mind until Mel said something. As far as Sasha was concerned she could trust Breezy. Breezy was like Sasha's personal bank without all the paperwork and long line ups.

"That's what you think," Mel continued. "Breezy's cut is the whole thing. You don't get nothing out of it. All you get is fine dining, VIP in the clubs and fancy clothes."

"I never been in the VIP before," said Sasha naively. "You are so sexy, but, you're so fucking stupid, I swear," said Mel as she rolled her eyes.

CHAPTER 9

Sasha spent the winter of 2004 travelling through Ontario with Mel, Breezy and two other white girls that worked for him. Sasha was Breezy's golden ticket. She made the most money out of all his girls, including Mel. Sasha brought in four hundred to eight hundred dollars a day while the other girls were lucky to bring in an even three hundred.

Mel continued to warn Sasha of Breezy's manipulative and sneaky ways, but Sasha ignored her. She was naive and caught up in Breezy's hyperbole of how to live luxurious and do it quickly. Sasha never lived a life outside of housing and crack pipes. Every meal at a nice restaurant was an aristocratic moment for her. When Sasha saw young girls shivering at the bus stop with their bubble jackets and knee high boots while she was sitting passenger side in Breezy's Audi, she felt like she was a queen. When Mel tried to talk to Sasha, she would brush Mel off and give her the cold shoulder. She would accuse Mel of being jealous of all the attention she was getting. Breezy had Sasha wrapped around his finger.

"You deserve it," he said one day while they were shopping at Eaton Centre. Sasha had questioned him on why she was getting all the special treatment. "You work the hardest. You got the drive in you."

Sasha took the bait and ran with it. Feeling special was a rare emotion. Anyone who was willing to acknowledge her in a positive matter was good in her books. As long as Breezy kept feeding her the luxurious life, Sasha had no complaints. The only thing on her mind was how to make more money and keep Breezy happy.

Sasha had her first case of homesickness in August of 2005 just after she turned seventeen. For Sasha's birthday, Breezy took Sasha and Mel out to a club downtown that one of his friends ran. They got a booth, a bottle of champagne and Grey Goose but it wasn't enough to truly make Sasha happy. Sasha missed Theresa and Deedee. She missed her old friends at school and she missed Genesis.

Sasha was so caught up chasing money she hadn't spoke to Genesis in months. Genesis was the only one who had Sasha's new number and the only thing keeping Sasha to her old life. She tried to call Sasha on numerous occasions, but Sasha always rushed her off the phone. Sasha was always too busy to talk and she never knew what to say. Sasha and Genesis had nothing in common any more. Genesis was a star basketball player at her school and already considering colleges to attend after she graduated. Sasha was a prostitute, and the only thing that was on her mind was money. As happy as she was with the lifestyle that came with job, Sasha still felt low and ashamed of doing it. She wasn't ready to tell Genesis or anyone what she was up to.

In December of 2005, Sasha stayed a hotel with Mel in

Brampton. It was their last night after a week stay. There were no calls coming in and the weather was crappy. There was thunder, lightning and even some hail from time to time. Sasha and Mel spent most of the day watching bootleg movies that were in theatres on Breezy's laptop.

Sasha's last client for the night was a young, Portuguese guy. He wanted an outcall with Sasha for an hour. He lived on a horse farm in Caledonia, a twenty minute drive from the hotel. Sasha hated doing outcalls, but it was a requirement if she wanted to continue working with Breezy. Whenever Sasha's nerves got the best of her, Breezy would shake her down and tell her, "outcalls make the most money. The further they are, the more you charge. The faster you make money, the faster you can reach your goals. These tricks out here are willing to pay you three to four hundred dollars an hour just so they can nut twice."

The young man was clean shaven with a young face and ocean blue eyes. Sasha thought he was rather cute and couldn't help but wonder why such a good looking young man like himself was paying for sex.

Sasha gave the man his first twenty minutes of pleasure. Not only was he attractive, he was good fuck too. Sasha enjoyed his long deep strokes as he heaved in her ears and had an orgasm when he called out for her as he climaxed. When they were done, he put on his boxers and grabbed his pack of Du Mauriers off the nightstand. He lay beside Sasha and stared at her with inquisitive eyes. Sasha stared back curiously with questions of her own.

"Can I ask you a personal question?" she asked with an innocent smile.

He nodded as he took a drag of his cigarette.

"How come you don't have your girlfriend?"

The man chuckled, amused at Sasha's choice of conversation. "I don't know. I'm too busy with work and school." He shrugged his shoulders. "I go to Humber full-time in business management and I work part-time with full-time hours at a bar downtown."

Sasha leaned into him wanting to know more. "So, why don't you find a girlfriend at school? You guys can study and have lunch together or something. I'm sure you don't have classes on Saturday and Sunday during the day."

The man gazed in Sasha's bold eyes and chuckled. He took another drag of his cigarette and shook his head to himself.

Sasha raised her eye brows and folded her arms. "What's so funny?"

"Don't take this the wrong way," he laughed. "I never thought I'd be getting relationship advice from a hooker."

Sasha was not at all amused by his comment. She could feel her blood boiling. She took a deep breath trying not to lose it. She tilted her head to the side. "And why not? Do you think because I fuck for a money I don't have a brain?"

"No, I'm saying the opposite." The man took Sasha's hand into his. Sasha was fuming, but something was telling her she needed to hear what he had to say. "You sound like a smart girl, so why are you out here prostituting?"

"Because I don't have a choice," Sasha looked at the floor, feeling embarrassed "I'm here because I have to be."

"Is someone forcing you to be here?" he asked with concerned.

"No!" Sasha responded quickly, grabbing him by his hands. "All I'm saying is right now this is all I have going for me." There was a doleful expression on her face. She looked away and took a deep breath. She collected herself and looked at him with a faint smile.

The man shook his head. "That's a shame. I don't understand why you feel like this is all you have. There is so much waiting out there, but you have to go and get it. It's not going to come to you. There is always a choice, Lisa. Don't throw your life away when you haven't even experienced it yet. You can still go to school, get a career and find a good man who will sweep you off your feet."

"It's not that easy."

Sasha wanted to tell the man everything that led her to prostitution, but there was no point. She knew she couldn't at the cost of putting Breezy in jail and her ending up homeless again. Her client didn't her pay to be a therapist. He was just trying to be nice.

It had been a while since Sasha considered her options. She knew the time would come when she would stop working for Breezy and get on with her life, but she never gave herself an actual date. Neither had Breezy. The young man gave Sasha something to think about.

They spent the rest of their session in the shower and then Sasha texted Breezy that she was finished. Before Sasha left, her client gave her an extra hundred dollars.

"You are better than this, Lisa," he told her as he hugged her at the door. "Save my number. Call me if you ever decide you want to change professions. Maybe I will take you out on a real date."

Sasha thanked him, but they both knew she would never call. She would never seriously date any of her clients, no matter how nice they were. Sasha wanted easy money but she didn't want an easy life. Sasha had no problems working for the lifestyle she wanted. She didn't need anyone to hand it to her. All she could do was appreciate their generosity and kindness to her and keep it moving.

Sasha returned to the hotel relieved that her outcall was successful and with a new perspective on life. She told Mel about their conversation. Mel was not the least bit surprised. She sat on the bed beside Sasha and relit her blunt. She had the I-told-you-so look on her face.

"You know that guy was right," said Mel as she coughed. She held her chest trying to keep herself from coughing again. "I keep telling you that Breezy is only in it for himself. You need to get up out of here and get your ass back in school."

"If Breezy is all for himself, why are you still here?" Sasha argued.

"Because I'm about to be nineteen, I have a grade seven education and I never had a real job. The streets is all I know." Mel had a distraught look on her face. "I've never had a real family. I got taken away from my mother by Children's Aid. I have been living in foster care ever since." She turned to Sasha with sad eyes. "As fucked up as Breezy and Cherry are, they are the closest I have ever had to a family."

Sasha hugged her friend, trying her hardest not to cry. She understood how Mel felt when it came to a sense of belonging. Sasha also craved for the family that she never had, but she wasn't settling as a prostitute to get it.

Sasha placed her hands on her Mel's shoulders. "You have the same opportunities I have. You aren't that much older than me. You can still go back to school and get your diploma or GED. That's what I am going to do."

A faint smile appeared on Sasha's face as she thought about advancing her life. Sasha made a lot of money since she started working for Breezy. Sasha craved for the independence and success, but she was still young minded. She liked the idea of Breezy handling all the responsibilities. She didn't have to worry about her rent, her cell phone bill or groceries. If Breezy didn't have a problem about accommodating her than who was she to complain.

Breezy collected for Sasha and Mel the following morning. He dropped Mel back off to the condo and took off with Sasha. As soon as they were on the highway Sasha took the opportunity to discuss the whereabouts of her money.

Sasha rolled up her window then took a breath and looked at him confidently. "So how much money do you have saved up for me?"

"Where is all of this coming from?" he asked in a monotone voice

"Well, remember when I first came here, you said—"

Breezy cut her off. "I know what I said. Everything would be taken care of."

His tone was austere and caught Sasha completely off guard. She had no intentions of upsetting him. She caught herself playing with her fingers and placed her hands on her lap. "I just want to know how much money you have put away for me. I have been working for you for a long time now and—"

"And what?" Breezy snapped.

She looked at him blankly. She tilted her head at the audacity of his attitude. "How much money do you have for me, Breezy?" Sasha demanded an answer.

"I don't have any money saved up for you," he said emotionlessly with his eyes on the road. His face tightened.

"What the fuck do you mean you don't have my money, Breezy?" Sasha snapped. Fury took over her as her turned to face him. "Where the fuck is my money?"

Breezy looked at her and pointed his index finger in her face. "You need to fix your mother fucking tone when you are talking to me." His eyes grew dark and his breathing became heavy. "I am not no little punk bitch like Dessy. I will fuck your shit up if you ever talk to me like that again."

"Where is my money?"

Sasha was not budging. She fought her tears back and stood her ground.

Breezy took a breath and refocused his attention on driving. "You have no money," he grunted. "Who do you think paid for all the hotels? Who do you think pays for you VIP and bottles of Hennessey? Who do you think is paying the rent for that condo you rest your head at when you are not working? Who do you think pays for you food? All those fancy restaurants, fillet mignon and shit?"

Breezy shook his head at Sasha.

Sasha felt her heart sink into her stomach. She took a deep breath and thought about all the men she had slept with. She cringed at the thought of the smelly, sweaty, drunken men she forced herself to sleep with for a few hundred dollars. There were even a few couples who came to her for a good time.

Breezy's cut is the whole thing. You don't get nothing out of it. All you get is fine dining, VIP in the clubs and fancy clothes.

Mel's words taunted Sasha. She felt foolish for not holding on to her money herself. Sasha made thousands of dollars and never touched any of it.

"You told me you would take care of everything!" Sasha waved her arms around like a mad woman.

"And that is exactly what I did." Breezy laughed evilly. "I invested your money back into you. You think I'm rich, eh? Money grows on trees? If I tallied up all the money I spent on you, you would owe me money right now."

"Owe you money?"

Sasha couldn't believe what she was hearing. She pinched herself on her arm to make sure she wasn't dreaming.

Breezy got off at the next exit and he jumped right back on the highway going the other direction.

Sasha rolled her eyes and sighed. "Where are we going now?"

"Back to the condo. I was going to take you to Cherry's so she could do your hair, but you are acting like a little child. You and Mel can relax for the day."

Sasha rolled her eyes and looked out the window. "I don't want my hair done. Especially if I am paying for it."

"You are about to get on my fucking nerves."

Breezy was trying his best to keep his cool, but he could feel himself about to snap. He squeezed the steering wheel with both hands.

"About I owe you money," Sasha continued. She tapped her chest with her hand. "I know how much money I make eh. The bottles, the weed, it doesn't even come close to half. Nigga you owe me money."

Without hesitation, Breezy slapped Sasha in the face. Sasha touched her face in shock. It was stinging in pain. Tears roll downed her face as she looked at Breezy in fear.

"Say something again!" he shouted almost crashing the car.

Before Sasha could duck, Breezy slapped her in the face again. Sasha jumped in her seat as she screamed in pain. She contemplated jumping out the car, but they were doing over a hundred kilometers on the highway. Sasha would be jumping to her death. If the tumble and roll didn't kill her, the oncoming traffic would.

"No, you are going to be sorry," he threatened.

Sasha trembled as she bit her lips. She wiped the tears from her face with her jacket. Sasha cried silently to herself, finally realizing that she had been played.

When they got back to the condo, Mel was sitting cozy on the couch watching reruns of *Gossip Girl* on Much Music. She got up to greet them, but stopped dead in her tracks when she saw the anger in Breezy's eyes and Sasha holding her face for her life.

Breezy said nothing as he stormed into the room. He slammed things around cursing to himself. Sasha was about to sit down with Mel when Breezy stormed into the living room. He took Sasha by the wrist and dragged towards the bedroom behind him. Sasha pulled away and tried to break free, but Breezy's grip was too strong.

Mel sat in the couch watching in tears with her hands over her mouth. She felt sorry for Sasha but there was nothing she could do. Breezy was a big guy and could easily take on the two teenage girls.

Breezy never shut the door behind him. He didn't care if Mel could hear the commotion. He backhanded Sasha in the face. Sasha shrieked as she fell to the floor.

"You thought you were going to act up like that in the car and I wasn't going to do nothing?" he said as he crouched over her. He cocked his head to the side and stared at Sasha with dark, evil eyes.

"I'm sorry! It won't happen again! I swear! I promise!" she cried.

Sasha turned on her back so that she was facing Breezy. He towered over Sasha making her feel small, and helpless.

"I have been nothing but nice to you and this is how you are going to treat me?" he asked. He placed his hands on his hips.

"I am sorry!"

"No you aren't. You are an ungrateful bitch!" Breezy slapped Sasha again. "I made you. I will break you before I let you run a nigga." Breezy picked her up by hair and looked her dead in the eye. "You are nothing but a crack baby with no education and no sense of direction. You are a worthless without me, Sasha. You would have never survived those streets without me."

Breezy stood over Sasha, panting with rage filled eyes. She lay on the floor under Breezy unsure of what to say or do. He planted a nerve-racking seed into her head and she was watering it. Sasha felt forlorn. She felt used. Her heart went stiff and grew heavy with humiliation. All those men. All those nasty men. Her dream life wasn't such a dream after all. It was more like a nightmare.

Breezy continued slandering Sasha as he beat her. Sasha kicked and screamed, cried and fought for herself, but she was no match for him. When Breezy felt like he got his point across, he spit on Sasha and walked out of the room panting.

Sasha lay on the floor in a pool full of tears holding her swollen face. She was in too much pain to move. Moments later, Sasha heard the front door open and slam shut. Mel came running to the room with a wet rag.

CHAPTER 10

Breezy was no longer Sasha's prince charming. He yelled at her all the time and often put his hands on her. Breezy made it his duty to enforce that he was the boss and Sasha was to do what she was told. Sasha hated the position that she was in but was too afraid to talk back to him.

Sasha felt stupid for not listening to Mel's warning. Even Genesis warned her that Breezy's helping hand was too good to be true. All the signs were there, but Breezy managed to cover them up with notions he knew Sasha would not question. He knew Sasha's weaknesses and strengths and used them to his advantage.

Sasha was in another bad situation and needed to get out of it quick. There was no one she could call. Sasha lost contact with all her friends. Without her old phone it was impossible for her to reach to them. As bad as her situation was, she refused to go back home. Anything was better than living in a crack house. The only option Sasha had was to run away again. This time she would do it more wisely.

With Breezy taking all of her money Sasha had to find away to make more through her clients. It wasn't hard for her to nip the extra cash out of them. Sometimes she didn't even have to ask. They tipped her generously up to a hundred dollars and she pocketed it all without telling anyone—not even Mel.

Outcalls creeped Sasha out, but it was what made her the most money. Sasha charged her clients an extra ten to twenty dollars whenever she could. She maximized her savings by not telling Breezy about all of her inquires for outcalls. Being alone was rare, but whenever Mel was preoccupied, Sasha would take the chance and hop into a taxi to see a client. She would leave and come back before Mel could even realize she was gone. Sasha never discussed with Mel how much she made, so it was easy for her to hand the cash over to Breezy without any suspicion. Nobody knew what was going on except her.

Sasha continued giving Breezy her money as if nothing had changed. She killed him with kindness. Sasha reverted back to the girl he loved and adored—the young, naive girl who used to wake up excited to make money. Sometimes, Sasha found it in herself to fuck him to satisfy his ego. It wasn't long before he was convinced he got his favourite working girl back. Even Mel was convinced Sasha was back under his spell. She didn't tell Mel anything. The more of a fool Sasha could portray, the more likely her plan would see through.

In April of 2006, Sasha was working by the airport in Mississauga with Mel. Four months had passed since she had been saving money to run away. It was hard to wake up and keep a smile on her face every day, especially when Breezy was having one of his temper tantrums. Sasha sucked up her pride and thought about the day she would disappear without anyone ever knowing. It was time for Sasha to set a date. She had more than enough money saved, but she wasn't sure what to do about Mel. Her and Mel had became good friends over the past few months and she felt bad for not saying anything to her. Mel was the only person she had in her corner. Losing her would break Sasha's heart.

Mel lay beside Sasha in the queen size bed. Her eyes were low and she was drifting in out of sleep. Sasha was wide awake watching reruns of *The Boondocks* on Breezy's laptop. Her mind flooded with thoughts of running away. With all her money saved and hidden, she was anxious to rid herself of Breezy.

"If you don't get some rest, you are going to regret it in the morning," Mel warned. She yawned as she stretched, pulling the sheets over her head.

Sasha leaned her back on the headboard. She took a deep breath and turned to Mel collectively. "If you had a chance to dip out of here would you?"

Mel turned over to lay on her side. She pulled the cover under her chin. She spoke with her eyes closed as if she were dreaming. "Girl, I would jump at the chance to get away from Breezy's stupid ass. But you know that shit would take a miracle."

"Why would it have to take a miracle. What would it take for you to leave?" Sasha pressed.

Mel sat up. She looked at Sasha with tired, suspicious eyes. She knew Sasha was up to something. Sasha never spoke of running away. The last time she did was the first time Breezy laid his hands on her three months ago. "What are you up to, Sasha?"

Sasha gave Mel a fortunate grin. "Why do I have to be up something? Seriously Mel, between me and you, what would it take for you to leave Breezy?

Mel thought long and hard to herself. She shrugged. "I

don't know. Money I guess. But even if I were to runaway. Where would I go? And how far am I really going to get without money? Breezy takes all of our money, remember?"

"Not all of it."

Mel opened her eyes and mouth wide. She sat up on the bed. "I know you are not keeping secrets from me, Sasha, especially after everything we have been through together."

Sasha took Mel's hands into hers. She looked into her friend's suspicious eyes. Sasha took a moment and debated on whether or not to tell Mel of her kept secret. Her initial plan was to leave quietly. Sasha wanted to runaway during an outcall with a client. Nobody would have seen it coming. Not even Mel. Sasha wouldn't have been able to survive alone long because she was only seventeen, and she still had five months until her birthday. She needed someone who was the age of majority that could sign for things she couldn't. The only person who she trusted to do that was Mel.

Sasha's biggest concern was what Breezy would do to Mel if she left without her. Breezy would accuse Mel of playing a role in Sasha's escape whether she was a part of it or not. If Breezy was to hurt Mel or even worse kill her, it would be on Sasha's hands. For that reason alone, Sasha couldn't bring herself to leave without her.

"Mel, you have to promise whether you like what I have to say or not, you will not tell anyone." Sasha was serious.

"Who the fuck am I going to tell?" Mel laughed. "Breezy? Cherry? Those other hoes working for his stupid ass?'

Sasha took a deep breath and took Mel by the shoulder, forcing Mel to look into her eyes. "Mel I'm not playing with you."

Mel stopped giggling and quickly pulled herself together. Sasha reached for her purse. She slipped her hand down a hole in the inside pocket of her bag. When she pulled her hand out she was holding a bulk of cash.

"Holy shit!" Mel jumped up and glared at the money in perplexity. "How much money is that?"

"It's about three or four thousand dollars." Sasha took a deep breath of victory. She was proud of herself for being able to save up all that money. If she wasn't coming out of pocket to Breezy she would have had way more.

"Where the hell did you get all this money?" Mel looked at it in bewilderment. There were five's, tens and twenty dollar bills all rolled up in rubber bands. She personally saw Sasha hand over her money to Breezy and she was with Sasha all day, every day.

"I charged the clients extra money here and there and I pocketed some of the outcall money," Sasha explained.

"You don't even like doing outcalls," Mel chuckled. She shook her head still amazed at Sasha's scandal.

Sasha found it hard to believe herself. The truth is every time Sasha went to an outcall, she was scared shitless. Even though all her outcalls were successful, her biggest fear was going to one and never coming back.

Sasha's story was engrossing. Mel felt stupid for not thinking of the idea herself. She had been working for Breezy for a few months longer than Sasha and it did not even dawn on her once to charge her clients extra.

"How long have you been doing this?" she questioned.

"Since the first time that mother fucker whooped my ass," Sasha confessed. The night that Breezy beat Sasha up at the condo antagonized her. It played in her head every day and made her blood boil inside every time she remembered it. "I'm ready to leave, Mel. Are you are coming with me?"

"Coming with you where? And what happens when we run out of money?"

Sasha laughed as if Mel should have already known the answer. "We make the money. We do the exact same thing we are doing, and we use our money to get our shit together. That's what the fuck we do."

Mel scratched her head as she thought long and hard to herself. "Yeah. You have sat with Cherry while she has posted our ads before."

Sasha took a mental note every time she had the opportunity to sit with Cherry while she posted their ads. When Sasha had the computer to herself she found all the sites Cherry posted on and reviewed all of her ads. She checked the process of how to make an ad for each site and was shocked at how easy it was. Surely she could prostitute independently without Cherry and Breezy. The only items Sasha required was a new phone number, new pictures and a credit card.

"But where would we go?" Mel pressed. She had to hear a conscientious plan before she was absolutely sure that she was down to ride.

"Do you still have your ID?" Sasha asked.

"I have my health card and my driver's licence."

"I didn't know you had your licence."

"Had it since I was sixteen. I just never had a car," Mel admitted.

"We can stay in hotels until we find ourselves our own cribs. We can book them out of town, far away, where Breezy won't find us and we can make real money!"

Mel shifted. She loved the idea of running away but she wasn't strong minded like Sasha. Mel was comfortable working with Breezy. She had no short term or long term goals. Mel had no thoughts of returning school and she never longed for a boyfriend. The only thing on her mind was survival and Breezy was taking care of that.

"We can do anything we want," Sasha persisted. She wasn't leaving without her friend. "I'm going to go back to school to get my GED or my high school diploma—whichever comes quicker. Then I am going to college."

Sasha began spending her nights planning her future. She couldn't wait to live freely. Sasha was always money driven, but she hated fucking for money. Sasha knew she was better than that. There was more to life than hotel rooms and horny men.

"I am going to go see my mom. It sounds fucked up but I miss her. I still want her to get better. I want her to change her life around before drugs kills her." Sasha cracked a faint smile. Her chest felt heavy. "To tell you the truth, I just want a normal life."

Tears came to Sasha's eyes as she thought about the broken relationship she had with Theresa. Theresa had been doing drugs since Sasha was a baby and had never been clean. The clean Theresa was a stranger that Sasha was eager to meet. Sasha quickly wiped the tears off her face with her hand. She directed her attention back to Mel. "Don't you dream of something outside of this shit, Mel?"

"I'm not going to lie you. I haven't. This is all I know." Mel admitted as she started at the bed. "I mean, I thought about maybe starting my own business one day. I love kids. I would definitely work with kids."

Mel looked at Sasha with dreamy eyes and chuckled.

"What's so funny?" asked Sasha in confusion.

"I don't know. This industry has a way of fucking with your head. Makes you feel low." Mel smiled sadly. "I would be a stupid ass not to come with you."

"You mean it?" Sasha jumped to her feet excitedly.

"You're going to come with me?"

"Of course I'm going to come with you. Fuck that nigga, Breezy. He doesn't deserve bitches like you and me. He don't deserve any bitches at all. He will get what's coming to him sooner or later."

Sasha pranced around the room. "We don't need him. We can do this shit ourselves. We know how to make money. We are bad bitches! We will survive."

Mel began to charge her clients extra money and gave the rest to Breezy as if nothing had changed. They saved every nickel and dime that they could. Sasha and Mel did everything they could to prepare themselves for the real world. They searched for apartments online whenever they were alone and researched GED and college programs. Sasha and Mel became obsessed with running away. The ability to do anything they could whenever they could was their motivation.

It was very important for Sasha and Mel to reach an amount that they were both satisfied with because once they rid themselves of Breezy, they would have to fend for themselves. They didn't care how long it would take to save enough money. Victory loves preparation. They hated being around Breezy, but they continued to be his puppets for the sake of their plan. They kept all their money well hidden and left no tracks that would give away what they were up to. Breezy was never skeptical of Sasha and Mel. He continued to act manipulative and abusive towards them, while they played the suckers.

By June 2006, Sasha and Mel saved a total of eight thousand dollars They were more anxious than ever to leave.

Sasha prepared a bag to go to a hotel in Vaughan and she felt a sense of triumph and couldn't help but smile to herself. She took a shower as she replayed the plan in her head over and over again. When she was done, she put on a pair of tight jeans and a white, fitted tee that sucked on to her. Sasha and Mel packed only what they needed. They decided it would be best to leave everything else behind. They saved enough money to buy back everything else.

Breezy dropped them off to the hotel at three o'clock in the afternoon. He left his laptop with them and a hundred dollars in case they needed anything. Breezy followed them to the room, smoked a blunt and took a shot of rum before he left. He barely got out the hotel before Sasha and Mel were scrambling around the room trying to get themselves together. Sasha took off the black heels she was wearing and put on a pair of sneakers. Mel did the same. They even switched their lacefronts and put on a pair of sunglasses so they wouldn't be recognized.

"I can't believe we are doing this," said Mel nervously as she put on a leather jacket. "My heart is racing right now."

"I know. Mine too."

Sasha wasn't scared. She refused to let anything stop her from leaving. She was one step away from freedom. She could almost taste it.

"I guess I will call a cab then," said Mel as she took her cell phone out her purse.

Five minutes later, the taxi waiting for them outside. Sasha and Mel looked at each other valiantly as they grabbed their bags.

"Do you think the guy at the front desk will recognize us?" asked Mel nervously.

"Who cares if he does. He doesn't know us and he doesn't know where we are going."

Sasha closed the room door quietly behind her. They

walked towards the lobby in silence. Sasha's heart was pounding profoundly. The adrenaline rushing through her made her want to volt through the doors, but she found it within herself to remain calm. The closer she got to the doors, the clearer her life became. Working for Breezy did Sasha more harm than good. She had no control over her life. She was told how to dress, how to speak, and how to fuck. Sasha was rarely given free time and free time meant going out with everyone as a group. She always had to be accompanied by a babysitter. She lost contact with everyone she cared about including Genesis and now, with the exception of Mel, Sasha was alone.

The taxi ride was tight-lipped. Sasha felt like she was right back where she started—in the back of a taxi on her way to an unknown destination, not knowing what awaited her. She tried not to let her emotions overwhelm her. She reminded herself she was doing the right thing. Breezy was no good for her. He was never going to help Sasha. He sold her a dream and Sasha bought it with ease. Breezy was manipulative, conniving and only in it for himself, just like Mel warned. Sasha smiled at Mel. Mel had been nothing but nice to her from the start. If she had listened to Mel, she could have left a long time ago. Mel looked out the window with a relieved but sad look on her face. Sasha placed her head on Mel's shoulder and held her hand for the remainder of the ride.

On the way to the hotel, Sasha and Mel stopped at a cell phone store. They bought new SIM cards and activated them on a prepaid plan under fake names. They snapped their old SIM cards in half and threw them in the garbage on the way back to the taxi. When they arrived at the hotel, Sasha waited in the taxi while Mel went inside to check-in. Ten minutes later, she came back to the taxi waving two passes in her hands. Sasha paid the taxi driver

$132.

The room was a standard smoking room with two double beds. Sasha dropped her bags on the bed closest to the front door and looked around. Mel peeped her head out the window to make sure there were no signs of Breezy. Once they were convinced they were safe, Sasha and Mel jumped up and down on their beds screaming in joy.

"I can't believe we really did it! And it was so easy too," said Mel as she jumped on Sasha's bed to hug her.

Sasha thought about everything she had been through. "I don't think I have ever been this happy." She sat down on the bed and took a deep flourishing breath. "I wish we had thought of this shit sooner."

Mel sat beside her. She placed her hand on Sasha's shoulder. "Fuck it! Everything happens for a reason. We got away and that's all that matters. Like you said, it's time for us to grow up and start living our lives like normal people do."

"Well not so normal," Sasha reminder her. "We still have to make money,"

Mel sat down on the bed. There was worry on her face. "You think Breezy has figured out that we are missing?"

Sasha looked at the time on her phone. An hour passed since they had left. Breezy wouldn't be checking in on them for the next couple of hours. "I don't want to waste any more time thinking about him. He is in the past so let's keep him there. He has no way to find us and no way to contact us."

Mel sighed in agreement. "You're right. I'm not trying to think about his stupid ass either. He can kick rocks. I hope karma bites him and Cherry in their fucking asses."

Sasha nodded her head. She was happy that Mel was

finally starting to see the bigger picture. "We aren't Breezy's first set of hoes and we won't be his last. He will look thirsty if he tries to come looking for us."

Mel rolled up a fat blunt for her and Sasha. They smoked it in silence as the reality set in that they were finally free.

CHAPTER 11

A week had passed since Sasha and Mel ran away. They spent less time working and more time having fun. They decided that they had more than enough cash to live off and turned to retail therapy to help boost their spirits. Sasha and Mel bought everything from new laptops to new lace fronts. They ate at fancy restaurants and ordered the most expensive meals. They even rented a limo to site see downtown. By the time their spending spree was over and they were ready to check out of their hotel, they had spent over three thousand dollars out of the money they had saved up.

Sasha and Mel booked themselves into another hotel in Scarborough. Mel washed Sasha's hair for her and gave her eight neat. Sasha threw on a twenty inch lace front that was light brown in the front and dark brown in the back and had a side part that covered her right eye. Mel had eighteen inch lace front that had black, Spanish curls that took to her round face. They spent two hours taking pictures in their new lingerie and heels. Sasha edited all the pictures the best she could, being sure to crop out their faces. The faceless pictures made it hard to identify the two young ladies. They were unrecognizable.

Sasha and Mel made an agreement to leave the address of every outcall they went to. It was a good idea for them to be safe rather than sorry, especially with Breezy probably out looking for them.

A couple days later, when Sasha' nerves finally settled, she posted ads for her and Mel on a few escort sites. Within a half an hour, Sasha's phone started ringing.

Sasha was doubtful about her first client. It reminded her of her first time on the job. Sasha saw her share of clients but her palms were warm and still managed to sweat and her heart was racing. Every day they spent at the hotel, Sasha was to push Breezy to the back of her thoughts. As she waited for her client, she couldn't stop picturing Breezy's thirst for money and Cherry's motherly smile as they molded her into the perfect whore.

Guys are willing to pay for that pussy and there is nothing wrong with that. There is no reason why you should feel ashamed of surviving.

A chill ran through Sasha's body as she remembered Breezy's words of wisdom about prostitution. She hated to admit it but he was right. Sex was one of the of oldest trades and Sasha was using it to keep a roof over her head, food in her stomach and clothes and her back. Was it because this time she was doing it on her own will? This time no one was talking her into it.

It wasn't long before Sasha's client called confirming he was in the hotel lobby. Mel took her bags and brought it to the room next door.

"Don't worry," she said as she hugged Sasha. "You will be fine. Remember, if you feel uncomfortable, knock on the wall three times and I will come."

Sasha sighed. She didn't want to be there at all. She

loved the fast money but hated what she had to do to get it. It made her head hurt when she tried to think of another way to survive but it felt like prostitution was inevitable. Selling drugs was not an option. Sasha had been around drugs all of her life. She knew firsthand how it affected its users and their families. Sasha didn't want to be the person supplying another young girls misery. Sadly, Sasha didn't feel getting a job was an option either. Sasha lacked basic skills and didn't even have a resume. A rush of embarrassment ran through her. Without escorting she felt worthless and now Sasha needed more. She needed life, a real one.

There was a soft knock on the door disrupting Sasha from her thoughts. She wiped her sweaty hands on a towel in the bathroom. She checked her makeup, making sure she looked flawless. When she opened the door, a tall, black man was awaiting her.

"Hello Jessica. My name is K'wan," he said in a deep, African accent.

Sasha opened the door wider, allowing him to come inside. She checked the hallway to make sure he wasn't being followed before closing the door. K'wan wasted no time. He took a crisp, hundred dollar bill out of his pocket and handed it to Sasha. She took the money and put it in her pouch. She smiled at him as she took out a condom and placed it on the bed.

K'wan sat on the bed and gave Sasha a creepy smile as he pulled her too him eagerly. His breath smelt like hot garbage and made Sasha feel lightheaded. Her face stiffened as he pulled her on top of him and planted a sloppy kiss on her neck. When he tried to kiss Sasha on her lips, she turned her head away. He sighed in disappointed at Sasha's refusal to kiss him, but she didn't care. The thought of putting her lips on his was enough to make her hurl. Sasha placed his head under her chin to keep him from seeing her discomfort. He obliged and sucked anxiously on her neck. He clumsily unzipped his pants and pulled out his hard piece.

K'wan got up and went to the bathroom. Sasha peaked at the time on the alarm clock. Only fourteen minutes had passed. Sasha smiled to herself as she put her g-string back on. She checked her phone, and she had four missed calls and three new text messages. Before Sasha could review her messages K'wan came out of the bathroom with a pleased grin on his face. He buckled up his pants and buttoned his shirt as he stared at Sasha with eyes of admiration.

"Do you feel better now? She asked as she put her phone back down.

"Actually I do," he said still out of breath.

Sasha got up and walked over to K'wan. His eyes trailed Sasha's body. She held her breath and hugged him tightly, allowing him to smell her sweet aroma once more. K'wan thanked Sasha for the great time and excused himself out of the room.

Sasha sat on her bed feeling triumphant. Now that she had gotten through her first client independently, the rest of them would again be a breeze.

Sasha and Mel continued posting ad's throughout the day. At one o'clock in the morning, a Russian man named Michael called Sasha's phone and asked if she had any friends that could join. Sasha charged him four hundred and fifty dollars for the hour and gave him an arousing description of Mel and he excitedly agreed to come. Sasha and Mel had been working together for over a year and it was their first duo. During the first half of his appointment they smoked, drank and watched Michael do rails as he told stories about his career as a motorcycle racer. Sasha and Mel spent the other half of his session fucking each other while he watched. Michael couldn't release when he was high off cocaine and didn't want to waste their time searching for a nut they were never going to find.

By the end of the night, Sasha and Mel made a total of thirteen hundred dollars, and it made them feel autonomous. With the five thousand dollars that they still had saved, they had a total of eight thousand dollars to split two ways.

Now that money was no longer an issue, Sasha was able to focus her attention on other things. Sasha had given much thought about calling Theresa. She always wondered whether or not Theresa ever thought of her. Was she still on drugs or did Theresa finally clean herself up? The last time Sasha saw her was the night she ran away. Although the night still taunted Sasha, she wanted more than ever to put it all behind her and work on building a relationship with Theresa. She needed her mother's support. Sasha needed to hear Theresa say that she was proud of her, even if it was just once.

Sasha took a taxi to her old building. She had no idea if anyone would be at the house, but she didn't care. If nobody answered, she would wait. When the taxi drove and exited on Jane street off the highway, chills ran through Sasha's body. She gazed at the familiar corner shops and pizza stores along the strip. The street was filled with cars and people competing to play their music the loudest. The smell of fresh BBQ jerk grazed Sasha's nose as they passed a nearby Jamaican restaurant. It smelt good. It smelt like home. They pulled up in front of Sasha's building. There was a group of guys standing by the front door. They stared long and hard at the taxi waiting to see who would step out. Sasha rolled her eye as she paid the taxi man. She hopped out of the taxi and hurried into the building, ignoring the group of guys as they tried desperately to get her attention.

The ride to the sixteenth floor was long and torturing. The elevator stunk of piss and garbage, and there was spilt juice on the floor. The smell of curry on her mother's floor was like a breath of fresh air when she ran out of the elevator. Sasha fumbled with her hands nervously as she approached the door. She hadn't given much thought about what she would say or do once she saw Theresa. She prepared herself for her stank attitude and braced herself for the questions and comments that were sure to come. When she got to the door she could hear music in the background. Sasha knocked twice and stepped back. She took a deep breath as she fixed her shirt and took her hair off her face. Someone came to the door and looked through the peephole.

"Who is it?" said a familiar female voice.

Sasha stepped forward so the person could see her. "It's Sasha. I am Theresa's daughter."

The door quickly unlocked and Deedee came running out the apartment. "Of course I know who you are! Come here and give me a hug!"

Sasha hugged Deedee fighting to hold the back the tears that were forcing their way out.

"Oh my baby. I thought something happened to you. I didn't know if you were alive or dead. I am so happy you are ok." Deedee burst into tears as she held Sasha tightly like a mother who had just found her lost child.

Sasha exhaled slowly and accepted Deedee's motherly welcome. Deedee was more of a mother to Sasha than Theresa ever was. If it wasn't for Deedee, Sasha would have ended up a lot worst. Sasha took a good look at

Deedee and tried her hardest not to frown. Deedee lost a significant amount of weight, and her face was blotchy. Her clothes were too big and were wrinkled. She smelt like cigarettes and smoked crack—a smell that Sasha desperately tried to forget.

Deedee looked at Sasha and smiled. She nodded her head in approval. "Wild Flower, you look good! I see things aren't that bad in the real world. Come inside. Your mom went down to the store to buy a pack of smokes. She will back in a few minutes."

Sasha followed Deedee inside the house. Not much had changed since Sasha ran away except there was a thirty six inch, flat screen television that sat on the floor in the living room. There was garbage everywhere and the double sinks in the kitchen were full of dirty dishes. The house smelt of stale cigarette and crack. Sasha cringed as she stepped further into the apartment. She didn't even think twice about keeping her shoes on.

"What's been going on since I left? How are you?" asked Sasha as she looked around in disappointment. She brushed the crumbs and snack wrappers off the couch with her hands before sitting down beside Deedee.

"Nothing much," Deedee replied casually. "Do you remember that fast girl you used to hang out with?"

"Stephanie?"

"Yeah, that's the one." Deedee lit a cigarette. She took a long, hard drag and exhaled it slowly. "That little girl got pregnant not too long after you left. She has herself a baby daughter now."

"Are you serious?"

Sasha wasn't the least bit surprised. In fact, if she hadn't ran away, she would have been hanging out with Stephanie. There was a good chance she would have ended up pregnant too.

"Mhmm," Deedee continued. She placed her hand on her lap and leaned in to Sasha. "One of them drug dealing boys over by Thretheway and Jane knocked her up. And I heard she might be pregnant again for one of these cornballs that just moved into the building."

"I should go see her and the baby. I haven't seen her since I left. I bet she would be happy to see me," Sasha thought aloud.

Stephanie was Sasha's right hand man after Genesis moved out of the building. They hung out with each other almost every day until Sasha split. Sasha felt she owed her at least phone call to see how she was doing.

"Don't get too close. I heard pregnancy is contagious," Deedee laughed.

Sasha put her hand on Deedee's leg. "And how are you doing, Deedee?"

Deedee broke a half smile. "Well, you know me already. Taking it one day at a time. Just trying to survive like the rest of the folks round here."

"You still on the pipe?" asked Sasha bluntly.

"Girl, you know I love my pipe. Nothing can take me away from it. It's what keeps my spirits up. It makes me feel alive," Deedee did a happy dance, but Sasha was not the least bit amused.

Their conversation was interrupted by a text message from Mel letting Sasha know she was going on a outcall. A text message with a Woodbridge address soon followed. Sasha smirked and put her phone in her back pocket. She sat up straight and redirected her attention to Deedee. Sasha glared at her in disappointment.

"When are you and my mom going to stop this nonsense? Don't you know that these drugs can and will kill you?"

Deedee shrugged her shoulders. She didn't look

concerned. "I'm not strong like those people who go to rehab. They come out clean. They go home to their families and friends and start new lives. I don't have nothing to live for. I have no kids, and I have no man. All I have is me, my one bedroom apartment and my pipe."

Deedee had gone to rehab twice before. The first time she got out of rehab was a typical success story. Deedee was a new found woman excited for the life change. Deedee searched high and low for a job but even McDonalds wouldn't hire her. She was embarrassed at her inability to obtain employment and blamed herself for not pursuing the necessary skills and education to work. Depression quickly overcame Deedee and she started doing drugs again.

The second time that Deedee relapsed, she was seeing a man named Wilson who was madly in love with her. Wilson was a former drug addict and had been clean for three years. Three months into their relationship, he convinced Deedee to readmit herself into rehab. Deedee stayed in the program for eleven weeks. She was released a week earlier because of her good behaviour and cooperation. Deedee left her early release a surprise for Wilson. She thought it would be romantic to pop in on him at home drug free and ready to give her life to him. When Deedee got home, she walked into Wilson fucking a young, blonde girl nearly half her age. Deedee beat the crap out of her and stabbed Wilson in his leg five inches away from his cock. Deedee left the same day and booked herself into a shelter. She got housing in the apartment she lived in five weeks later. Soon as she moved in she started hitting the pipe again.

"You have me to live for," said Sasha. She wiped the tears that trailed down her face. "I love you like a second mom. It really hurts me to see you guys like this."

Before Deedee could respond the front door opened and Theresa came strolling into the house. She dropped her purse on the floor and stood dead in her tracks when she saw Sasha. They looked at each other in an awkward silence. Neither of them knew what to say.

Theresa looked unkempt. Her clothes were filthy and wrinkled. Her hair was dull and looked like it hadn't been combed in days, and her skin was noticeably dry. Yet somehow, despite how rough Theresa looked, she was still beautiful. Sasha could still see the mother in her.

"Hi mom," Sasha nearly choked on her words. She cleared her throat, trying to calm her nerves.

"The angels have heard my prayers!" Theresa cheered as she ran towards Sasha.

Theresa pulled Sasha to her feet and hugged her daughter tightly. Sasha was taken by Theresa's excitement to see her. She was expecting to go head to head with her. Sasha held her mother, ignoring her bad odour and cigarette stench.

Theresa spun Sasha around, checking her out. There was no doubt that Sasha deserved full commendation for her ability to keep strong and out of trouble after she ran away from home.

"You look good, girl. I see the streets been on your side," Theresa complimented.

Sasha sighed as she thought about Breezy. "If you only knew."

"Why are you here?" Theresa asked suspiciously.

Sasha stopped laughing and became serious. Her heart felt like it was trying to pound its way out of her chest. When Sasha arrived there she felt like a strong, independent girl who was ready to take on her mother and her nasty drug habit. Sasha stood in front of Deedee and Theresa and felt like a little girl again. For a split second, Theresa was no longer the junky – she was a concerned parent happy to see her daughter safe and sound. Theresa and Deedee were engrossed as they waited for Sasha to respond.

"I am here because I love you and I miss you," said Sasha.

Theresa looked at Sasha with doubting eyes. She tried many times to call Sasha and not once did Sasha pick up the phone. Theresa knew she wouldn't get the award for perfect mother but she still loved her child. She slandered Sasha's name everyday when she ran away, but the feelings that consumed Theresa were not anger and betrayal. There were feelings of hurt and worry. The fate she called for Sasha was not the fate Theresa wanted for her.

When Sasha ran away it made Theresa realize how fucked up of a mother she was. Her underage teenage daughter was out on the streets and no one knew where she was. If anything had happened to Sasha, Theresa would have been held responsible.

"Then why did you leave? Was it because you fucked him and you were ashamed?" asked Theresa. She didn't want to bring it up, but it was a thought that taunted her every time she thought of Sasha. Theresa had a good feeling of why Sasha left, but she wanted to hear Sasha say it.

Theresa's words were harsh and cut Sasha like a knife. She couldn't believe Theresa's audacity. "I didn't fuck your man. He raped me!"

Deedee jumped out of her seat nearly choking on her breath. It was the first time Deedee heard Sasha's side of the story. "What do you mean he raped you?"

Sasha told Deedee everything that happened between her and Suave from start to finish. She made certain not to leave anything out. She wanted them to know and understand that she wasn't the one to blame. Suave was just a pervert and a pedophile and there was nothing more to it.

"Why didn't you tell me?" asked Deedee. Her eyes began to water. She got up and held Sasha in her arms. "You know I would have done something."

"What would you have done, Deedee?" Theresa snapped. "When I walked into Sasha's room, Suave had her bent over her bed and she looked like she was enjoying it. It didn't look like a girl who was being raped by no man."

Theresa's heart was beating a million miles a minute. She held her chest and sighed as she stared at Sasha long and hard. For a moment Theresa wished Sasha never came back. She wasn't prepared to deal with Sasha.

Theresa huffed as she cut her eyes at Sasha. "You have some nerves coming in here, acting like you're brand new, wearing all those fancy clothes with your hair done up all pretty." She scanned Sasha from head to toe and smirked. "I know you too well Sasha Brown." Theresa sat down beside Deedee who watched the commotion in silence. "So what are you selling? Drugs or pussy?"

Sasha turned away and looked at the floor. She didn't want Theresa to see the truth in her eyes. Theresa was right that Sasha was selling her pussy to make ends meet, but Sasha would never give Theresa the satisfaction of knowing. She looked at Deedee and Theresa. They stared back at her with questioning eyes.

"He came into my room while I was sleeping," she continued. "He woke me up and—"

"And you fucked him!" Theresa cut her off.

She jumped out of the couch to her feet. Tears came to Theresa's eyes. Suave was the only man that Theresa had genuine feelings for since Silva died. She didn't want to believe the only man she was attracted to after Silva was a pedophile.

"Let me find out Suave was touching Sasha," Deedee warned. She glared at Theresa, hoping there was no truth to Sasha's story. Deedee knew as well as Sasha that the drugs had total control over Theresa. She would sell her soul if she could to get high.

Sasha felt irritated. A headache was slowly creeping up on her. She had enough drama for the day. "I'm not here to argue with you, mom. I came because I am at a point in my life where I need you and Deedee more than ever." Sasha smiled at the two woman who hung on to her every word. "I need you to clean yourselves up and act like real women." Sasha took Theresa's dry, rough hands into hers. "Mom you are such a beautiful, smart lady. I am the way I am because of you."

Theresa fluttered as she twirled her knotted hair in her fingers. A faint smile surfaced as she gazed at Sasha.

"It's not too late for you guys to get your acts together." Sasha continued. She took a stack of brochures and pamphlets out of her purse. They all had detailed information about drug rehabilitation centres across the GTA.

"All you have to do is pick one." Sasha split the stack of brochures and pamphlets in half and handed them to Theresa and Deedee. "Don't worry about anything else. I will do all the work. All I need you guys to do is be serious. Be serious about wanting to change your lives."

Deedee barely looked at the brochures. She skimmed through a couple of the them quickly and then placed them beside her on the couch. She looked around the room shamefully, refusing to make eye contact with Sasha. Sasha rolled her eyes at Deedee and watched

Theresa look through a few of the brochures with a great deal of interest.

"These look like they cost a lot of money, Sasha. Working part-time at the mall can't pay for this," Theresa told her doubtfully.

"I can only imagine what my dad would say if he were alive right now," Sasha laughed.

Sasha heard many stories of her notorious father. It was a pity he died when she was so young. Sasha had no memories of Silva before he passed. She couldn't even remember the break-in that lead to his death.

"He would be so disappointed in you," she continued. "I never knew him, but if there was one thing I do know, he never wanted you on drugs."

Sasha directed her attention back to Deedee who was still refusing to look her in the face. Sasha placed her hand on Deedee's shoulder. Deedee turned away as she wiped the tears from her eyes. "Deedee, as I said before, you are like my second mother. I am tired of being embarrassed by you guys. If you don't accept this offer, I am going to walk out of your lives and I promise you, I am never coming back."

Sasha took Deedee and Theresa`s numbers and left them feeling embarrassed and ashamed of themselves. Deep down inside Theresa knew Sasha was right. If Silva were alive, Theresa would have been a long time ago. If she continued doing drugs there was no doubt in her mind that he would have left her and took Sasha with him. Theresa knew she was partly to blame for Sasha turning to the streets and eventually running away. All of Sasha's life, Theresa didn't care what Sasha did as long as she didn't bring police to her door or come home pregnant. Theresa`s only concern was getting high and for the first time in her life, she felt disgusted with herself.

CHAPTER 12

Sasha and Mel devoted their time to making money and apartment hunting. They searched across the Greater Toronto Area from Scarborough to Mississauga. Instead of saving money and getting a cheap apartment, they agreed it would be best to find a condo to both live and work out of. Finding apartments was difficult at first. Neither of them had proof of income, established credit or rent history. Condo owners and apartment rental agents were reluctant to give two, young girls with cash a condo to rent. They sensed bad news.

Finally after three weeks of searching, Sasha and Mel found an ad for a three bedroom condo available for rent for eighteen hundred dollars on Bathurst. Mel called the owner Marcello to make arrangements to view it the next morning. After having a brief conversation with Marcello, Mel was convinced that with the art of seduction they would get the place. The following day, Sasha and Mel dolled themselves up and went to pay Marcello a visit.

Marcello was waiting for them in the lobby. He was a good looking, middle aged, European man dressed in cargos and a button up shirt. He had on Burberry sandals and Versace sunglasses. When he saw the two, young women, he shifted, trying to hide his noticeably perverted grin. His demeanour was far from professional.

"Hello. I'm Marcello," he said in a thick accent as he ran his hands though his greyish-brown hair.

"I'm Mel. You spoke to me on the phone," Mel took his hands into hers. She rubbed it gently before letting it go. "This is my cousin, Sasha. We will be living together if we get the place."

"Hi," Sasha chirped as she licked her lips at Marcello seductively. She reached her hand out to shake his.

"This is going to sound so unprofessional, but you two are very gorgeous women," he smirked. "You're boyfriends must be proud."

Marcello took no shame in undressing Sasha and Mel with his curious grey eyes. He motioned towards the elevators. "Come, I'll show you the place."

The suite was on the nineteenth floor facing downtown Toronto. It was empty and smelled like air freshener and cleaning products. It had brand new stainless steel appliances, hardwood floors and a nice balcony. The master bedroom had an ensuite bathroom and a walk-in closet. The other two bedrooms were medium sized and had decent sized closets. The condo also had a personal washer and dryer and an electrical fireplace.

"This is beautiful, Marcello. How could you rent this out? If I owned it, I would want to live in it," Sasha complimented in awe.

"It is a beautiful place but not the only one I own," Marcello confessed as he looked out the window. The sun was shining into the condo, brightening the living room with its natural light. "I have a couple of condos downtown and a house in Thornhill," he said nonchalantly. He was not fervid about his properties.

"I'm impressed. You're wife is a lucky woman to have a man who works so hard." Mel walked up to Marcello and gently placed her hand on his shoulder.

"I have no wife," he admitted profoundly. "No wife, no girlfriend. Just work."

Marcello was blushing. He looked at Mel with dark, grey eyes. The arousal was so dense in the room it could be sliced with a knife. Mel had him right where she wanted him—horny and vulnerable.

Sasha and Mel got lucky. They didn't know Marcello was weak for beautiful women and paid for sex all the time.

"So, what do you do when you're horny and want to fuck?" asked Sasha proceeding to join Mel into leading him astray.

Marcello was caught off guard by Sasha's blunt attitude, but he was quickly turned on.

"I don't know. I make my own arrangements."

He rubbed his legs together. He hardened at the thought of fucking the two, young ladies. Marcello cleared his throat and took a deep breath as he gazed at Sasha and Mel long and hard.

"Good. Then you could understand why we have thirty six hundred dollars cash in our purses right now," Sasha smirked as she unbuckled his pants.

Sasha and Mel made certain they made an impression on Marcello. He tasted and fucked the both of them all day in every room. He agreed to give them the condo for twelve hundred dollars a month if he could come over and fuck them every once and a while. It was a win-win situation, an offer they couldn't refuse. They gave Marcello twenty four hundred dollars in hundreds and fifties and in return he gave them two sets of keys.

Sasha and Mel left the condo feeling victorious. The condo was not only a home, it was an accomplishment. It made their independence authentic. They set their move-in date to July 1st 2006 and booked themselves into a hotel in Richmond hill.

They spent the next few days devoted to planning the decor and furnishing their new home. Sasha and Mel bought cookware, dishware, pots, pans and linen – anything they could carry back to the condo. They ordered a black leather sectional, a forty two inch plasma television and a bedroom set for the master bedroom. They agreed they would both take the smaller bedrooms and use the master bedroom for work.

Sasha and Mel were an unbeatable team. They were bringing in six hundred to a thousand dollars each a week. Mel took advantage of her new found independency. She never realized how long it had been since she had sole control of her money. Mel went shopping every other day and spent hundreds of dollars at a time. Sasha accompanied Mel on her shopping ventures from time to time. However, she was very strict about her own spending habits. She had other plans for her money.

Fixing up the condo took up a lot of Sasha's time, but she still committed herself to checking up on Theresa. Sasha called everyday and left numerous messages for her, but Theresa never returned any of them. Theresa was deliberately ignoring her but Sasha refused to give up. After Sasha and Mel moved and settled into their new place on July 15th 2006, Sasha jumped in a taxi and headed straight to her old building.

When Sasha arrived, there were three cop cars and an ambulance in the front of the building. Two police officers were controlling the crowd of neighbours that surrounded the building lobby. Those who were not outside stood on their balconies trying to catch a glimpse of the scene. Sasha made the taxi let her out on the street to avoid having to drive through the frantic crowd. As she walked towards her mother's building, a nosey neighbour wasted no time to tell Sasha about the stabbing that had just taken place. A teen boy was stabbed multiple time to the body and was brought to the hospital with fatal wounds.

Sasha stood in front of Theresa's door and took a long deep breath. She could hear Patti Labelle "If Only You Knew" was playing in the background on the radio. Sasha knocked the door three times, but no one answered. She rolled her eyes as she turned the door knob and opened the door. When Sasha stepped inside, she was amazed at how clean the apartment was. The garbage was thrown away, all the tables were wiped down, and the floor was swept. There were dishes in the sink but not nearly as much as when Sasha first visited.

The bathroom door opened and Theresa walked out humming along to Patti Labelle. She nearly had a heart attack when she saw Sasha standing in the living room.

"For fuck sakes, Sasha!" Theresa held on to her chest heaving. "How the hell did you get in here? And why didn't you knock? Are you trying to kill me?"

"I did knock. I knocked three times," Sasha chuckled. She was trying her hardest not to laugh. "That's what you get for leaving the door unlocked all the time."

Theresa gave Sasha a hug. They sat on the couch silently, waiting for someone to say something. Theresa knew why Sasha showed up unexpectedly. She saw everyone of Sasha's calls but she was still embarrassed by the way Sasha confronted her about using drugs.

Sasha got straight to the point, killing the awkward

silence. "So, which rehab centre did you pick? Or would you like me to pick one for you?"

Theresa shifted. She took a deep breath. Theresa had looked at every brochure and pamphlet that Sasha left for her. The more she read, the stronger she felt about giving up drugs for good. It was the fear of the unknown that scared Theresa. She was afraid of who she would become once she was clean. Doing drugs was all she knew. Theresa hadn't worked in over fifteen years and all she had was a high school education. She didn't feel like she could fit into the real world.

Theresa stared at Sasha with weak, brown eyes. Her little girl had grown up so much, and despite Sasha's secrecy about her whereabouts and source of income, Theresa was proud of Sasha's strength and independence.

"You are my only child," said Theresa softly. She took Sasha's hands into hers and looked deep into Sasha's eyes. She could still see her old self in Sasha—sassy, fierce and without a fear in the world. "This is not the life I dreamed for us. The 80's was a crazy decade full of crack and AIDS."

Theresa smiled gracefully as she wandered into her thoughts. She took Sasha's hands into hers. "Robert Da'Silva was a charming man. I was lucky to be his woman. He loved me religiously. He took care of me. He did drugs too, but I didn't have control like he did. The drugs just took over me.

"When he died, I felt like I had died too. I was so weak and vulnerable. Your grandparents basically disowned me and I had dropped all my friends for your father. There was no one. All I had was myself. I should have stayed strong. I let you down."

Sasha's face tightened. She couldn't remember her dad. She couldn't remember the day he died.

"You were about two years old at the time," Theresa recalled sadly. "I'm glad you don't remember that day. It's not a good memory to have, trust me."

Sasha choked on her words. "I just wish I had something to remember him by."

Theresa shook her head in disappointment as she stared at the ground. "Drugs are nothing but the devil in disguise." Her eyes grew dark as she thought about all the hurt she caused to herself and her family. "I want to stop doing drugs. I want to rid myself of these demons."

Sasha hugged Theresa tightly and they burst out crying together. For the first time Sasha felt like she had a mom. They spent the next couple hours laughing and talking like old friends. Sasha told Theresa about Mel and the condo. She didn't tell Theresa how she was making money and Theresa never asked. Sasha knew if there was anyone she could speak to about the game it was Theresa, but she felt like a little girl looking for her mother's approval. She didn't want Theresa to be disappointed about the choices she had made to survive.

Sasha visited Theresa every other day. They researched different rehab centers across Toronto and the surrounding area together. Sasha had unlimited data on her phone so they were able to check out their websites for more information. Theresa didn't care which one she went to as long as it had a bed and food.

By the beginning of August, they finally decided on Greengrass Rehabilitation Center. Greengrass offered a forty-five day residential program to its patients. Their Live Sober program included counseling, group meetings, mentoring and activities geared to transitioning back into a normal life. It also offered access to exercise, volunteer and/or paid work and housekeeping services.

Sasha thought long and hard about the investment she

was about to make. It would cost her $431 a day plus a $750 deposit for Theresa's bed. She was looking at a total of approximately $19,400. Truthfully, Sasha didn't care how much it would cost. She was determined more than ever to get Theresa sober again. Sasha was a natural born hustler and she already had a lump sum of money saved up.

Sasha made the phone call to Greengrass right away. After a twenty minute telephone assessment on Theresa, it was determined that she was eligible to enroll in their Live Sober program. Sasha agreed to put five thousand dollars down, including the deposit for Theresa's bed. The administrator put Sasha on a two-year financing plan that would allow her to pay five hundred dollars a month for twenty four months. Sasha registered Theresa to begin the following Monday.

CHAPTER 13

"Are you ok?" asked Sasha. She took off her Christian Dior sunglasses, put them in her purse and threw her purse on the coffee table.

"I'm really nervous," Theresa admitted. She fiddled with her hands. "What if I don't make it through the whole program?"

"Well, they have a eighty-seven percent success rate. Let's burn that bridge when you get there. If you are as serious as you say you are you shouldn't have a problem." Sasha smiled. She could only imagine how hard it was for Theresa. Sasha appreciated Theresa's effort and was happy to be there to support her. "Just think of how proud I will be. For the first time I can talk about you with my head held high."

"I'm feigning right now, Sasha," Theresa scratched her arm and shook her leg uncontrollably, ignoring Sasha's words of encouragement. "I don't know if I can do this."

Theresa took the initiative not to smoke any crack the night before. It was a long, lonely and laborious night. She hadn't slept. Theresa spent the night curled up in her bed under the blanket, shivering, sweating and talking herself out of taking one last hit.

Theresa looked at Sasha with anxious eyes. She really wanted to buy a ten dollar piece of rock, lay in her couch and get high. She started fidgeting and sweating profoundly. She closed her eyes and took a long, deep breath. She reminded herself this wasn't just for her, it was for Sasha. Theresa didn't want to disappoint her again. She wanted to show Sasha that was she trying, but her colossal craving and nauseating feeling that was slowly creeping up on her was making it unbelievably hard.

"I feel sick to my stomach and I think I have a fever," Theresa complained. "Maybe I should wait it out and go tomorrow."

"There are doctors for all of that. Don't worry, mom. You will be fine."

Sasha hugged Theresa tightly. She hated seeing Theresa in such a sick state, but it was for the best. No one said that the road to recovery didn't have curves and bumps.

Sasha held Theresa in her arms for the whole taxi ride to the rehab center. Neither of them said a word. They were both lost in the thoughts and thinking the same thing—would Theresa complete the program? When they arrived at the rehabilitation center, Sasha went inside to register Theresa. Two nurses, a tall, blonde haired woman and a middle-eastern male accompanied Sasha back to the taxi.

Sasha took a deep breath then tried her best to smile as she opened the car door for Theresa. "Mom, these two nurses are going to escort you inside."

"Hello Mrs Brown. Welcome to Greengrass Rehabilitation Center. My name is Stacey and this is

Noah. We are you intake nurses," said the blonde woman. "We will be working with you for your first couple of days here to make sure everything goes as smooth as possible."

Theresa reached her hand out to shake their hands but suddenly held her stomach and threw up outside of the taxi. The two nurses went to her aid immediately. They wiped her face with a wet cloth and helped her out the taxi. The taxi driver gave her a bottle of water to wash the excess vomit out of her mouth.

"When was the last time you used your pipe, Miss Brown?" asked Noah as he took a pen out of his pocket and started scribbling on his clipboard.

"I hit my pip last night around 10:00 P.M then I smashed it and threw it in the garbage," Theresa answered trying not to gag. "I don't want to do this anymore. I want my pipe!"

Sasha had to keep herself from crying. She had no idea the process would be so dramatic.

"She is just going through withdrawal," explained Noah. "Don't be alarmed. Fever, vomiting, cold sweats and anxiety are all part of the physical withdrawal."

"How long does it last?" asked Sasha. She couldn't bear to see her mother in so much pain. A part of her wanted to throw Theresa back in the cab and bring her home. *She needs this,* Sasha kept saying to herself.

Noah jotted down some more notes as he observed Theresa. "It all depends on your mother. According to her profile she was a strong user. Once we bring her inside we can evaluate her and determine the best method of detoxification."

Theresa let out a loud shriek and tried to make a run for it. Noah dropped his clipboard and ran after her with Stacey. They caught a hold of Theresa as she kicked and screamed for her life, trying to break free. One of her loosely worn sandals went flying in to the air and nearly hit another car.

Sasha stood beside the taxi as the nurses restrained Theresa. Sasha never saw Theresa act out like that before and it frightened her. She nearly choked as she tried not to cry.

"You fucking cunts, let me go!" Theresa yelled. "Fuck you!. Fuck you, Sasha. How could you put me through this shit? Fuck you!" Theresa spit in Noah's face. "Male nurses are fags. Are you a faggot? Do you like it in the ass, cock sucker?"

Stacey was struggling to keep a hold of Theresa's arm. "Should we inject her?"

"No. Restrain her until we bring her inside," Noah instructed as he led her towards the building's entrance.

"Do you know who the fuck I am?" Theresa yelled as she tried to break free. She looked at the building with fear in her eyes. "Do you know who my dead husband is? Let me go or I swear you will not see Christmas. God himself will not be able to save you from my wrath."

Sasha quickly wiped the tears away from her eyes when they passed her. She locked eyes with Theresa, but neither of them said a word to each other. Sasha wiped her face as she watched the two nurses drag Theresa away. She sighed in relief when they were finally inside.

CHAPTER 14

Sasha and Mel spent a week trying to figure out what to do for Sasha's eighteenth birthday. Sasha wanted to keep it simple and go out for dinner. Mel suggested going to the strip club because dinner was an everyday thing. They had been to almost every restaurant in Toronto. It was Sasha's first birthday as an independent, young lady. Her birthday was supposed to be fun and memorable.

They decided on going to a party that was going on downtown. The most respected men and women of the streets were expected to be there. The VIP would be flooded with gangsters, drug dealers and bad bitches popping the clubs most expensive bottles. The dance floor would be swamped with local party heads working up a sweat. The bar would have clusters of people squeezing in to buy drinks.

It was the type of party Sasha and Mel would have rolled to with Breezy. The thought of Breezy made Sasha cringe. She could only pray that he wouldn't be there, and if he was, that they would never cross paths.

Celebrating her eighteenth birthday wasn't the only

thing Sasha was excited about. Sasha had an appointment to see Theresa in a couple days. Spending her birthday night in the VIP with her best friend and seeing her mother clean for the first time were the best gifts Sasha could ask for.

Sasha carefully put her red lipstick on as she hummed the words to R Kelly's "Down low". She fixed her skintight, red dress and twirled in front of the mirror. Mini wasn't the word to describe Sasha's dress. It barely covered her ass. Thankfully, her breasts fit her dress perfectly, and they weren't popping out like two water balloons being squeezed by a five-year-old. She wore a pair of six inch, black heels and accessorized it with a black waist belt and a black Coach clutch. With her eighteen inch, bone-straight lace front and green contacts, Sasha looked like an exotic video vixen.

Sasha strutted into the living room. Mel was sitting on the couch in her red, sleeveless mini dress and black high heels waiting. When she saw Sasha, she pulled a bottle of Hennessey from behind her. "First let me say you look sexy as fuck."

Sasha smiled as she sat down beside Mel. "Thank you."

Mel licked her lips then quickly gained her composure. "You look way too sober right now. We need to take some shots and smoke a blunt before we leave."

Sasha smirked. She pulled out the Ziploc of weed she had in her clutch and took out a piece of bud. She rolled the blunt while Mel grabbed two shot glasses from the kitchen. They took four shots each and practically swallowed the blunt in the process. By the time their taxi was downstairs, Sasha had a serious buzz. She was already tripping over her feet and slurring her words.

When they arrived at the club, it was packed outside.

Male and female high rollers stood beside their customized cars and motorcycles parked along the street. Girls, wearing nothing but pieces of fabric, walked up and down the sidewalk, waiting to be noticed. Sasha frowned at how desperate those girls looked as her and Mel hopped out the taxi. She scanned the crowd for Breezy, but he was nowhere in sight. Sasha let out a sigh of relief.

The two girls strolled down the sidewalk confidently. They passed a long line of thirsty men and envious ladies who rolled their eyes and whispered to one another as they passed them. Sasha and Mel didn't pay them no mind. There was a reason why those girls were in line and they weren't.

Andre, one of the bouncers, saw Sasha and Mel and smirked. Andre was a tall, good looking man who was affiliated with Breezy. He heard about the stunt the girls pulled, but luckily for Sasha and Mel, he didn't care much for Breezy. Andre had to hand it to the two girls. They looked better than ever. Breezy got caught slipping.

Sasha pulled down her dress. She could feel it riding up her ass as she walked towards the club entrance. When she saw Andre she tried her hardest not to frown. *Just be cool,* she thought to herself as she faked a big smile. "How are you doing, hun?"

Mel nodded and smiled unpleasantly at Andre. She had nothing to say to him. She didn't like him because he was cool with Breezy. That meant he couldn't be trusted.

"Sexy ladies," he said as he checked them out. He licked his lips and rubbed his hands together. "Looking good as usual. Where is that nigga Breezy at?"

"Who knows," Sasha replied nonchalantly.

"Ya'll don't fuck with him anymore?" he pressed for confirmation.

"Nah," Sasha retorted as she rolled her eyes

impatiently.

The club was packed inside considering it was just after midnight. The music was so loud, Sasha couldn't hear herself think. She bobbed her head to Ne-yo's "So Sick" as she looked around the club in search for Breezy.

Sasha and Mel went straight to the bar and ordered themselves a shot of tequila and a bottle of Hennessey before they headed to the VIP section. They could feel the frowns and nasty glares in the crowd as a young, blonde bartender brought the two ladies their bottle in a bucket of ice accompanied by orange juice and glasses.

It wasn't long before they were completely drunk. They laughed and danced together feeling fortunate and care-free. Mel raised her drink as she swung her hips from side to side.

"Cheers," she slurred as she motioned to Sasha to pick up her drink.

"What are we cheering to?" Sasha yelled over the music. The DJ had switched the mood and was now playing reggae. She placed her hand on Mel's shoulder, struggling not to fall on her face.

Mel waved her drink around and spilt it on the floor as she spoke. "To your mother fucking birthday, to your mom being in rehab and to me and you getting this money."

"I'll drink to that," said Sasha as she touched glasses with her friend.

They chugged their drinks down in one shot and poured themselves another. Sasha was having the time of her life. She couldn't have asked for a better celebration. In good time, Sasha was sweating out her dress and their bottle of Hennessey was almost done.

Sasha tapped Mel on the shoulder. "I have to use the bathroom or I am going to have an accident. Are you coming?"

"Of course I am coming. We stick together," Mel slurred as she followed Sasha out of the VIP.

They walked through the steep crowd to a narrow hall that lead to the bathroom. Sasha's heart skipped a beat when she saw a tall, dark skin man walk around the corner towards them. When he finally noticed Sasha grinned at her and she blushed.

Mel nudged Sasha. "He is sexy. You better talk to him."

Before Sasha could answer, Mel stopped dead in her tracks and folded her arms. She gave the man a thank-me-later smile.

The man nodded as he stood in front of Sasha. He gazed into Sasha's brown eyes and smiled. "How is your night going, shorty?"

His voice was deep and tranquilizing. He had perfect, straight, white teeth and dimples that made Sasha's love mountain jump.

"It's good. It's my birthday so we are celebrating," Sasha's voice squeaked. She cleared her throat. "Trying to get wasted."

He laughed. "Happy birthday—"

"Sasha," she cut him off. She looked long and hard into his hazel eyes. They were hypnotizing.

He reached out his hand. "Happy Birthday, Sasha. I'm Jahkai."

Sasha took his hand into hers expecting a handshake, but he pulled her into his arms to give her a hug. Jahkai was a lot taller than Sasha. Even in her six inch heels she was just under his chin. She allowed him to place his hands on her waist. She wrapped her arms around his neck as if he were her man and hugged him tightly, snuggling her face into his neck. His cologne was strong and teasing. Sasha stepped out of his arms. His heavy breathing matched hers.

"I need to tell more people it's my birthday," she panted as she looked towards Mel.

"I'm going to use the bathroom and leave ya'll to talk." Mel grinned as she eyed the both of them excitedly. "Come to the bathroom when you are done or I will meet you back here."

Jahkai stared at Sasha with adoring eyes that made Sasha flutter nervously. She looked around to see if anyone was waiting for him. "Who are you here with?"

"Some of my boys. We are also here celebrating a birthday. You know how it goes." He looked at Sasha collectively and grinned. "You know you're fine as hell, right?"

"I don't want to sound cocky, but I have been told." Sasha twirled her hair with her fingers, trying not to blush.

Jahkai laughed. "You aren't being cocky. It's the truth."

"Thank you."

Jahkai reached for his pocket and pulled out his cell phone. "I'm going to take your number so you can do your thing with your girl. You can come find me later if you want."

Sasha gave Jahkai a dreamy smile as she gave him her number. She hugged him and nearly melted in his arms again. "What kind of Cologne is that?" she asked before letting him go.

"Versace," he whispered into her ear.

Sasha closed her eyes and exhaled. She wanted to stay in his arms forever. She kissed him on the cheek and glided to the bathroom grinning from ear to ear.

Mel was leaning over the bathroom counter fixing her

makeup. She looked at her blushing friend through the mirror. "How did it go?"

Sasha blushed as she stared at herself in the mirror. She was glowing from head to toe.

"I will take that as it went great," Mel laughed playfully as she eyed Sasha suspiciously. "Don't fall in love on me, Sasha. You look like you are ready to jump off a cliff and let that nigga catch you at the bottom."

"We exchanged numbers. He said that we could come hang with him if we wanted to."

"You know I got your back, Sasha. But if I don't find myself a boy toy in his little posse, don't expect me to be your wingman for the rest of the night," said Mel.

They parted the crowd and hit the dance floor. Sasha wined her body seductively like a snake. She could feel everyone's eyes on her as she twirled around and moved her waist to the beat of "Déjà-vu" by Beyonce. A young man squeezed his way through the dance floor to dance with her. Sasha looked around for Mel. She spotted her dancing with a young, light-skin guy with long cornrows. Mel waved to Sasha and smiled. She looked at the guy Sasha was dancing with and nodded her head in approval. Sasha was too drunk to care. Even if he looked like Shrek, Sasha would have given him his one dance. It was her eighteenth birthday and she was feeling good.

She looked back at the skinny, caramel guy she was dancing with. He grinned at Sasha and placed his arms around her waist, pressing himself onto her. Sasha grinded on him slowly. He breathed heavily in Sasha's ear as he danced with her. Sasha bent over and placed her hands on her knees. She was working up a sweat when Jahkai popped up out of nowhere and interrupted their dance.

"Excuse me!" he said sternly.

Sasha jumped when she heard Jahkai's voice. Her heart was pounding. She stood straight and pulled her dress down. She wasn't sure why, but a flush of guilt swept through her. Her eyes met Jahkai's alert, hazel eyes. She smirked at him, waiting to see what he was about to say next.

Jahkai and the caramel guy caught eyes. They glared at each other. The guy nodded as he took two step backs. He didn't even say goodbye to Sasha. He vanished into the crowd like a ghost.

"So, we are interrupting each other's dances now?" Sasha slurred trying to sound pissed. She rolled her eyes, but she had butterflies in her stomach.

"I don't like to share."

"I didn't know that I was yours to share," Sasha challenged. She tilted her head to the side and placed her hand on her hip.

Jahkai gave Sasha a handsome, collective smile. "You're too cute for your own good. Did you know that?"

He pulled Sasha into him and she started moving her hips slowly with his. They danced to "Smack That" by Akon. Sasha leaned her head into Jahkai's chest and pushed her butt into his groin. He kissed her on her neck as he ran his hands down her side. Sasha exhaled slowly. She was enjoying every moment.

When the song was over, Mel shooed the sweaty guy she was dancing with away. She rolled her eyes and shook her head, directing her attention to Jahkai. "I know you just seen that fat fuck I was dancing with and I know you have some sexy friends."

"Yeah, my boys are in the VIP," he laughed. He shook his head slowly. "I don't know about them being sexy though. That's all on you."

"Well, show me where they are," Mel pushed. "You're going to have to set me up if you want me to put in a good word for you to my home girl."

Sasha and Mel followed Jahkai to his booth where three of his friends sat with full cups in their hands. One of them was short, fat, and dark skinned. He had a scar under his left eye. He was too busy texting on his cell phone to notice the two girls. Another guy was tall, thick and caramel. He was a pretty boy. The third guy was also dark skin. He was tall and thick like a football player. He nodded to them politely and sipped on his drink.

"Jay, you always get the bad bitches," the caramel friend teased. He smirked as he checked the girls out thoroughly.

"I'd like you to meet my thirsty ass friends." Jahkai joked. He kicked his foot in his friends direction. "This pretty motherfucker is Jason. He is my older brother."

Mel smiled seductively and stepped forward "I'm Mel."

Jason nodded his head and motioned her to sit down beside him.

Jahkai took Sasha by the hand and pulled her to sit with him at the end of the booth. He poured two glasses of Grey Goose and cranberry juice.

"So you always get the bad bitches, huh?" Sasha questioned him.

Jahkai chuckled and shook his head. "It's not even like that." He put his drink down and looked Sasha in the eye. "I just know what I want."

Sasha took a gulp of her drink nearly finishing it. She raised an eyebrow. She was unmoved by Jahkai's slick talk. "And you want me?"

"Maybe."

"Maybe is not an answer."

"Maybe is my answer."

Sasha bit her lip to keep herself from grinning. Jahkai came across as a smart ass but ironically, it turned Sasha on. He spoke with confidence. He cut the bullshit and went straight to the point. Sasha glanced at Mel and Mel looked like she was in her own world with Jason. Sasha smiled. She was happy to see Mel having fun and not worrying about money.

"So, what's does a guy like me have to do to see you again?" Jahkai asked.

Sasha directed her attention back to Jahkai. She looked at him with curious eyes as she sipped on her drink. She exhaled slowly as the Grey Goose burned the back of her throat on the way down. "What do you do for a living, Jahkai?"

"What difference does it make?" he looked at her unwelcomingly.

Sasha didn't really care what he did for a living as long as he wasn't a pimp. She didn't want anything to do with them. She thought about Breezy and Cherry's relationship. She couldn't understand why Cherry as a woman would want to manipulate and con young girls in to prostituting. What if her son was a daughter? Would she still have the same views about it then?

Sasha snickered to herself and took another sip of her drink. "It makes a big difference."

"I make money." Jahkai's eyes met Sasha's. "How are you paying for you bottles, Sasha?"

He picked up his cup and gulped the last of his drink. He gave Sasha the same look she had just given him only his hazel eyes were dark and daring and made Sasha feel slightly timid.

"I make money too," she replied nonchalantly.

Jahkai chuckled and poured himself another drink. "Would you like another one too?"

Sasha place her glass beside his. Jahkai poured half the cup with Grey Goose and a little bit of cranberry juice. He slid the glass to Sasha.

Sasha raised her glass to Jahkai's. "To my mother fucking birthday!" She took another sip an made a face as she forced the Vodka down. "Are you trying to get me drunk, Jahkai?"

"I'm not trying to make you do anything you don't want to do, shorty," he smirked.

Sasha laughed and patted her thighs. "I'm not coming home with you, Jahkai. It's going to take a lot more than a VIP booth and some vodka to get up in this."

"You think I'm trying to fuck you? You must have mistaken me for one of them niggas." Jahkai pointed to his two friends who looked desperate as they scanned the crowd of half naked women. "Bitches aren't a problem. I thought we established this already."

Sasha raised her left eye brow at Jahkai. She wasn't sure if he was joking or being serious, but she didn't care. Regardless of the reason, she was upset by his statement. As offended as she was, when she glared at Jahkai with angry, brown eyes the butterflies in her stomach still managed to do a drunken Tango. That pissed her off even more.

"If bitches aren't a problem, what the fuck do you want with me? Do you want to add me to your list of bitches?" she hissed.

Somehow the liquor was able to surpass Sasha's rationality and took over her whole train of thought. She stood up and grabbed her clutch off the chair.

"Man, you're fucking tripping!" Jahkai fanned her off and shook his head.

"You're the one that's tripping," Sasha twisted her neck and glared at him. "I'm not one of your bitches. Get it straight."

Mel heard the commotion and snapped out of Jason's love spell. She looked at Sasha who was towering over Jahkai. "Sasha what's wrong?"

"I'm ready to go." Sasha didn't want to leave but the liquor was now working fulltime. She couldn't think straight. She wanted to be out of Jahkai's presence and home seemed like the best choice.

"Are you serious?" Mel pouted as she got up reluctantly. She wanted to stay with Jason. She was hoping they would all leave together.

"Yes, I'm serious." Sasha slurred. She tripped over her foot and grabbed the table to keep from falling. "I am ready to go home."

"Well, you heard the girl," said Mel, directing her attention to Jason. "I guess I will call you tomorrow."

"No doubt, shorty. You got my number. Hit a nigga up." Jason pulled Mel to him and hugged her.

Sasha watched with envy as Mel sank into Jason's arms. She wanted to leap into Jahkai's arms. She rolled her drunken eyes and turned towards the entrance of the VIP.

"So, you aren't going to say goodbye?" asked Jahkai as he cut his eye at her.

Sasha gave him a devilish grin but didn't respond. Jahkai watched in disappointment as she left club.

CHAPTER 15

Sasha woke up with a nasty hangover. Her head was pounding and her stomach was on the verge of coming out of her mouth. She rolled onto her back and looked up at the ceiling trying to recall the night before. She smiled when she remembered meeting Jahkai. She remembered the smell of his cologne when he hugged her by the bathroom. Sasha frowned when she thought about their pointless argument. It was another example of liquor at its finest.

Sasha reached for her cell phone to check the time. It was just after nine in the morning. She checked her text messages and was surprised see a new message from Jahkai. After her drunken fit, Sasha was sure Jahkai didn't want anything to do with her. She took a deep breath as she read it slowly:

Hey shorty! It's Jahkai. I hope you had a good time last night. If you don't think I'm an asshole anymore, give me a call. I would like to take you out for lunch and talk to you on a more sober note.

The butterflies in Sasha's stomach started doing

acrobats. She sighed in relief as she reread the text message. She was thankful she never made herself look like a complete idiot. Even though she was drunk, she still felt offended by what he said. She didn`t want him to compare her to the local hoes trying to get a piece. She genuinely liked him and wanted to get to know him better. She reread his text message a couple more times then finally figures out what to reply:

Jahkai, u r a smart ass not an asshole and that is why I had my temper tantrum. But I'm glad that u aren't a push over. I'm starving and will take u up on that lunch offer today if u r free.

Instantaneously, he text her back:

Hahaha! A smart ass I am. I'm free at 1:30. I will call you then to get your address. What's your major intersection?

Sasha couldn't keep herself from smiling as she texted back:

K. 1:30 is fine with me. I live at Bathurst and Sheppard. Call me when you are in the area.

Sasha jumped out of bed and headed for the bathroom to brush her teeth with her phone in her hand. Just as she had hoped for, Jahkai texted her back:

Ok. I will do that. You know you are sexy as hell right? I can't wait to see you again. I think I may be tempted to kiss you.

Sasha placed her phone on the counter. She looked at herself in the mirror and smiled. The feeling of genuine happiness was blissful. Her curiosity about Jahkai was at its peak. She was fond of the hazel eyed man that took her breath away on her birthday. Sasha washed her face and brushed her teeth and headed to the living room. Mel was on the couch watching *Scooby Doo*.

"How are you feeling?" Mel asked as she took a sip of

her tea. "Like horse shit," Sasha whined as she flopped herself on the couch beside Mel.

Mel put her cup down. She looked at Sasha with churlish eyes. She was still upset about leaving the club on a bad note. There was attitude in her voice when she spoke. "Did you talk to that dude from the club?"

"Yes. He is coming to pick me up at 1:30." Sasha bit her lip to keep from smiling.

Mel raised her eyebrows at Sasha. "After that shit you pulled last night, this nigga still trying to talk to you? Where are you guys going anyway?"

Sasha shrugged her shoulders. "I don't know. We'll probably just go eat and talk. Did you talk to his brother?"

Mel softened at the mention of Jason's name. She placed her hand on her cheek and she smiled as she lost her self to her thoughts. "I really like him, Sasha."

"I can tell. Look at you. You're glowing."

"I'll be seeing him later on tonight."

Sasha tilted her head to the side. "Oh?"

"Yea, I'm going to go to his place and—"

"You guys are going to fuck?"

"And you have no intentions of fucking Jahmoi or whatever his name is?" Mel giggled.

Sasha shook her head in disbelief but didn't say anything. Mel was grown. If she wanted to sleep with Jason, Sasha wasn't going to stop her.

1:30 came too quickly. Sasha barely had enough time to get over her hangover much less get herself together. She threw on a long, white, button up shirt, a pair of black leggings, gold and black Versace shades, and a pair of six-inch, black, Guess heels. She completed her outfit with a black and gold Guess city bag that matched her shoes.

"Mel, I'm leaving now. I will call you later," yelled Sasha as she headed for the door.

Mel jumped off the couch and flew into the kitchen to see Sasha off. She smiled in approval as she checked out Sasha's outfit. "You look good. Have fun and don't forget to wrap it up."

Sasha threw her house keys in her purse and smirked. "Unlike you, I don't give it up on the first date."

"Unless they are paying," Mel joked.

Sasha waited anxiously for Jahkai in the condo lobby. She played with her sweaty hands as she scanned every car that pulled up to the front. She thought about what she would say to him. She wondered if they would still like each other now that they were both sober and attentive. Everyone seems charming in the eyes of a drunk.

After ten minutes of waiting, a shiny, black Mercedes with chrome rims pulled up to the front. The passenger window went down and Jahkai appeared in the driver's seat. Sasha's heart skipped a beat when his eyes met hers. He smiled at her as he motioned for her to come. Sasha waited for him to come around and open the door. He hesitated for a second but then came out, strolled around the front of the car and opened the door for her.

"A man with taste. I like that," said Sasha as she hopped into the car. It smelt like fresh pine and leather.

"I can say the same about yourself." Jahkai looked at the condo with commendation as he pulled out. "I like the stone layout they got going in the front. It makes the place look classy. How long have you been living here?"

"Me and my friend you seen me with last night live here. We moved in a couple months ago."

"Two bedrooms?"

"Three."

"How much are you guys paying for your spot? I know it costs at least sixteen hundred," Jahkai pressed.

"We pay twelve hundred. That's only because we know the owner. He is a friend of ours."

Jahkai smirked. "Yeah. I bet."

Sasha chuckled as she checked him out from head to toe. He had on a pair of khakis and a white and gold golf shirt. His watch, bracelet and chain were thick, heavy gold.

"Looks like you guys are doing well for yourself," he continued. "What do you do again?"

Sasha looked out the window. She wondered if he could see the shame in her face. "I make good money."

Jahkai traced his hand up Sasha's lap. Sasha fluttered. Her heart started beating like it was trying to escape out of her chest. She exhaled slowly, trying to keep her composure.

He drove to the outskirts of the city and parked in front of place called Don Valentinos. They walked in and were greeted by a waiter dressed in all black. The restaurant was dimly lit and had three levels. The lower level had a fireplace.

"Have you eaten here before?" asked Jahkai. He opened his menu and scanned through it quickly.

"Plenty of times."

"So you know what you want already?"

"What are you having?" Sasha could tell by his clothes and car that he wasn't cheap but she didn't want to come off as a gold-digger.

"I'm having a steak with mash potatoes."

"Then I will have same."

Sasha took their menu and rested it on the side of the table. Jahkai leaned back and gazed at Sasha with curious eyes. Sasha squirmed in her seat. His bold stare made her feel timid.

"What?" she said softly trying not to blush.

"I like you," he said in a serious tone. "I don't know why, but I do."

"Lucky me. A man who knows what he wants."

Jahkai leaned towards her. He placed his hands on the table. "So tell me about yourself."

Sasha sighed. She didn't know what she could say that wouldn't turn him off.

"I was born in Scarborough, and I grew up in Jane and Finch. I am a lover, a fighter and a survivor. How about yourself?"

"I was born and raised in Regent Park. I still live downtown but in a nice condo on Yonge street." Jahkai kept his eyes fixed on Sasha. "What about your parents? Are they dead? In jail? Alive? Do you speak to them?"

Before Sasha could answer, a young brunette dressed in a black shirt that read "stop staring at my breasts" in small writing and a black, mini skirt came to their table.

"Hello. My name is Jessica and I will be your server this afternoon!" The young lady scribbled her name on the brown paper cloth that was spread over the table. "Have you decided what you will be ordering today?"

"We will take the pan bread with cheese to start." Jahkai looked at Sasha. She nodded her head in agreement. "We will both be having the New York Sirloin steak. Make them both well done please. I want mash potatoes with mine."

The server turned to Sasha "And what would you like?"

Sasha nodded her head. "I will have the same, thanks."

"Would you like any drinks with your meals?"

"I will have a rum and coke," said Jahkai

Sasha wanted to have a rum and coke but she didn't have her fake ID, and she didn't want to risk the embarrassment of having to tell the server she was underage. "Ice tea is fine for me."

The server scribbled their order on her notepad and then rushed off, leaving them to their privacy.

"How old are you?" Jahkai asked if he was reading her mind. "And don't lie to me either."

"I'm eighteen."

Jahkai smirked. "Eighteen, huh?"

The server came back with their drinks just in the nick of time. Sasha took a deep breath. Jahkai didn't seem disturbed about her age. He didn't show any emotion at all.

"How old are you, Jahkai?" asked Sasha finally breaking the awkward silence.

"I'm twenty-two."

"Twenty-two with your own condo and a Mercedes. And you talk about me being well off." Sasha drank her ice-tea as she tried to read Jahkai. "What did you say you do again?

Jahkai leaned back into his seat. He gave Sasha an expressionless glare. "I make money. That's all that matters."

They were interrupted by Sasha's phone. It was a number she didn't know. She knew it was a call from a potential customer. Sasha wanted to kick herself for not putting her phone on silent. She knew she had to answer it. She didn't want to raise any suspicion about who was calling.

"Hello...I won't be available until later this evening...ok...I will talk to you soon." Sasha hung up the phone and exhaled. She took another drink of her ice-tea. "And I make money too. That's all that matters."

Jahkai looked at Sasha blankly. Sasha smiled and battered her eyes at him. Jahkai laughed. "What you know about these streets, Sasha?"

"My daddy was a drug dealer and my mom is a junky." Sasha responded. "I know what I need to know."

Jahkai frowned. "I'm sorry. I didn't mean to offend you. I just can't believe a pretty girl like you is out here hustling."

Sasha's voice cracked as she spoke. "You do what you have to do to survive."

Sasha wished she had memories of her father. He died long before she could develop any. Sasha never had any good times with Theresa worth remembering. She was always high and fighting with Sasha. She never took Sasha's side on anything, no matter how much Sasha pleaded. Sasha always got her comfort and support from the streets. She was a product of her environment.

"Both my parents were drug dealers," said Jahkai as he drifted into his own thoughts. "My dad got deported back to Jamaica when I was thirteen and my mom was murdered when I was seventeen."

"Do you still talk to your dad?"

Jahkai grinned like a son proud of his father. "Yeah. We keep in touch. He taught me everything I know now about survive in this fucking jungle."

The waiter came back with their food. It looked and smelled delicious. The mashed potatoes were fluffy and the steaks looked juicy and tender. Sasha's stomach began to talk to her. She hadn't eaten since the night before.

"Does your mom still do drugs?" he asked as he took a bite into his food.

Sasha took a bite of her steak and moaned to herself. It melted in her mouth. "She's actually in rehab right now. I'm going to go and see her tomorrow."

"That's a good look right there."

"It's costing me an arm and a leg that I don't have. If it will get her back to normal, whatever that is, I will find a way to make it happen."

Sasha sighed as she thought about the nineteen thousand dollars she was about to fork up to Greengrass. Sasha had never seen that much money before in her life. She knew it wasn't impossible to make, but she never imagined she would be spending it on rehab. The five thousand dollars that she had to put down was almost everything she had saved, and it still wasn't enough.

They enjoyed the rest of their lunch and they talked about everything from dumpsters to the illuminati. Jahkai couldn't stop telling Sasha how beautiful she was. The more he made her laugh and smile, the more Sasha fell for him. Drug dealer or not, he was definitely a keeper.

They left at 4:30 P.M. She was upset their date had to end so soon, but Jahkai had some business to attend. Sasha never realized how much fun she was having until she was home

"Thanks for lunch. I'm stuffed," said Sasha as she rubbed her belly.

"I'm full too. I'm about to go do some stuff then go home and take a power nap,"

Sasha looked at him in a trance. There were so many things that were intriguing about him. She reached over to give him a hug and he surprised her with a kiss on the cheek. She look at him with dreamy eyes as their lips met. Sasha opened her mouth and allowed his tongue to enter. Sasha placed her hands around his neck.

When they finally parted, Jahkai was breathing heavy. He shifted in his seat, trying to fix his erection. Sasha licked her lips and blushed. She was taken by his kiss. Not even Dessy kissed her like that.

"Call me," she whispered as she stepped out the car.

"You know I will."

He waited until she was through the main doors before he pulled off.

Sasha changed from her black, silk rob to a red, baby-doll lingerie set. She put on a pair of black heels and clear chopstick on her lips. Her client arrive while she was fixing her hair. Sasha welcomed the middle aged, white man inside. He looked at Sasha with praise as he reached into his back pocket. He paid her one hundred and twenty dollars for the half hour. Sasha placed the money on the kitchen island and they went into the master bedroom.

"This is a fine place you have here, Lisa." he commented as he looked around the bedroom.

Sasha closed the door behind him and walked over to the bed. "Anything to make you feel right at home."

The man made a clumsy attempt to take off both of their clothes. He laid Sasha on her back and put a condom on. He pushed himself in her and grunted as he found his groove. Sasha wrapped her arms and legs around his body. He flipped her on her back and pushed her face down in the bed, pulling her ass up in the air. He put one hand on her waist as he slipped himself back inside her. Five minutes later, he pulled himself out, ripped the condom off and groaned in pleasure as he spit out a large load over Sasha's lower back. Sasha squirmed in discomfort as he heaved his way to the bathroom. She picked up the towel on the night stand, trying not to let the liquid on her back drip onto her sheets. She wiped the thick, sticky liquid off her back and threw the towel on the floor beside the bed in disgust.

The man came out of the bathroom looking refreshed.

He smiled at Sasha as he put on his clothes. "Thank you, Lisa. I will call you again sometime."

Sasha threw on her robe and walked him to the front door. Sasha gave him a loose hug. "You have my number. You can call me anytime. I look forward to seeing you again."

She took the money off the kitchen island and brought it with her to her room. She threw it on her bed then headed to the bathroom to take a long, hot, shower. Sasha felt drained. She could barely keep her eyes open to lotion herself when she was done. As she curled into bed, her cell phone vibrated on the nightstand. Sasha made up her mind she was done working for the night and picked up her phone to see who was calling. She exhaled in relief and smiled when she saw Jahkai' name:

Hope you had a good time today baby. Damn your lips are soft. They had me thinking some dirty thoughts. How are you getting to the rehab centre tomorrow?

Sasha fluttered. She licked her lips as she thought about submitting herself to him as he bent her over her queen sized bed and fucked her from behind. She grinned devilishly as she replied:

Hey papi. I had an amazing time with you today. I loved kissing you. I hope you know those lips are MINE. I'm glad I wasn't the only one thinking nasty. I'm taking a taxi.

He replied back:

Nah, fuck that. I'll drive you. What time do you have to be there for?

Sasha was flattered that he offered to take her, but she didn't think it was a good idea. Seeing her mother for the first time was a personal matter, and she didn't want to let him into her life like that. She had no idea what to expect and she didn't want Jahkai to witness any vulnerable

151

emotions:

Aww ur so sweet. I have to be there for ten, but you don't have to drive me. I don't know how long I am going to be there. It's my first visit. I'm sure you have things to do and I don't want to keep you outside waiting.

He texted her back:

Don't worry about all of that. I insist. I'm taking the day off tomorrow, but if I have to bounce you can take your taxi home.

Sasha squirmed. He was persistent. She wasn't sure why he wanted to wait outside of a rehab centre for a girl her barely knew. It wasn't something she was used to. It had been a long time since anyone had any interest in Sasha who wasn't paying for her time. She texted him:

Ok you can drive me. It's in Richmond Hill. Please make sure you are here no later than 9:15 AM. It's my first visit, and I don't want to be late. Taking the day off. huh?

He responded:

Lol! I make my own schedule ☺. Ok baby. Imma go take care of some shit right now. I'll holla at you tomorrow.

Sasha smiled blissfully at her phone. Jahkai seemed like a gentleman. He could take care of Sasha if he wanted to. Sasha wasn't sure how she felt about that. Breezy was the last person to extend his hand out to her. Breezy seemed like a saint at first. He seemed so concerned for Sasha's wellbeing and manipulated her into trusting him with her life. Although Sasha only knew Jahkai for a mere few days, he didn't come off as a manipulative, eccentric dickhead. Jahkai had the demeanor of a real man. He made Sasha nervous when he spoke and flutter when he complimented her. It had only been a few days since they met and Sasha already felt like she valued his opinion.

Sasha replied to his last text message:

<u>You won't take no for an answer, and I won't let anyone boss me around. We might have a problem, Jahkai. I'll talk to you tomorrow. Xoxo</u>

Sasha put her phone on silent and curled herself under her comforter. She closed her eyes and fell asleep within minutes.

CHAPTER 16

Sasha woke up at seven feeling revived. She sat up and stretched her arms in the air as she yawned. Sasha rubbed her eyes as she climbed out of the bed, opened her bedroom door and peeped out into the hallway. The condo was silent and in the same condition Sasha left it before she went to sleep. Sasha knocked on Mel's door but there was no response. Sasha waited a moment before she turned the knob and stuck her head inside. Mel's room was spotless. Candles were set neatly on the dresser. Her bed had a purple duvet and was made neatly. The window was cracked open for fresh air. Sasha knew Mel was with Jahkai's brother and didn't have to worry but still made a mental note to text her later on in the day.

Sasha washed her face and brushed her teeth then made herself two fried eggs, bacon and toast for breakfast. She turned on the TV and found an old episode of *Nikita* to watch while she ate. When she was done she rolled herself a blunt.

Sasha sighed to herself as she thought about what she was to going to say to Theresa. The rehab centre was very strict on their "no contact" rule. Sasha had no idea what to expect of Theresa. She wasn't sure if Theresa would be grateful Sasha saved her life, or if she would hold a grudge against Sasha for bringing her to rehab. Sasha only dreamed of the day she would get Theresa cleaned up. She never thought that day would really become a reality.

It was only a shame that Deedee wasn't as enthusiastic about going to rehab as Theresa. Sasha wanted Deedee to get clean just as badly. Deedee's addiction was strong, and it would take more than Sasha's cold words of reality to convince her to change.

Sasha decided on wearing a pair of denim jeans and a white fitted tee. She wore a pair of a black flats and a black pair of shades. Mel texted her letting her know she was fine. She was still with Jason and they were out for breakfast. Sasha sighed in relief and smiled. Sasha enjoyed Mel's company more than anything, but she was happy to see her friend finally having fun of her own. Sasha and Mel were always joined by the hip. They could have easily been mistaken for a couple. Sasha wondered from time to time if Mel was too dependent of their friendship. She worried if Mel would be able to take care of herself whenever Sasha decided to move out.

Jahkai was waiting downstairs for her at 9:15 A.M. as promised. Their eyes met as Sasha sashayed to the car. She tried her hardest to hold her smile in, but a faint grin still managed to escape as she opened the passenger door. Jahkai looked comfortable in his gray sweatpants and white wife-beater.

When she jumped in the car Jahkai greeted Sasha with a kiss on the cheek. He was wearing the same cologne he wore the night she met him. Sasha inhaled the familiar scent and sunk in her seat.

Sasha closed her eyes and allowed herself to get lost in

his smell. "What's the name of your cologne? I remember you were telling me it was Versace."

"How are you baby? It's Versace Pour Homme."

Sasha took another deep breath before sitting back in her seat. "You smells amazing." Jahkai chuckled and Sasha smiled benevolently. "I am excited to see my mom. It feels like I haven't seen her in forever."

"I'm sure she will be happy to see you."

Sasha frowned. "I'm not so sure. You haven't met my mom yet. She is a hothead, she is stubborn and she has a mouth dirtier than a baby's diaper."

Sasha could only pray that drugs weren't the only thing Theresa gave up in rehab. She hoped that somewhere down the line that they would be able to fix Theresa's crude attitude. "I'm not sure about anything right now. I have never been this nervous in my life. I feel like I am meeting my mom for the first time."

Jahkai gave Sasha a prudent stare. "In many ways you are."

She leaned into her seat and somehow relaxed. Jahkai placed his hand on her knee and pulled out of the condo. They cruised up the 400 without saying a word. Jahkai hummed along to the songs on the radio while Sasha stared out the window. She was lost in her thoughts about seeing Theresa. The last time Sasha saw her, she was being dragged inside by two in-take nurses. Sasha barely got to say goodbye. She shifted in her seat as she sighed.

"Are you ok?" asked Jahkai.

He moved his hand up Sasha's thigh. Sasha stared blankly out the window. She was far from alright. She was a nervous wreck. She dreamed of this day since she was a little girl. Her hands were sweaty and her heart was racing faster than a employee on probation late for work.

"I'm just a little overwhelmed," she choked on her

words.

Sasha was drenched with thoughts. She wondered how Theresa would look. Did she gain weight or was she still as skinny as a tooth pick? Was her hair still messy and dull or did they take Theresa through an extreme make over? Sasha wondered how Theresa was taking rehab? Was she really serious about living a drug free life or would she relapse as soon as she got out?

"I'm sure your mom is doing just great," Jahkai reassured her. "I'm sure you're mom is just as nervous as you are right now."

Sasha frowned. "I highly doubt that."

"Are you kidding me? You're mom is probably over there sweating as we speak. You were the one who put her in rehab, so it's you're approval she seeks."

Sasha nodded her head in agreement. She hadn't looked it from that perspective. If Sasha never demanded that Theresa go to rehab, Theresa would have been home with Deedee smoking her pipe.

"You don't have anything to worry about," Jahkai continued. "Be yourself and don't be afraid to ask her any questions. It's part of their healing process to be able to face the ugly truth."

"How do you know all of this?"

"Because I been around my share of buckets," he said flatly.

They made one stop to a cheque cashing shop so Sasha could buy a money order. Sasha nearly cried when she gave the teller one thousand dollars in hundreds. She quickly braced herself because that was just the start of a two-year journey. Although Sasha was only obligated to pay five hundred dollars a month for twenty four months, she decided that she would pay a grand instead and have it paid off within a year. She didn't like the idea of being locked down into a contract and having to owe money. If it was up to her, she would have paid it in full. Coming up with fourteen thousand dollars in a year or less would seem impossible to any average person but not to Sasha. As long as she continued prostituting and putting two hundred and fifty dollars a week a side, she could see her goal through.

They arrived at the rehab centre's parking lot at 9:45 A.M. Sasha rubbed her hands together. They were cool and moist. Sasha couldn't understand why she was so nervous. She was the one who put Theresa in rehab in the first place. It was Sasha who wanted the change more than anything. Why did she feel so tense about seeing Theresa?

Jahkai gave Sasha a comforting smile. Sasha was happy she took Jahkai on his offer to drop her off. Lord knows that his words of encouragement were helping. There was no way Sasha would have been able to face Theresa alone.

Jahkai leaned over to hug Sasha. "Just be yourself, and don't forget to tell her how proud you are."

He kissed Sasha on her forehead. She crawled out of the car reluctantly. Her heartbeat quickened as she read the gold plated words on the front of the building "Greengrass Rehabilitation Centre". Sasha took her time walking towards the wooden double doors.

Greengrass looked like a hotel inside. There was a sitting lounge larger than Sasha's whole condo that had a flat screen TV hanging from the wall. There was a waiting area for visitors that had two leather sectional couches and a large coffee table covered in magazines. The front desk sat in front of a grand staircase that led to the second floor.

Behind the front desk was a young, mulatto woman

with curly, brown hair. She was watching the news. Sasha cleared her throat so that the young lady would notice her. The woman looked up at Sasha and smiled.

"Welcome to Greengrass. How may I assist you." Her voice was perky and quick when she spoke.

Sasha leaned on the desk and placed her elbows on the table. "I'm here to see my mother. Theresa Brown. My name is Sasha Brown."

The woman typed something into the computer and smiled. She pulled out a stack of forms, shoved them neatly on a clipboard and handed it to Sasha. She pointed to the waiting area. "I will have someone escort you to your mother. In the meantime, take a seat over there and fill in these consent forms. Someone will be with you shortly."

Sasha sat in the waiting area. She looked out the window. Jahkai was nowhere in sight. Still, the thought of him made her heart flutter. She skimmed through the documents on the clipboard and cringed at the one that outlined the fees and her payment plan in fine details. She looked at her purse that sat on the chair next to her. The money order was in an envelope zipped up in a inner pocket. It was funny how a piece of paper smaller than a dollar bill was worth so much money.

Sasha signed the documents and gave it back to the receptionist. She sat back down in the waiting area and skimmed through the magazines on the table. She spotted a *Time* Magazine and got lost in an article on Hilary Clinton. She barely noticed the tall, middle age, redhead woman that approached her. Her name was Megan Carcilli. She was Theresa's in-house worker. Megan was assigned to Theresa a week after she was admitted. Sasha got up and shook the woman's hand. She tried her best to smile but her heart was pounding in her chest and her stomach twisted with anxiety. The redhead gave Sasha a welcoming smile, exposing her straight, perfect, white teeth.

Sasha followed Megan through an open corridor. Megan stepped swiftly as she flipped through the papers on her clipboard. "Theresa has been doing extremely well. It was rough for her during her first week as it is with most of our patients. But since she has completed her detox, there has been a drastic change in her attitude."

Sasha let out a big sigh of relief. Megan told her exactly what she wanted to hear. There was hope for Theresa after all. If she knew that rehab was all it took to get Theresa sober again, Sasha would have made the effort to admit Theresa a long time ago. It filled her heart to know that Theresa was drug-free, but she refused to get her hopes up so soon. If Theresa was unable to complete the program or relapse, Sasha was prepared to cut her out of her life completely.

"How does she look?" Sasha questioned.

"Amazing," Megan replied. "The drugs did a number on Theresa`s physical appearance, but even I can say that your mother is a gorgeous lady. The weight she has been putting on is doing her justice." They turned into another hallway. The walls were collaged with pictures of the facility`s staff and patients. It led to a set of glass doors that led outback. "It's a beautiful morning. Your mother requested that you guys sit outside in the gazebos."

Greengrass truly reminded Sasha of a resort. Outside was even more beautiful than the inside. There was an outdoor pool lined with chaise lounges, a tennis court and a basketball court. In the distance, there was a group of people doing yoga and another group of people doing tai chi

"This is quite some place," Sasha commented.

"Just because it's a rehabilitation centre doesn't mean it needs to look like a hospital."

Sasha couldn't help but frown. It was costing her over four hundred dollars a night for Theresa to stay there and she could finally see why. She wasn't paying for the treatment, she was paying for the accommodations. "Well, you're right about it not looking like a hospital. It looks like a first class hotel. No wonder you guys are so expensive."

"We like our patients to feel tranquil and relaxed. The staff, the activities and everything they do here is a constant reminder of why they are here. Everything is an incentive to make them want to a better life."

"The program or the amenities?"

"Both."

They walked down a trail that led to group of gazeboes. Theresa was sitting on a bench with her back facing them. Her black, French-braid looked healthy. Her hair shimmered in the sun. Theresa was reading *To Kill A Mockingbird* by Harper Lee. Sasha nearly choked on her breath when she saw the classical novel in her hand. She never saw Theresa read anything in her life.

"Ms Brown?" said Megan. "Your daughter is here to see you."

Theresa folded the page she was reading. She got up and spun around quickly. Sasha was amazed at how different Theresa looked. Her skin looked soft and moisturized. Her face was clear and her teeth were white. She wore a clean, black t-shirt, a pair of boot cut jeans and a pair of white, no-name sneakers.

Sasha ran into Theresa's arms. Theresa smelt like a citrus body spray. It was refreshing compared to the smell of alcohol, cigarettes and smoked crack Sasha was used to. Sasha held her tightly as tears of joy came to her eyes.

"Mom, look at you!" she commented. "You look great!"

"Thank you," Theresa blushed. "I can't remember when I have felt so alive without having to take a hit." Theresa's face saddened. Sasha could see the shame in Theresa's eyes and it weighed her heart down. "I can't believe I went through all those years on the pipe."

Megan smiled gracefully at the two women. She placed her hands on Sasha and Theresa's shoulders. "Now that you guys have been reacquainted I will give you some privacy. Someone will come and get you in a hour when visitation is over. Sasha, I can answer any questions or address any concerns you may have at that time."

Sasha and Theresa hugged Megan then continued down the trail and searched desperately for an empty gazebo to sit in. It was 34°C and the sun was out and ready to burn anything in its rays. Sun block and shade was necessary for anyone who planned on being outside.

"So, how are things in the real world?" asked Theresa. "I hope you have been keeping yourself out of trouble, Sasha. Maybe I'm not the only one who needs a change in life, huh?"

Sasha breathed out heavily. If only Theresa knew the lengths Sasha was going through to survive and to pay for her treatment. Sasha never told Theresa that she was prostituting because she didn't want to give Theresa the satisfaction of saying that she was right. Now that Theresa was sober and showing a motherly concern, Sasha felt embarrassed and ashamed about her affairs. She felt an emotion inside her that she never felt before. She feared that Theresa would be disappointed in her. Nevertheless, it was weird and yet comforting hearing her mother lecture her about life. That was something she was going to have to get used to.

Sasha gave Theresa a reassuring smile as she twisted around uncomfortably. She fanned herself off with her hands. "I'm not getting into any trouble. I work hard every day and I pay all my bills."

"What about school? You stopped going long before you left, but you're only eighteen. It's not too late for you to go back."

Sasha sunk in her seat. She didn't feel in control of the situation anymore. She felt like a daughter being penalized by her mother about going to school. Sasha couldn't help but grin. Theresa never took any interest in Sasha's academics. No matter how good Sasha's grades were, they were never enough for Theresa's appraise and now Theresa sat beside Sasha with worry in her eyes for her child's future.

Sasha couldn't blame Theresa for being worried, but everything was ok—at least that is what Sasha told herself every day. She had an end plan and she was going to see to it after she was done paying off Greengrass and Theresa had her own apartment.

"I plan on going back to school," she said out loud. "But I didn't come here to talk about me. How are things going with you. Are they treating you ok in here?"

Theresa fluttered at the thought of her success. "Its fucking amazing. Every Wednesday we have woman group meetings and every Friday we have co-ed group meetings."

"What do you guys talk about?"

"We talk about everything. Janet is our group meeting coordinator. She doesn't fool around with us. She makes us go face to face with our demons and tackle each one of them face to face."

"That's good. I heard it's good to talk about things like that."

"My dietitian is a cunt." Theresa frowned, folding her arms. "She put me on this bullshit diet—asparagus, unseasoned chicken, white people shit. I need real food like oxtail, jerk chicken, curry goat and chicken foot soup."

"Where are you going to get that from? You don't cook," Sasha laughed still stunned at her mother's enthusiasm. She nodded her head in approval. She had to give Greengrass a hand. Four hundred dollars a day, but they were doing a fantastic job with Theresa.

"Fuck, I'm going to learn." Theresa slapped Sasha on the thigh playfully as she laughed out loud. She quickly became serious again. "I am going to buy a computer and get the internet. I want to look up recipes and type up a resume. I need to get a job and keep myself busy when I get out of here."

Theresa got lost in her thoughts. Her eyes began to water. She looked away from Sasha and wiped her tears. "This program, it makes me see life in a whole new perspective. That's what I'm trying to do, see life in a whole new way. I made the wrong decisions in a very low time in my life. I remained in the past, dwelling over your father.

"I remember my first meeting. Kathy, our counsellor told us that we were not bad people. She said that if we were sick, the cure was within our hearts. Change only happens when the pain of holding on is greater than the fear of letting go. It hurt me to see you look down at me. It made me disgusted with myself. I wanted to change more than I wanted the dope."

Sasha was lost for words. She took Theresa's hands into hers. She took a deep breath to keep herself from crying. "Mom, you have no idea how proud I am of you. Seeing you and hearing you speak like this, I feel like you

164

are a whole new person."

"Oh, I'm still me," Theresa intervened. "The loud mouth, stank attitude and all. I'm just drug, liquor and smoke-free."

Sasha looked at Theresa in shock. "You quit cigarettes too?"

"Well, it's a smoke-free centre so I didn't really have a choice," Theresa frowned. She fanned herself off with her book. "But hey, the healthier the better, right?"

An hour into their visit, Megan came walking towards them. She was out of breath and her face looked like it was about to break out in a sweat. She knocked on the side of the Gazebo before she entered. "I hate to be the bearer of bad news but your visiting time is up."

Sasha and Theresa smiled at each other, but there was hurt in both of their eyes. Theresa's demons were exposed and put to rest but the wounds still throbbed with pain.

"Megan, am I allowed to see Sasha to her taxi?" asked Theresa as she took Sasha's hand into hers.

Sasha cracked an uncertain smile. She didn't want Theresa to meet Jahkai. At least not so soon. Sasha didn't even get a chance to tell Theresa about Jahkai much less introduce them. "You don't have to do all of the that, mom. I never took a taxi. I got a ride," she said, trying not to sound suspicious.

"A ride from who?" Theresa pushed.

"A friend of mine."

"Your boyfriend?"

Sasha struggled to keep herself from smiling. "He's not my boyfriend?"

Theresa waved Sasha off in disbelief. "Please. I'm your mother and I'm sober as a kite. I know a girl in love when I see one."

Theresa and Megan walked Sasha through a gate at the side of the building. They walked around the building to the front. Jahkai was parked up waiting. His windows were down and the music was loud enough for anyone on the property to hear.

Theresa frowned as she gazed at Jahkai's Audi. Even Megan couldn't hide her smirk as they walked towards his car. Sasha rubbed her hands together nervously. How stupid could she be to bring a drug dealer to a rehabilitation centre? She could only imagine what Theresa was thinking. Funny enough, if it was the same time last year, Theresa would have been thrilled.

Jahkai came out his car and leaned on it nervously. He took off his shades exposing his seductive, hazel eyes and smiled as they approached him. Sasha gave him a look letting him know that she was just as much on the spot as he was.

"Jahkai, I want you to meet my mom, Theresa Brown."

Jahkai stepped out extending out his hand to the ladies. Megan blushed as she shook Jahkai's hand. Theresa eye-balled him before she shook his hand.

"The pleasure is all mine." she said sternly. She held his hand while she spoke. "You are a friend of my daughters?"

Jahkai smiled. Theresa grinned back at him, but she was looking at Sasha. Sasha looked away to hide the huge blush on her face.

"Hmmm," Theresa sang. "Well, I won't keep ya'll. It was pleasure meeting you, Jahkai. Next time Sasha visits you should come."

There was an awkward moment of silence. Jahkai looked at Sasha hoping she would take control of the conversation, but Sasha shrugged her shoulders like a child, refusing to say anything. Jahkai was not a child. He could fight his own battles and make his own decisions.

"If it is ok with Sasha, I will definitely be here," he promised.

Theresa laughed out loud and let his hand go. She raised her eyebrow and looked him in the eye. "Take good care of my daughter. Keep her off these streets and out of trouble."

"I will try my best."

Jahkai said goodbye and slid back into the car. Sasha gave Theresa a hug and kiss goodbye. She loved how fresh Theresa smelt when she hugged her. It was refreshing and definitely something Sasha could get used to. "I love you, mom. I am so proud of you."

Theresa kissed Sasha on her cheek. "I love you too, baby and thank you for believing in me."

"Thank you for believing in yourself."

CHAPTER 17

"So, that's Theresa?" Jahkai asked, keeping his eyes on the road.

Sasha shifted in her seat. She still felt awkward about Jahkai meeting her mother. Sasha knew Mel would be pissed once she told her. Mel was Sasha's roommate and best friend. She hadn't gotten a chance to meet Theresa yet. Sasha wasn't purposely keeping Mel from Theresa. She wanted to wait until Theresa was out of rehab. Theresa was just as much as a stranger to her as she was to Jahkai and Mel.

"Yup! That's my mom," she replied nonchalantly.

"She is beautiful. Now I see where you get it from."

Jahkai grinned and put his hand on Sasha's lap. Sasha's heart fluttered. There was no doubt that Theresa was a gorgeous woman. All her natural features were slowly coming back. Sasha smirked at thought of telling people she looked like her mother, a first for her.

An accident on the 400 caused a traffic backup. Jahkai rolled up the windows and turned on the AC. They hot boxed his Audi and bumped their heads to Busta

Rhyme's "In The Ghetto". By the time they actually passed the two-car accident, they were both hungry.

"I could always cook at my house," Jahkai offered.

Sasha looked out the window and sighed. There was too much going on for one day. "I appreciate your offer, but I am going to have to decline."

"Why? You think I am going to try and take advantage of you?" he looked at Sasha with a devilish grin. "What kind of nigga would I be?"

Sasha tried her hardest not to smile. She didn't want to go to his house. She was still too vulnerable to be in a private surroundings with him. She wrapped her hair nervously around her index finger.

"What kind of a nigga are you?" she challenged.

"I'm the type of nigga that feeds a woman when she is hungry."

Jahkai's condo was on the eighteenth floor. The walls were a deep burgundy and the floor was hardwood throughout the whole place. There were another set of doors that led to a sunken living room that opened up to the balcony facing the heart of downtown. A black, leather sectional couch sat in the middle of the living room alongside a set of black chaise lounges. His fifty-one inch LCD television hung nicely on the wall. The kitchen was open concept, and it had granite counters and stainless steel appliances. It also had a kitchen island that separated the kitchen from the living room.

"Fine place you have here," Sasha commented as she looked around. She took off her flats at the front door and placed them neatly by the closet.

Jahkai disappeared through the corridor and into the bedroom with his shoes on. When Jahkai returned he was wearing a pair of black, basketball shorts. He gave Sasha a piece of bud, as well as a Century Sam and a pair of scissors. He was a lot more relaxed now that he was in his comfort zone. Sasha rolled a spliff as she watched Jahkai scan his cupboards for something to eat. He pulled some pots and pans out of the bottom cupboard and a pack of ground beef out of the fridge. They smoked the blunt while Jahkai made homemade burgers and fries.

"Why don't you have a girlfriend?" asked Sasha as she bit into her burger. Sasha licked her lips as the beef patty melted in her mouth. "Did you put the cheese in the beef?"

Jahkai grinned. "That's a trick I learned while watching the food network one night. I love to cook."

Sasha took another bite into her burger. It also had lettuce, tomato, bacon, mayo, ketchup, onions and relish on it. She moaned as she swallowed her food and pointed her burger at Jahkai. "As I was saying, why don't you have a girlfriend?"

"I don't know. Haven't found someone really worth me taking seriously," he said nonchalantly.

"I find that hard to believe. You are a good looking guy, you can cook and you seem like a gentleman."

"You know how bitches get. When they see a young nigga like me with shit like this," Jahkai pointed around the house. "Bitches will sell their soul. It's not genuine."

Sasha nodded her head in agreement. She knew exactly what Jahkai was talking about. He was a gold diggers dream man. Sasha was sure he caught the eyes of all the girls in views way. His hazel eyes were hypnotizing. He was charming. He made money and he had the house and the car to show for it.

"Do you think I am being genuine?" she asked while enjoying her home cooked food.

Jahkai huffed as he picked up a bunch of fries out of

his plate and stuffed them all in his mouth. "I know you don't need a nigga to take care of you," he said with a matter-of-fact attitude. "You are a real bad bitch. I could be asking you the same thing. Why don't you have a man?"

"Because money is the motive. And that's all its ever been."

"So what changed?" Jahkai leaned back into the couch engrossed by Sasha.

Sasha smiled timidly. She played with the fries in her plate. "I got money. Now I can play with the boys."

Jahkai pointed a fry at Sasha, impressed by her answer. "That's why I like you. You know what time it is. Money before pleasure."

Sasha laughed with Jahkai but her heart was starting to hurt her. It was beating with loneliness. It had been beating that same song for a while, but Sasha put in great deal of effort to ignore it. Sasha had been touched by many men but loved by none. She wanted to be truly loved. She wanted Jahkai to really love her. Sasha wondered how he would feel if she told him that she was a prostitute. She had a gut feeling he already knew, but she refused to say anything about it until she knew what she wanted to do with him for sure.

They fell asleep shortly after they ate. Sasha woke up forty-five minutes later laying on Jahkai. He had one hand around her and the other hand over his head. He slept so still. Sasha slid herself out of his arms. He wiggled in his sleep but didn't wake up.

Sasha took all the dishes out of the living room and put them in the sink. She washed all the dishes and she took the garbage out of the kitchen and placed it at the front door. She swept everywhere but his bedroom. When Sasha was done, it was after five and Jahkai was still knocked out on the couch. Sasha sat down beside him and watched him as he slept peacefully. She contemplated on waking him up but decided to call Mel first. Sasha hadn't spoke to Mel since she left in the morning. She was out with Jason, but Sasha still wanted to make sure everything was fine. She picked up her phone and called Mel in the kitchen.

"Hello stranger," Mel answered with an attitude.

"What's up?" Sasha spoke in a low voice.

"Let me guess. You are with Jahkai?"

Sasha laughed, ignoring her question. "How was your date last night?"

Mel smiled through the phone. "It was great. Jason is a real womanizer."

"Do you actually like this guy, Mel?"

"We will see. I'm not really one for relationships," Mel told her flatly.

"Maybe a real man is what you need. All we do is chase paper. You need someone to cook for and cater to."

The line went silent for a moment. Then, Mel burst out laughing. "Listen to you! This nigga dick whipped the shit out of you."

"We haven't even done it yet," Sasha snapped, trying to keep her voice low. She looked over her shoulders to see if Jahkai was still sleeping. The thought of his hands all over her body sent chills down her back.

"We will talk more on it when you get home," Mel laughed. "How was your trip to visit your mom?"

Sasha sighed in relief. She was happy Mel changed the topic to something other than Jahkai. "It was great. My mom is like a whole new person. She looks different and she talks differently now. She is happy. I can't wait until she gets out."

"Me too. But like I said, we will talk more when you get home. I'll let you tend to your new man."

Sasha hung up the phone with Mel and went back into the living room. Jahkai was still laid out on the couch. She sat on the edge of the couch and kissed him softly on his cheek. He wiggled around before he finally opened his eyes. He smiled at Sasha and pulled her to lay on top of him.

"How long was I knocked out for?" he yawned.

"For almost an hour."

Jahkai sat up and rubbed his eyes. "Shit! Why didn't you wake me up?" He pulled his phone out his back pocket.

"I just cleaned up for you," she told him nervously. "I did the dishes, wiped the counters and swept up."

Jahkai raised an eyebrow. "You cleaned up my spot?"

Sasha sat up. "Sorry. I thought it would be a nice gesture."

"It isn't even like that," he said. He palmed Sasha's face. "No one has ever cleaned up my spot for me before."

She was ready to grab her bag and run out the front door for making an idiot of herself. She imagined the girls he brought to his house had no home training—that is if he brought any there at all. Sasha couldn't imagine going to someone's house and not cleaning up for herself.

"Well I'm not just anyone," she said defiantly.

Jahkai pulled her towards him and kissed her on the lips. Her breath staggered as she allowed Jahkai's hands to explore her body. Sasha felt like she could orgasm on the spot. She was so aroused by his touch, she felt weak in the knees. Their kiss grew passionate and a moan escaped from her lips. Jahkai picked Sasha up as if he was reading her mind. He wrapped her legs around his waist, still kissing her and carried her into his room.

When Sasha opened her eyes and peaked around his bedroom, he had a king size bed and a forty-two inch TV on the wall. Jahkai carefully laid Sasha on the bed. He stood up and gazed at her in awe and she blushed. He had a way of making her feel like she was the prettiest person he had ever laid eyes on. He sat Sasha up and pulled off her shirt in one motion. Sasha smiled and sat on her knees at the edge of the bed in front of him. She pulled his arms around her. They kissed passionately as they fumbled around the room ripping each other's clothes off.

Jahkai pinned Sasha's naked body on the wall. His hands trailed across her body and made her quiver. Sasha watched him panting as he took a condom out of his back pocket and pulled his pants off. Sasha did the same. Jahkai put the condom on and pulled Sasha to him.

"Are you ready, baby?" he whispered in her ears.

Sasha closed her eyes and nodded her head. She had no regrets. Sasha wanted him just as bad as he wanted her. She took him into her hands and led him to her hot, wet opening. She gasped as he inserted himself inside of her. He stood there for a moment with his head rested on Sasha's shoulder. She bit her lips as she trailed her hands down his back. Jahkai started to penetrate her slowly. She wrapped her legs around him as she slid up and down the wall moaning in his ears.

"Fuck me, daddy," she whispered as she curved her back and moved her hips in sync with his.

Jahkai carried Sasha to the bed and lay her on her stomach. He fucked her with strength and power. She screamed out loud and gripped anything she could get in her hands.

"Just like that daddy!" she yelled as he flipped her on

to her stomach.

He lifted her ass in the air and pushed her face down into his pillow. Sasha took his cotton sheets into her hands as she prepared herself for him. Jahkai slammed himself inside Sasha and fucked her until they climaxed together and fell asleep in each other's arms.

CHAPTER 18

Sasha was finally starting to feel content with her life. She continued to make money with Mel. Their home was their private goldmine. The two young ladies brought in three hundred dollars each on a bad night. Sasha was grateful for every penny she made. She cut down on her spending and saved a majority of her earnings. Her first monthly payment was due in the middle of September. Sasha already had a grand put aside but she wanted to give them more.

Sasha continued checking up on Theresa as promised. The program was going extremely well for her. Sasha was surprised Theresa actually joined the cooking class she had talked about. Theresa also discovered a new liking for public speaking and volunteered to be a mentor to new patients. Surprisingly, she made Sasha promise that the next time she visited she would bring Jahkai. Sasha was hesitant but agreed to bring him.

Sasha and Jahkai became inseparable. Sasha spent a lot of time at his house playing housewife. She always cleaned and although Sasha wasn't the greatest cook, she put in an exceptional amount of effort to try. Sasha was never taught how to cook. The majority of the home cooked meals Sasha ate growing up were at the courtesy of Deedee. In fact, Deedee was the only one who taught Sasha something in the kitchen. Sasha would never forget Deedee teaching her how to toast bread and spread peanut butter and jelly. Thankfully, Sasha was a quick learner and was able to cover the basics in no time. Jahkai never complained. He was flattered that he was the reason Sasha was trying so hard. Sometimes he would offer to help her and they would cook together side by side. Jahkai couldn't have come into Sasha's life at a better time. He had his own money and wasn't shy to spend it on Sasha. Sasha wasn't a user but she was grateful. It made it easier for her to save her own.

On the last weekend of August, Jahkai took Sasha shopping. They pulled into a dense parking lot five minutes from the mall. Before they got out of the car, Jahkai pulled a stack of twenties out of his pants pocket. He handed it to Sasha.

"Buy yourself something sexy," he said as he kissed her on the forehead.

Sasha kissed him on his neck and thanked him before she took the money. "Aren't you coming with me inside?" she asked in confusion as she put the money in her purse.

"I have some shit to take care of first. I will be back in about an hour or so to come and get you."

Sasha frowned.

Jahkai slapped her on her ass playfully. "If it was up to me, I'd be shopping with you."

"You always have a choice," Sasha whined.

Sasha went in all her favourite stores including Guess and H&M. She bought everything from shoes to accessories. By the time Jahkai picked her up, she had less than twenty dollars out of the stack he had given her. They had lunch at a nearby cafe and then Jahkai dropped her home in a rush. Sasha struggled upstairs to the condo with her hands full of bags. She dropped them at the front door and knocked twice. Mel opened the door and looked at the bags.

"All these bags, I hope you bought something for me," Mel joked as she picked up some of the bags. She grinned devilishly at Sasha. "Jason is here."

Sasha followed behind Mel into the living room. Her back was starting to hurt from carrying all the bags. Sasha put the bags down in front of the couch and took a moment to catch her breath. She flopped herself on the couch and placed her hand on her chest.

"I see my brother has been spoiling you," Jason smirked as he eyed the shopping bags.

"I sure wish I could get spoiled like that," Mel frowned as she sat in his lap.

Jason rolled his eyes as he put his hand on her thigh. "Baby, everything will come to you in due time." He kissed her on the cheek and she fluttered.

Sasha picked up two bags and handed them to Mel. "You know I got you, Mel. You can thank me later."

Sasha bought Mel two outfits from H&M and pair of boots from Guess. She also picked up a couple pair of jeans and tops to bring to Theresa so she didn't have to continue wearing used clothes.

"I'm wearing one of these the next time I go out," said Mel as she folded up the clothes and put them back in the shopping bag.

They finished the small bottle of Appleton Mel and Jason were drinking then Jason excused himself for the night. The night quickly became slow and boring. Mel figured it made sense that they tried to get a couple calls, but Sasha wasn't in the mood. Mel was under the impression that laziness finally got the best of Sasha. She was wrong. Sasha wasn't as excited to work as she was before. The thrill was gone now that running tricks was a requirement in order for her to live her everyday life.

If that wasn't enough to get Sasha looking in another direction, she was baring the weight of not telling Jahkai. Things were going good between them, and Sasha didn't want to hold any secrets from him. The longer she kept it a secret from Jahkai, the more vulnerable she would become to losing him, but she still couldn't bring herself to tell him. It was a job Sasha was not proud of.

After ten minutes of going back and forth, Mel finally talked Sasha into working. Sasha got on her laptop and posted two ads for her and Mel. A Russian man named Sergio called Mel's phone for a duo within the hour. She confirmed a price of five hundred dollars for the hour then happily gave Sasha the OK to start getting ready.

"I hope he isn't a prick about the time." Mel yelled from her room. Sasha was doing her hair in the bathroom "You know the ones that literally count the clock."

"There is fifteen minutes left. We finished fucking a long time ago and the dude is still trying to stay until the hour is up."

"Get the fuck out. Your time was up when you bust a fucking nut!"

Sasha laughed as she looked at herself in the mirror. So much had changed since she started prostituting. She remembered when she was a foreigner to the game. She used to sit down and listen to Mel's stories about some of the clients she came across. Now Sasha had stories of her own. Sasha was grateful that she still had Mel by her side. She didn't have any friends outside of Mel. All of her old friends slowly faded away with her old life.

Mel answered the door wearing a black, laced g-string set. Sergio could barely take his hungry, grey eyes off Mel as he followed her into the living room. Sasha soon came out of the bathroom to join them.

"You are both very beautiful," he complimented. His accent was heavy.

Sergio gazed at Sasha and Mel and smiled letting them know that he was pleased. He took his wallet out of his pants pocket and took out five hundred dollars in hundreds and fifties, and placed it on the coffee table.

Sasha smiled at Sergio seductively. She trailed her hands along his chest. She could feel the print of his pecks. "Have you ever fucked two black girls before?"

"No this is first time for me," he admitted with excitement.

He explored their bodies with his hands. He groaned in pleasure while he groped their asses and breasts. Something about him made Sasha feel uncomfortable. His hands were dry and rough and he touched the girls with aggression. He kissed Sasha on her neck. It was wet and sloppy, and he sucked on her like a vampire.

Sasha tapped Sergio on his shoulder. "Please do not leave any marks." She could feel the blood drawing to the spot he sucked on.

"Don't worry. I leave no marks on you," he told her reassuringly.

They quickly undressed themselves and threw their clothes on the living room floor. Sergio sat on the couch and pulled Sasha to him. He lifted her onto his face and Mel slapped a condom on Sergio and began sucking him off. When Sergio was rock hard, he pulled Sasha to her feet and bent her over the couch. Sasha rolled her eyes. The fun was over in her eyes and a rush of guilt spread through her as her mind ran across Jahkai again. Sergio slid himself inside of her effortlessly, distracting Sasha from her thoughts.

Sasha pulled Mel to sit down on the couch in front of her. Mel grinned at Sasha knowing exactly what was about happen. Sasha spread Mel legs apart and planted her face in Mel's pussy. Sergio tried to slip inside Sasha's ass but she wasn't having it.

"Please, baby. I give you two hundred dollars," he whined as he tried to push himself in her ass again.

No matter how much extra money clients were willing to pay, Sasha never provided Greek services. If they wanted to fuck someone up their ass, they had to call someone else.

Sergio pulled out of Sasha after he got frustrated. He pulled her legs to his shoulder and shoved himself inside of her. He then hovered over Mel and took a handful of her hair into his hands. She grabbed onto the couch and took every inch of his swollen meat. Sergio slid his hands around Mel's neck and choked her as he penetrated her. Mel tapped on Sergio's arm for him to release. Sasha grew nervous as Mel's face drenched with worry. He looked at her with dark, grey eyes and squeezed harder on her neck. Mel looked like she was unable to breath. She slapped his arms again frantically and widened her worried eyes. As Sasha got up to pull him off her, he mumbled something in Russian and then pulled out of Mel as he released into the condom. Mel held her neck coughing as she sat up on the couch.

The two girls watch nervously in silence as Sergio put on his briefs panting out of breath. He looked at his watch and smiled. "I know I said an hour, but I am tired." He wiped his face with his undershirt. "I am going to go home and go to bed."

"Well you have our number now. Call us anytime," said Mel in relief.

Sergio put the rest of his clothes on and took a bottle of water to go. He thanked the girls and gave them an extra fifty dollars each for tip. When he left, Sasha gave Mel two hundred and seventy-five dollars.

"Did you fucking see that shit?" asked Mel as she rubbed her neck. It was dark red from Sergio's choke hold.

Sasha cringed at the thought of Sergio. She took a sip of her hot chocolate. "I thought we were about to have a situation."

"I had a customer like that before. He was way too aggressive. Border line rape if you asked me."

Sasha rolled her eyes in disgust. Thoughts of Bill, the trucker who took her virginity, crept into her mind. She could still feel the tearing pain as he forced himself inside of her. Losing your virginity is a milestone in life. He took that special moment away from Sasha and turned it into a traumatizing experience. Sasha wondered if she would offer Bill her services if he called. After all, wasn't it the same thing? A sexual barter or monetary system—the client offers money, goods and services in exchange for sex. Sasha huffed at herself. What was she doing with her life?

"We live the street life. Everyone has to pay homage at some point," Mel reminded her, breaking her away from her thoughts. "Take drug dealers for instance. There is a risk in every dollar. They could get robbed, shot or put in jail."

"Or killed," Sasha added.

Mel nodded her head. "Exactly. Tricking is a risk in itself. We could get robbed by a hungry nigga, kidnapped by pimps, killed by clients or even worse, we could catch a disease. It's part of paying homage."

Sasha took a deep breath. She hadn't really taken the time to think about all the risks she was taking being a prostitute. At the same time, Sasha hadn't been in much danger outside of her fall out with Breezy. Sasha and Mel had a solid game plan, and their condo had a concierge, security and cameras everywhere. Everyone visiting had to sign-in and out. Sasha felt secure as she needed to be. She didn't plan on prostituting much longer anyway. She had every intentions of quitting while she was ahead. She took another sip of her hot chocolate. "I'm just glad Sergio bust a nut and got the fuck out."

Mel put her arms around Sasha. She placed her head on Sasha's shoulder. "Don't worry, Sash. That was one bad experience. And it wasn't even that bad. I was just caught off guard."

Sasha eyed Mel suspiciously. Mel was only trying to comfort her. Sasha could still see the worry in Mel's face.

They finished their hot chocolates then separated into their own bedrooms. Sasha climbed into her bed and texted Jahkai:

As intimidating as you are, sometimes you make me feel safe. Goodnight, daddy.

Sasha curled under her comforter. He replied instantaneously:

I hope so. I'd rather you feel safe than scared of me. You are one of the most beautiful woman I have ever laid eyes on. Next to Halle Barry of course ☺. But there is pain in your eyes. I want to change that. I wish I was there with you right now. I want to put it on you so bad.

Sasha blushed at the thought of him in her bed beside her. It didn't matter how many clients she serviced in a day, thought of Jahkai always made her horny. She texted him back:

I wish u were here to u have no idea. And Halle Barry's old ass ain't got shit on me. After we go see my mom, maybe I'll let you stick your hand in my cookie jar.

He sent her one last text:

It's not my hands that I want to stick inside your cookie jar :p. Goodnight shorty. I will talk to you tomorrow.

Sasha clenched her phone in her hands before she turned it off. She threw the comforter over head and fell into a deep sleep.

CHAPTER 19

On October 27th 2006, Sasha woke up to Mary J Bilge's "Sweet Thing" blasting on the radio in the living room. Mel was in one of her grooves. She was giving the house a good cleaning. Sasha yawned and stretched her arms in the air as she climbed out of bed. She dragged her feet to the living room. Mel was singing along with Mary J Bilge as she wiped down their glass coffee table.

"Morning slut," she said as she sprayed Windex on the table.

"Morning to you too, hoe," Sasha yawned still half asleep.

"Are you going to see your mom today?"

"Yeah. Jahkai is coming with me."

Mel stopped what she was doing, giving Sasha her full attention. There was envy in her eyes. "Oh! He is really coming?"

"So he says. I'm kind of hoping that he chickens out. Rehab isn't really the place you bring your people to meet your mother."

"Well it's not like you're mom gave you much of a

choice," Mel reminded her. She failed to hide her frown. "I can't wait to meet her."

"Just like you said, Mel. I didn't really have a say in this. If it was up to me, you would have met her a long time ago. Don't forget when we met, I wasn't even talking to my mom much less bringing people to meet her."

"You're right," Mel said nonchalantly.

Sasha made herself some toast and hot Milo then got ready. She wore a pair of True Religion jeans and a Ed Hardy fitted T-shirt that she bought the night before. She put on a brown, wavy lace front over her cornrows.

Sasha and Jahkai were on the 400 to Richmond hill by 10:45 A.M. Most of the drive was silent. Sasha was nervous about the visit. She still felt just as much of a stranger to Theresa as Jahkai. The Theresa Sasha knew was a heartless junky not a mother concerned for her daughters innocent heart. Theresa was almost two months clean—the longest Sasha had seen her go without her pipe.

"I'm pretty cool with parents," said Jahkai, breaking Sasha from her thoughts. "Everyone's mom loves me. I have manners and I respect my elders."

"Yeah, whatever! Who are you trying to impress?" Sasha pushed him playfully as she stared out the window. "My mom is mad cool. If you want to impress my mother just be yourself."

Sasha sighed and looked out the window. She wasn't sure if she was talking to Jahkai or herself. She hadn't come clean to either of them about what she was doing to survive, and it was killing her.

"I'm not worried. Once she see's my pretty dimples again she will fall under my spell like every woman does."

"Be careful, pretty boy," Sasha warned him. "Even

roses have thorns."

"I can handle your mom," he smirked.

Jahkai sat in the waiting area while Sasha checked them in. She brought him a clipboard of papers for him to sign. "It's just saying you will obey the rules of the centre. No smoking on the property, no drugs on the premises, blah, blah, blah," she explained.

"Not even this fat blunt I have in my pocket?"

Sasha punched him in the chest. "Jahkai don't play around. Why didn't you leave that in the car?"

He covered his mouth to keep himself from laughing. "I'm just playing with you, ma. I left it in the car."

Jahkai skimmed through the papers before he initialed and signed them. Sasha brought the forms back to the receptionist then joined Jahkai in the waiting room. They waited silently for a few minutes before Megan, Theresa's worker, greeted them.

"Hello, Sasha. It's good to see you again," said Megan as she checked out Jahkai. Her face grew red as she tried her hardest not to blush. "I see you brought your friend with you."

Sasha's blood boiled as she got up from her seat. "You remember Jahkai, my *boyfriend*?" she smirked. Sasha wondered if Megan realized her face resembled a ripe strawberry on a summers day. Sasha took Jahkai by the hand and pulled him to his feet. "Baby, you remember Megan, my mom's worker?"

Jahkai got up to shake Megan's hand. They followed Megan into a private lounge set up for the visitation where Theresa was waiting. Sasha ran and hugged Theresa as if it were her first time seeing her. The familiar smell of a citrus body spray pierced Sasha's nose. She inhaled deeply and smiled. She could get used to Theresa smelling fresh She loved seeing Theresa so vibrant. Theresa was clean, sober and happy still.

Theresa kissed Sasha on the cheek. "Hey, baby. Jahkai, it's good to see you again," she said in a stern motherly tone.

"The pleasure is all mine, Miss Brown," he said as he reached to hug her. "You look even more beautiful than the first time I saw you."

Theresa blushed as she played with her hair. "Well, I still have plenty of work to do. My goal is to put on fifteen pounds before I leave here. I've already put on ten."

Once everyone was settled, Megan excused herself, leaving the threesome to their matters. Theresa sat down on a black arm chair and Sasha and Jahkai sat in the loveseat. Sasha looked at Theresa nervously anticipating what she was going to say. Theresa stared at Jahkai long and hard before she started questioning Jahkai about his background.

Jahkai wasn't shy to tell his story. Sasha listened attentively. A lot of the facts he shared was known to her also. Jahkai looked up to his father, Money Moe, like he was the king of the streets. Technically, he was. Money Moe was a high rolling drug dealer and a stone killer, but people still respected him because he protected the neighbourhood and treated everyone associated with his business with respect, even those that weren't. He was a business man, a good dresser, a charmer and a lady's man. It explained a lot about Jahkai. Jahkai loved and adored his mother, Jackie. She was also a drug dealer but she managed to maintain her class and be a lady. She had a sophisticated style and only dressed in name brand clothing. She was fierce and a force to be reckoned with.

Megan interrupted them shortly after Jahkai's story.

She peeped her head through the doors. "I came to come and grab you guys. Group is going to start in five minutes."

Sasha looked at Theresa in confusion. Theresa never mentioned anything about a group meeting when she spoke of their visit.

"I wanted you guys to hear me speak." Theresa confessed once she seen the dumbfounded look on Sasha and Jahkai's faces. "That's why I invited you to bring Jahkai. I figured that letting him hear me speak would make you proud of me."

"I'm already proud of you, mom," said Sasha as she hugged Theresa.

They followed Megan into a small auditorium filled with other patients and visitors. It was easy to differentiate which patients had been there the longest. Those who had been their longer sat confidently with their loved ones in the front. They looked healthy and carried a glow that matched Theresa's. The newer patients looked nervous and afraid. They scanned the room with suspicious eyes as they fidgeted in their seats.

Sasha, Jahkai and Theresa in the middle behind a white girl who didn't look much older than Sasha. Her shoulder length, blonde hair was in a high pony tail. Her clothes were wrinkled and dirty. Sasha couldn't help but feel bad for her. She looked as rough as Theresa did when Sasha first brought her to Greengrass. Sasha exhaled as she took Jahkai's hands into hers. He kissed her on the forehead and gave her a reassuring smile.

A tall, skinny, Jewish man wearing a navy blue sweater and a pair of jeans stood at the front of the auditorium. "Hello, my name is Steve Norman." He shouted. The crowd of people stopped talking amongst themselves and directed their attention to Steve. "I run the group sessions here at Greengrass. How is everyone doing?"

"This guy is mad cool," Theresa whispered. "And sexy too. He is only a few years younger than me."

Sasha huffed as she twisted in her seat. The only boyfriend Theresa had since her father was Suave. Suave was the worst thing that could have happened to their relationship. He was Sasha's final straw. Somehow, despite Sasha's discomfort, she managed to crack a smile and embrace Theresa's enthusiasm. "Mom, you are looking for a man already?" she chuckled.

"And now I would like to call up Theresa Brown to the front," said Steve. They missed his opening speech about change and how proud he was of the Greengrass patients for making it so far.

The crowd clapped as Theresa made her way to the front. She placed her sweaty hands at her side and took a deep breath. As confident as Theresa looked, she couldn't hide the secrecy in her eyes. She was about to make an announcement. She smiled nervously at Sasha who stared back at her attentively.

"There is no such thing as a good excuse to be a dope fiend." Theresa paused and looked through the crowd. She took the microphone off the stand began to pace around from side to side. "I was not born nor was I raised in the streets. My father was a doctor and my mother was a stay at home wife. I graduated high school with honors and went to medical school at U of T. My dad always told me that I would follow in his footsteps and I would always tell him I don't want his job, I want his bosses."

The crowed chuckled in sync. Sasha hung onto Theresa's every word. Sasha never met any of her grandparents. She had always wondered if they were alive or dead and why Theresa rarely spoke of them.

"My man was drug dealer. I didn't know anything about crack-cocaine until I met him. I was introduced to a lifestyle that was foreign to me. I remember it like it was yesterday." Theresa drifted into her thoughts. A slight smirk appeared on her face. "I was twenty three when I did my first rail. Man, the feeling that took over me was euphoric. I wanted to feel it all the time, and with the ol' man that I had, I was able to. When I got pregnant with my daughter, it was his eye opener. It was mine too until she was two when he was shot and killed in a raid."

Theresa took a moment to gather herself. She squinted her pain filled eyes trying to hold back her tears. Sasha took Jahkai's hand into hers. Her face matched Theresa's. It hurt to hear Theresa speak of her father. Sasha didn't have any memories of him. She couldn't remember him if she wanted to, but she could still feel him in her heartbeat. After sixteen years without him in her life, hearing his name still made her emotional.

"I never felt so alone in all my life," Theresa continued. "When you are a constant user like myself, dope becomes your life. Nothing else mattered to me. I didn't need a man because crack-cocaine became my man. I didn't need faith because crack-cocaine became my god. I didn't care about my daughter because crack-cocaine became my baby."

Theresa looked at Sasha with apologetic eyes. Sasha couldn't look back at her. She looked into the crowd of people who were hanging on to Theresa's words with their lives. Theresa wasn't herself when she as on drugs, but the scars and wounds that Sasha got in the process still throbbed with neglect and pain.

"I used to do everything to get high. I used to rob, steal and hustle. I sold myself and neglected my daughter. My beautiful, baby girl spent her whole childhood alone and I didn't care. The only thing I cared about was getting high." Theresa wiped a tear from her face. "We had our share of fights believe me. My baby girl has the Brown blood. She left me when she was sixteen. I will never forget that night. I chose a man over her when I should have been there for her as a mother. That night should have been my wake-up call but like many other nights, I was scared to face reality and my rock was the only thing that could help me escape it."

Jahkai turned to Sasha in shock. Sasha had told him that she ran away but she never got into details why. He put his arm around Sasha and pulled her close to him. She wiped a tear from her eye and leaned her head into his shoulder. Sasha's heart grew heavy as she replayed the night she ran away in her head. It was the first and only time she gave up on Theresa.

"I left him a while after that. I spent every night worried about her, wondering if she was ok or if she was dead or alive. I called her phone every day until the line was cut. For the first time, I felt really fucked up and disgusted with myself as a mother. How could I do that to her? She didn't ask to be here. She deserved a fair shot at life and I took that away from her.

"When my daughter came home to me it was as if my prayers had been answered. She spared me no sympathy. She told me if I didn't quit doing drugs, I would lose her forever. The night before I came here was the last night I touched my pipe. I took my last hit then I smashed it and threw it in the garbage."

The crowd roared for Theresa. She smiled and waved to them. Theresa took a breath and became serious again.

"It's crazy how something so simple as smashing a pipe felt like the hardest thing I have ever done. It's like I woke up one morning thinking 'I'm tired of this shit'. I mean, I could have been a fucking doctor for crying out loud." Theresa chuckled with the crowd but the hurt was evident in her eyes. It was an opportunity not many people have and she let it slip away at the tip of her fingers. "I want a normal life and a real relationship with my daughter. Coming here changed my life. It made me remember that there is more to life than a piece of rock and a pipe. There is more to life than these streets. I spent twenty years of my life as a slave to dope and now I am finally clean, but just because I am clean, doesn't mean I am fully blessed. Everything in life comes with a cost. The cost for my drug usage is HIV."

Sasha' heart sunk to her stomach. For a moment, she felt like she couldn't breathe and she gasped for air. Sasha had no idea Theresa had HIV. She wondered why Theresa hadn't told her sooner. Sasha burst into tears before she could stop herself.

The young, blonde girl sitting in front of them turned her head. She looked at Sasha with sad eyes "I'm sorry about your mother. Look at it as a blessing in disguise. At least she won't die a dope fiend."

Sasha and the girls eye met, and ironically, their face expressions matched. Sasha had no recollection of the female who sat in front of her yet she could feel her pain. She too had been hurt by someone she loved. Did her mother neglect her too?

"You're mom is a great woman. She has been helping me through recovery. She is like a mother to me."

Sasha eyes widened as the young girl went on to speak highly of Theresa. Theresa was never known to be the helpful type. If there was one word to truly describe her it would be selfish. Theresa didn't care about anyone or anything but herself. At one point she didn't even care for her only child. Now Sasha was sitting in an auditorium full of recovering drug addicts listening to a white girl young enough to be her sister talk about Theresa as if she was a saint.

"You obviously never met the real Theresa," Sasha smirked. Those were the only words she could bring herself to say. She placed her hand on her chin and took a breath in attempts to control her emotions.

"It doesn't matter who she was before. This is the real Theresa now, and this is her story." The young blonde girl cracked a grin at Sasha then turned back around.

"You didn't know?" Jahkai whispered.

Sasha shook her head. She took another deep breath, this time to control herself from bursting into tears again as she listened to Theresa speak, unsure of how she should feel.

"I am sixty-five days clean and I am loving each and every second I spend with her. She is the reason why I am here today—the reason why I will stay clean. I did this for my daughter, but most importantly I did this for me."

"Mom, that was amazing," said Sasha once Theresa rejoined them. She sniffled and wiped the tears off her face with her hands. "I have never heard you speak with so much passion."

Sasha cracked a faint smile as she hugged herself tightly. Theresa's announcement was still ringing in her head like a church bell at noon. She wanted to talk to Theresa about it but she didn't know what to say or how to bring it up.

"That was great, Ms Brown. I felt everything you were saying," said Jahkai in amazement.

Theresa blushed. "Please call me Theresa." Her eyes sparkled as she spoke. "I get so emotional every time I get up there. But it's all a part of the process—being able to speak about it openly."

The young, blonde girl who sat in front of them turned to Theresa and caught her attention. Theresa smiled gracefully as she placed her hand on the young girls shoulder.

The girl grinned and placed her hand on top of Theresa's. "You were great, Theresa. I wish I had the guts to speak the way you do." She turned to Sasha and cracked an envious smile at her. "I wish my family would come visit me."

"Amy, I would like you to meet my daughter, Sasha." Theresa placed her other hand on Sasha's shoulder. She looked at them both with excitement. "Sasha, this is Amy. She checked in about a week ago. Her mother is this cold-hearted, rich bitch from Richmond Hill that don't give a flying fuck about her."

Amy looked down at the floor in embarrassment. Theresa was telling more than she needed to. She gave Amy an apologetic glare. She sat down in her seat, folded her legs and tucked her hands in her lap. "Anyway, I have been helping Amy with the first part of her recovery. I think helping others that are going through the same thing as I am is very self rewarding."

Sasha and Jahkai nodded their head in agreement. Sasha and Amy's eyes met for the final time before Amy turned to face the next speaker. Sasha cracked her an empathetic smile. Sasha knew how it felt not to feel loved by her mother. Up until a couple months ago she was a victim of it herself. Growing up, Sasha was always free to do what she wanted, when she wanted to. Sasha did a lot of things growing up just to get a reaction out of Theresa, but she never got the reaction she wanted.

The car ride back to Sasha's house was silent. Sasha leaned her head on the window and stared off into the distance on the verge of tears. It was hard feeling happy and sad for Theresa at the same time. It was hard feeling happy and sad for herself. Sasha's heart felt heavy and her head was pounding. She felt emotionally exhausted by everything that was going on. Jahkai held her hand the whole ride. He didn't know what he could say or do to make her feel better. When they got to the condo, Jahkai had meant to follow her upstairs but a business call came and he had to leave. Normally Sasha would have made a fuss about it, but she needed the time alone to gather her thoughts and begin coming to terms with her mother's condition.

Mel left a note for Sasha saying she was on an outcall. She didn't leave the address. Sasha frowned as she tore up the note and threw it in the garbage. Mel knew the rule—always leave the address of the client when you are going on an outcall. Sasha poured herself a tall glass of juice and made her way to the living room. She didn't turn on the TV, nor did she turn on the radio. She let out a stressful sigh as she flopped herself on the couch. Theresa's words replayed in her head like a broken record.

I spent twenty years of my life as a slave to dope, and as a result, I am HIV positive.

Sasha burst into tears at the thought of Theresa having HIV. Sasha had no idea. She was oblivious to the signs and the symptoms—then again, she wasn't checking. Sasha paid so much attention to the drugs that she forgot about everything else that came along with it. She knew Theresa was having sex for drugs, but she didn't imagine she would be so sloppy. Sasha curled into a ball and cried as horrific thoughts flooded her mind. How bad was it? How long did Theresa have to live?

There is more to life than these streets.

Sasha wanted to change more than ever now, but she

felt like prostitution was all she knew. Like Mel, Sasha didn't posses any real education, job experience. After seeing how much money she could make in an hour, never mind a day, Sasha couldn't see herself working at the mall for ten dollars per hour. To Sasha, who charged her customers at least two hundred dollars per hour, that sounded like a joke. A joke it was, but it was also her reality. If Sasha wanted a normal life she would have to start at the beginning, just like Theresa was doing.

CHAPTER 20

Sasha squeezed into her tight, black plants. Alberto, her rich, Italian customer, was in the bathroom rinsing off. She just finished a two-hour, candle-lit session with champagne, massage oils and hot, sweaty sex.

"I'm going to call for my taxi," Sasha yelled, putting on her cream blouse and black blazer.

Alberto stormed out of the bathroom anxiously. He shook his head. "Do not call a taxi. I have arranged a ride for you." He gave Sasha a devilish grin as he freed himself from his towel and slid back into his boxers.

Sasha eyed him suspiciously before placing her phone back in her pouch. She had nothing to fear. Alberto was what girls in her profession would consider a good client. He always stuck to the rules and tried his best to make Sasha feel as comfortable as possible. He even offered to help pay for Theresa's rehab, but Sasha kindly declined. It was a generous offer but too personal for Sasha's liking. She learned a valuable lesson about accepting help from strangers.

When they were done getting dressed, Sasha followed

Alberto out of the master bedroom, down the stairs of his four thousand square foot house and into the laundry room that led to the garage. They stood in front of the stainless steel washer and dryer. Alberto looked at Sasha with his deep, grey eyes and smiled. Sasha squirmed. She hated when he looked at her like she was a child. It made everything they did a while ago seem awkward. Alberto told her many times that she reminded him of his daughter who was around the same age—the reason for his fatherly gestures.

"Sasha, you know I care a lot for you, right? I wish you would let me take care of you," he told her softly as he placed his hand on her shoulder.

Sasha smiled back at Alberto unsure of what to say. "I appreciate your concern, but I can take care of myself, Alberto. I'm not struggling you know."

"I'm sorry if I offended you," he said, regretting his choice of words. "What I meant to say was, I want to be that person that helps you through your journey. You won't let me get you an apartment. You won't let me pay for your mother's medical bills." He gave Sasha the fatherly stare again before he softened his gaze and smiled at her.

Sasha smiled back. "Alberto, you are such a good man. I wish there were more guys like you."

Alberto took a step back from Sasha and checked her out. She truly was a beautiful possession, but even he could see the pain and struggle in her eyes. Sasha's pretty looks couldn't hide the fact she was hurting. Sasha had been through hell.

"Come," he ordered as he pulled her in front of him. "I bought you something and I will not take no for an answer."

Sasha fluttered. "Alberto you shouldn't have."

Alberto opened the garage door and there was a black, 2006 BMW 323i wrapped in a huge, red bow. Sasha placed her hands over her mouth and gasped. It was sleek, shiny and brand new. The butterflies in her stomach weren't just dancing. They were going nuts. How could she say no to a brand new BMW?

They walked down the steps that led into the garage. Sasha exhaled as she hugged herself to keep from the cold. The car was so shiny, Sasha could see her reflection. Sasha stepped closer so she could look inside. The windows were tinted. It was too dark to see, but she was able to make out the beige, leather interior.

Alberto pulled a key from his pocket. He pressed a button and the car doors unlocked. "Open the door so you can see better."

Sasha opened the car door reluctantly and sat in the driver's seat. It smelt like leather and pine. The front panel was dark wood and had a nine inch touch screen. In between the driver and the passenger seat were individual heating controls. She opened the glove box and there was another thousand dollars in it.

Sasha wanted to accept the car but she didn't know how. Outside of Jahkai and Mel, nobody had given her anything without wanting something in return. "How much did this cost you?"

"You have no debt to me," he stated as if he was reading her mind. He folded his arms and leaned on the garage door. He called for Sasha and she came to him nervously, unsure if she was going to accept his gift. He hugged her tightly and kissed her on the forehead. "When you get lucky don't question it. Accept it and be thankful."

"What did I do to deserve a car?" she asked suspiciously. Sasha felt so overjoyed she could cry.

"Listen, gal," Alberto took her by the shoulders and looked at her with burning eyes. "I'd be lying if I said I didn't want you outside of the sex, but you are too young for me." He laughed at himself before letting Sasha go and giving her that fatherly stare again. "Fuck, you look like you could be my daughter and sometimes I feel bad calling you for sex."

"Don't feel bad," Sasha assured him. "If I didn't want to be here I wouldn't come. We are both adults with a mutual understanding."

Alberto looked at the car and back at Sasha feeling sure of his decision. "I cannot give you my heart. I have my wife and my daughter. I love my wife with all my heart. I would not leave her for the world, but I can give you this car to help you out. It's paid in full. If you want to sell it, you sell the piece of shit. Or you keep the car and you drive. I don't know." Alberta shrugged as he looked at the car and grinned.

Sasha knew she shouldn't have accepted the car, because she barely knew how to drive and she didn't have her licence. To make matters worse, it was November and they had just gotten their first taste of snow. Sasha wasn't keen on the idea of learning how to drive in the winter. A BMW was not the ideal car for a first time driver. Her reason's weren't enough to make her decline Alberto's gift. Alberto drove Sasha home in her new car and then took a taxi back to his house. Mel was not the least surprised. She was relieved that they could do more outcalls and save money in the process. Sasha and Mel spent a lot of money on taxi's. Depending on how far they were going, they spent up to one hundred dollars on a single ride as opposed to taking the bus.

They agreed on letting Mel be the designated driver because she had her license. She was a driver for Breezy her first year working with him. He stopped making her drive after Cherry got pregnant and was unable to work anymore. Sasha felt a sense of relief knowing she would now be accompanied to her outcalls by Mel. Even though she never had any issues, she hated going their alone. Sasha preferred working within the comfort and security of the condo.

The next day, they filled the tank up with sixty dollars worth of premium gas. Sasha bought a G1 study guide inside the gas station to study for the test. She wanted to start driving legitimately as soon as possible. She couldn't afford for her car to be towed, or getting a ticket for driving without a license.

"I've never driven a BMW before. This is hot," said Mel as she hit 120km in the left lane down the 427 highway.

"Hotter than Breezy's Audi?"

"Way hotter because it's yours," Mel laughed. She looked at Sasha and gave her a thankful smile. "I'm so happy I left with you. I don't know what I would be doing right now if I was with Breezy."

"Selling your ass," Sasha laughed back.

"Yeah, basically the same thing only he would be taking all of my money. I don't know how I could ever thank you."

Sasha raised her eyebrow. "Thank me? I don't think I would have lasted this long by myself if you weren't with me." Sasha looked outside the window. They were zooming past the cars like they were racing to a finish line. "Lord knows what I would be doing now. I'd probably be selling drugs."

Mel howled, "I can't imagine you sitting at a table bagging weed and coke. You weren't made for the drug game."

Sasha laughed along with Mel but what Mel said stood out to her. She wasn't made for the drug game, but surely enough, prostitution wasn't her destiny either. Sasha was good at what she did, but she was ready to start putting together her end plan. She had her place, she had her car, her mom was getting ready to get out of rehab, soon it would be time for her to start looking for a new means of making money.

They parked the car and strolled along Woodbridge Ave, stopping at a few boutiques as they searched for somewhere to eat. Nothing beat the authenticity of an Italian restaurant in Woodbridge. It was the city of the Italians, Siberians and Portuguese. The October weather was too cold to sit on the patio so they found themselves at a booth by the windows facing the main roads.

"So, have you figured out what you are going to tell Jahkai?" asked Mel as she stuffed her fork into her fettuccini alfredo.

Sasha slouched into her seat. She played with her food. She lost her appetite while they were window shopping. "I have no clue, Mel. How am I going to explain the car without explaining what I do?"

"I don't know why you haven't told him yet. I told Jason up front that I am tricking." Mel took a loud slurp of her rum and coke. "He was actually cool with it."

"Even if Jahkai's cool with it, he isn't going to be happy with me telling him now."

"Well that's all on you, baby girl. You can't lie and say you bought the car because you can't drive."

Sasha sighed and finally took a bite out of her chicken Alfredo. The sauce was creamy and tasted homemade, but she wasn't sure it was worth fifteen dollars. "And it's a car. It's not like it's clothing or a piece of jewellery. It's a fucking car!"

For a moment Sasha regretted accepting Alberto's gift. Her car left her vulnerable to losing Jahkai. It had only been twenty four hours since she pulled out of Alberto's driveway and already Sasha felt attached to it. Even though it was a gift, Sasha was beginning to feel like she was one step closer to her success. It was *her* car.

"He did give me the option of selling the car," Sasha thought out loud.

Mel screwed her face at Sasha. "Don't be fucking stupid, bregrin. You're not broke. Money isn't an issue. You need a car. Everyone needs a car. Jahkai is going to be mad but he is just going to have to accept it. I wouldn't be surprised if he knew already. Don't forget, him and Jason are brothers."

Sasha cringed. "That would be even worse. If he knew and didn't say anything. That means he has been waiting on me to tell him all this time."

Mel took another sip of her rum and coke and finished the last of her pasta. "Don't sweat it. Keep the car if you want to keep the car. Sell it if you want to sell it. I got your back either way."

"You always do."

When they were finished eating, they headed over to Orfus Road to do some shopping. Orfus Road was the place Torontonians went if they wanted to get more for less. It was right down the street from Yorkdale Mall— one of Toronto's major, upscale shopping centers. Sasha wasn't keen on the idea of spending any money so Mel paid for everything, hoping that some retail therapy would cheer her friend up.

By the time they got home the sun was setting, and they were both exhausted. Sasha took a shower then rounded up the courage to finally call Jahkai. God must have heard her prayers and granted her some time because he hadn't called or text her all day. When Sasha told Jahkai about the car he wasn't too pleased to hear that someone bought his girlfriend a brand new BMW.

"No motherfucker in his right mind is going to buy you a car just like that," he scowled. He breathed heavily over the phone. "You either fucking around or tricking. Which one is it?"

Sasha's heart was beating laboriously. She regretted telling him anything. She should have just followed her gut instincts and sold the car but there was no turning back. Now she had to tell him the truth.

"One of my buckets," she said nervously as she clenched her cell phone in her hand

"One of your buckets or one of your tricks?" Jahkai snapped. "I'm not an idiot, Sasha. You think I didn't see your ads on those sites? Huh, Lisa?"

Sasha huffed frantically. She closed her eyes in attempts to hold back her tears. Her heart felt like it was trying to break through her chest. She should have known better than to try and keep something like that from Jahkai. Just because he wasn't a pimp didn't mean he couldn't find out.

"I wanted to tell you," she chocked.

"I wanted you to tell me to," he said disappointingly.

There was a moment of silence that cut Sasha in the chest like it was cutting a hole for her heart to break free. Sasha held her chest and exhaled slowly. A tear fell from her eye.

"I don't give a fuck if you tricking these dudes, Sasha." Jahkai continued. There was hurt in his voice. "I can never knock anyone of their hustle, but it doesn't change the fact that you didn't tell me. I knew the day I picked you up for lunch. At your age, a girl might have her own apartment not her own condo. A trill chick has a condo, and she is either stripping, tricking or selling drugs. You are too young to buy, so obviously your renting. I love the strip clubs, and I have never seen you in the clubs, and if you were a drug dealer, we would be doubling our money making these wops. That leaves one thing."

Sasha's blood boiled as she burst into tears. "I'm sorry. It isn't the easiest thing to confess."

"And you think selling drugs is?" he shouted. Jahkai was beyond livid, and there was nothing Sasha could do about it. "We have been together for over a month. How long did you think you were going to keep it a secret? Until you got hurt? Until you got AIDs? Until you gave me AIDs? Were you not going to tell me? Am I a sugar daddy? Another paycheck?"

"No! I would never think of you like that. I love you."

There was silence on the line. Sasha said it before she could stop herself. She may not have admitted but there was no doubt in her mind that Jahkai was indeed her first love. He meant the world to her. He was her king and the thought of losing him scared her to death.

"And you have the audacity to tell me you love me," he growled. He groaned as he banged on the walls. "That doesn't mean shit to me right now. You don't love me."

Sasha felt could feel her heart shattering. She bawled over the phone as she tried to beg for his forgiveness. She knew she should have told him sooner. She had plenty of opportunities to.

"I don't let bitches into my life because they are always on some snake shit," he told her angrily. His voice was cracking. "My father always told me never trust bitches." There was another moment of silence. Jahkai listened to Sasha sob over the phone as both of their hearts broke. "You are suppose to be my girlfriend, Sasha. How are you going to wait for a trick to buy you a car to tell me that you are a hoe?" Jahkai laughed to himself in disbelief.

"I wanted to tell you, Jahkai I swear," Sasha snapped. "But if you already knew, why didn't you just tell me? Why did you wait for me to tell you that a trick bought me a car to get at me? Doesn't that make you just as shady?"

"This fucking bitch," Jahkai laughed at Sasha's blustering. "Let me tell you something, Sasha Brown. A nigga like me doesn't respond to bitches like you. It was your responsibility to tell me, not vice versa. You didn't even consider the fact that I know you selling your pussy and I'm still here. Bitches I tell you. Bitches."

Before Sasha could respond, Jahkai disconnected the call leaving her alone in her tears. She squeezed the phone tightly before she threw it on the bed. Mel knocked on the door and stepped inside.

"Sasha, are you ok?" she asked as she sat on the bed beside Sasha. She wrapped her arm around her, and Sasha leaned her head in Mel's shoulder.

Sasha cried to her friend and told her about the conversation she just had with Jahkai. Mel grabbed a tissue paper off the night table and wiped Sasha's tearful face.

"I don't even know what to tell you, baby girl. All I can say is the cat is finally out of the bag. Like I said before, Jahkai is going to have to accept it or move the fuck on." Mel told her in all honesty.

Sasha sobbed silently, too heartbroken to say anything. She felt sick and light headed. Her heart hurt. She felt like she could physically hear her heart breaking. She squeezed her eyes shut and held her chest.

"He knows you weren't trying to hurt him, Sasha," Mel continued. "If he thought you were trying to hurt him, I think he would have left a long time ago. He's just jealous that someone gave you a car, and he had to buy his."

As mad as Sasha was, Mel succeeded in making her laugh. Sasha hugged Mel tightly. "I can never be mad around you," she whispered.

"I will always be there for you."

When Sasha looked up, Mel was gazing at her seductively with her dark, brown eyes. Mel took Sasha's chin into her hands and pulled her face to hers. She planted a soft kiss on Sasha's lips as she lay Sasha on her back. Mel kissed down to Sasha's navel making Sasha wiggle in anticipation.

Sasha thought about what Jahkai would think if he knew she was about to have sex with her best friend. He would probably be livid, but at that point Sasha didn't care. Sasha needed healing. Sexual healing, and Mel was already one step ahead of her.

CHAPTER 21

It was eight in the morning. Sasha was in bed with her favourite book "The Coldest Winter Ever" by Sister Souljah. Sasha loved to read. It was always her escape from the real world, but she never had any time too with everything going on. After trying to contact Jahkai everyday for a week, Sasha took the hint and started reading again.

Sasha had more than enough money put away for a rainy day, but she desperately wanted to work. Turning tricks kept her mind off of everything. It forced her to smile and be happy. It made her feel loved and wanted, even if it was only her body they lusted. It was a beautiful, November, Saturday. There was no snow on the ground, it was over zero degrees Celsius, and the sun was shining brightly in the sky by its lonesome. The only problem was her phone wasn't ringing and a dead day forced Sasha to stay at home, drowned with thoughts of an ex-boyfriend and a HIV positive mother.

Mel spent the night at Jason's house. She was with him a lot, helping him with his line of business. They were like a power couple when they were together. Sasha thought it was only a matter of time before Mel stopped tricking and went back into her old ways of selling drugs again. They would be the drug dealing Bonnie and Clyde of the new millennium. Sasha envied their relationship.

She tried calling Jahkai numerous times, but he never answered any of her calls or returned her texts. It burned Sasha's chest every time she got his voicemail or when her phone chirped, but the new message wasn't from him.

Sasha read three pages before she threw the book down beside her and hopped into the shower for a hot bath. The water was soothing, but it could never compare to the touch of Jahkai's hands all over her body. Sasha showered herself quickly as she fought herself from crying. She refused to cry again. She got out and looked at herself in the foggy, bathroom mirror. She was such a beauty to look at but she was a mess inside. Her heart and head were hurting. She sighed to herself and started to lotion her body when her cell phone rang. The number looked familiar, but she couldn't remember who it was. She let it ring a couple times, trying to put a name to the number before she finally answered it.

It was a young, white man. His voice was also familiar. "Hello. Is this Lisa?"

"Who is speaking?"

"My name is Alex. I met with you a while back in Brampton." He sounded relieved to have found her.

Sasha sat down on her bed. "You have my attention, but you are going to have to be more specific than that, Alex."

"I gave you my number and told you to call me when you were out of the business."

"Oh, wow! Hi!" Sasha remembered exactly who he

was—the sexy, business student from Humber. He was one of the very few clients Sasha had that were good looking, and Sasha wondered why they were calling her for services. His looks alone could get him any girl he wanted. She also remembered him telling her that she was better than prostitution.

"I tried calling you a while back, but you changed your number. I was just skimming through the escort sites, and I found your ad. I could never forget a body like yours."

"Yeah. New phone new number," she said nonchalantly.

"I see your still in the business," he said with a hint of disappointment.

"Get it where you can, right?"

"Hey, I don't judge. I just thought..." There was an awkward silence on the phone that made Sasha feel even worst about still being in the business. Alex sighed over the phone. "Never mind. Anyway, are you available?"

"I'm actually going to see my mother today. If you want, you can give me a call back later in the evening or tomorrow."

"No worries. Now that I know this is your number, I will save it."

Sasha really wanted to see Alex again. She would never forget the conversation they had during their session. It brought Sasha back on track. She was actually disappointed that she was still prostituting despite the things she was able to accomplish.

The sex trade only took care of materialistic things. In reality, it was eating Sasha alive. She was renting a nice condo, owned a brand new car and was paying for her mother's rehab, but she lost her boyfriend in the process. Not all cut corners have smooth edges.

Sasha threw on a pair of jeans and a brown knitted

sweater. She grabbed her bags and headed out the door. It felt weird going to see Theresa without the company of Jahkai. He had been her ride since her first visit. Surely Theresa would be asking about his whereabouts.

It took Sasha an extra twenty minutes to get to Greengrass. Her inexperienced driving left her no choice but to take the main roads to Richmond Hill. Sasha was slowly becoming better at driving but she still took her sweet and dandy time driving up Yonge street and made it safely. Sasha met Theresa in the same visitation lounge. It was amazing how much healthier Theresa looked every time Sasha visited. Theresa was sitting in the arm chair. She was wearing a pair of Guess jeans and a sweater that Sasha bought her. It showed off Theresa's curvy hips and long legs. Even as a recovering addict, Theresa looked like she could walk the runway.

"Something is wrong," said Theresa as she eyed Sasha suspiciously.

Sasha sat down in the arm chair across from her and sighed. She debated about telling her mother the truth. "Honestly, so much shit has happened since I last saw you."

"Where is Jahkai? Did you guys break up?"

Sasha felt her heart crack. She took a deep breath, trying to hold in her tears. "Yes, mom. We broke up, but it wasn't his fault. It was mine."

Theresa gasped in shock. "You seem so self-oriented now, and mature. How did you manage to fuck that up?"

Sasha shook her head in disbelief. "Someone gave me a gift that I shouldn't have accepted."

"What kind of gift?"

"An expensive one."

"Were you sleeping with another man?" Theresa pushed.

Sasha leaned over placing her elbows on her knees. "I might as well have been. The announcement of the car led to secrets being shared. Secrets that cost me him."

A tear fell from Sasha's eye. She wiped her face quickly as she stared at the floor.

"Well, you know what they say; all things come to the light. I don't know what secret was so big that he would break up with you, but at least it's out now. If he loves you, he will be back."

"That's what my best friend said."

"Then you're best friend is smart."

Sasha got up and hugged Theresa. What a foreign feeling for Sasha—getting relationship advice from her mom.

Theresa got up and walked over to the counter. She picked up the piece of cake wrapped in plastic and handed it to Sasha. "I baked this cake yesterday during cooking class. I saved this piece for you."

Sasha took the cake and unwrapped it. It was a marble cake with chocolate icing. She took a big bite and it melted on her tongue.

"Mom, this is good. Are you sure you made this?" Sasha moaned as she took another bite.

"I sure did. I put the icing on myself," Theresa responded proudly. She watched as Sasha stuffed another piece of cake into her mouth. "There is another piece here. I was going to give it to you to give to Jahkai, but since you guys are broken up, maybe you can give it to your roommate."

Sasha cracked a fake smile as she ate the last piece of cake. If it was up to her, she would have personally dropped off the cake to Jahkai herself. "I will give it to Mel. I'm sure she will love it."

They spent the rest of the visit walking the corridors

of the facility. Theresa showed Sasha the squash court, massage beds, chapel, meeting rooms and the Helen Bloomingdale Hall—a memorial for the founder of Greengrass. It had the names of all the graduating patients who were clean for over five years. Theresa made a note that one day her name would be on the wall also.

"So, how does it feel to be a sober woman?" asked Sasha once they finally made their way to the front lobby.

"I don't ever want to get high again. I will tell you that much," Theresa laughed.

"I hope not. You look better than ever. You even sound happier. I am so proud of you."

"Don't be proud of me yet," Theresa grinned. "Be proud of me when I get out of here and I make it in the real world."

They hugged each other goodbye. Sasha held her mother tightly, not wanting to let go. She didn't want to go back into the real world.

"Everything will be ok," said Theresa, sensing Sasha's discomfort. "I will be out in a couple of weeks. You can come stay with me if you want."

Sasha wiped her watery eyes. "Thanks, mom. I might have to take you up on that offer."

"You know I can accept phone calls here too, right? Don't hesitate to call me. I may not have been around before, but I am here for you now."

Sasha squeezed Theresa before letting her go. She left Greengrass with a small weight off her shoulder. She couldn't have had her mother sober at a better time in her life.

Mel was still out with Jason when Sasha got home. She flopped her purse on the kitchen counter, poured a strong glass of rum and coke and sat in the living room. Sasha held her phone tightly in her hand. It was killing her not being able to see or speak to Jahkai. She missed him so much. She wished she could turn back the hands of times to when they went to eat on the way to visit Theresa. She wished she told him straight up she was a prostitute when he asked her what she did for a living.

Thoughts of Jahkai were turning Sasha's heart numb. She skimmed through her contact list to his number and clicked the send button. Each time it rang her chest burned with anticipation. She wanted him to answer but was unsure of what she would say. Sasha let it ring a few more times before she hung up. She didn't want to hear his voice mail or an automated message saying the caller she was trying to reach was unavailable. As Sasha was about to put down her phone it began to ring. She checked the caller ID and her avidity quickly turned to let down when she realized it wasn't him. Sasha closed her eyes and clenched her phone in hand, feeling stupid for even attempting. She took a breath and answered the phone.

"Hello. My name is Jonathan. I was calling about your ad." He had a deep voice. He sounded like he may have been drinking.

Sasha curled into her bed as the familiar emotional exhaustion she was used to crept up on her. "How can I help you?"

"Are you available for an outcall?"

Sasha took a deep breath. She was already in bed, and Mel was out with Jason. Sasha hated going to outcalls alone, but she hated skipping out on money even more. Her phone wasn't ringing as much since the school year had started. Paying Greengrass was an expense in itself never mind her own personal expenses. Sasha felt like she had no choice. "Where are you located?"

"Downtown. What are you rates? I wanted an hour if

215

possible."

"It is one hundred and forty dollars for the half hour and two hundred and twenty dollars for the hour," Sasha replied nonchalantly. She was hoping that he was just inquiring or that her price was too expensive. She really didn't want to go anywhere.

"That's not a problem," he slurred. "Can you come now? I will give you some time to get yourself ready if you aren't ready now. In the meantime, I will text you my address, and you can call me when you are leaving."

Sasha yawned and stretched her arms in the air as she jumped out of bed. She skimmed through her closet for something to wear. She took out a red mini dress and a pair of a black, leather, knee-high boots. She took off the bone-straight lace front she was wearing and switched it to a wavy one. She texted Jonathan when she was on her way.

Sasha fumbled around with the built-in GPS for five minutes before she was able to figure out how to input his address. Her chest grew heavy and her blood boiled when she realized Jonathan was down the street from Jahkai's house. Sasha turned off her GPS and drove through the crowded streets of Toronto. She parked on the side-street by Jonathan's condo as instructed and walked up to the lobby.

An older, white man was waiting between the lobby doors. He was wearing a white, button up shirt, beige business pants and black shoes. "Lisa?" he said as she walked through the door.

Sasha nodded as she reached to hug him. His cologne was strong and overpowering, and his breath reeked of alcohol.

He took a step back and checked her out. "You are even more beautiful in person."

Jonathan stared at Sasha all the way up to the twenty-fourth floor with dark, anxious, green eyes. Sasha usually would have engaged in a conversation, but for some reason she felt extremely awkward.

Jonathan's condo reminded Sasha of a bachelor pad. There was a huge, flat screen television on the wall in the living room in front of a black, leather sectional. He omitted the dining table and replaced it with a pool table. There was a kitchen island separating the kitchen from the living room and a fully loaded bar. A large, black and white portrait of a young, naked blonde woman hung on the wall across from the television. Sasha looked at the painting and rolled her eyes. Jonathan had a nice place, but her spirit just wasn't there.

"Would you like a drink?" he asked as he strolled to the bar. "I have my own fucking LCBO back here."

Sasha faked a smiled as she continued looking around the condo. "No thank you."

Something about Jonathan was creeping her out, and it didn't help that he had been drinking. A rum and coke would have relaxed Sasha, but she wanted to be on point in case anything went wrong. There was a small knot in her stomach. She wish she hadn't' taken the call without Mel.

Jonathan pointed at Sasha frantically. "I get it! You don't like Jack Daniels." He poured himself a glass and took a sip. "It really is a fine whisky. You're missing out."

Sasha tried her best to smile as she fidgeted with her bag nervously. She was lost at words.

"You are a cognac lady," he said as he stood beside her. "I understand. I love cognac too. Hennessy is my favourite."

"I like cognac, Hennessy too," she said dryly. "Do you mind paying me so we can get started?"

Jonathan took another sip of his drink. "What you think I'm not going to pay you? Look at this fucking place. I'm a fucking millionaire!" He took a bunch of twenties out of his pocket and threw them on the couch. "I spend two hundred dollars on my fucking underwear."

Sasha stepped back, frightened by his demeanor. "I wasn't trying to offend you."

Jonathan slurred his words. "Offend me? You cannot offend me. You're a whore! You're disgrace to woman. You have no morals, no self-respect, and no class. You are just a stupid, fucking whore."

Sasha took another step back. Her heart was racing, and her hands were shaking so hard she could hear the zipper on her clutch dangling.

Jonathan finished the rest of his drink in one gulp. His face turned red as the whisky burned his chest. His eyes were dark green. "Say it," he ordered.

Sasha was too frightened to say or do anything. She stood in her spot as stiff as a statue, crying and praying to God he wouldn't hurt her.

"Say it!" he screamed, making Sasha jump. "I'm a whore! Say it!"

"I'm a whore."

"And I deserve to be punished."

"What?"

Jonathan grabbed Sasha by the hair, almost ripping off her lacefront. "And I deserve to be punished. Say it!"

Sasha burst into tears. "And I deserve to be punished. Now please let me go!"

Jonathan took a deep breath. He gulped the last of his drink and placed it on the coffee table as he watched Sasha with dangerous eyes. He squinted his face and rubbed his hands through his hair.

"Do you believe in god, Lisa?" he asked.

Sasha nodded.

"I am a man of god," he said proudly. "I have read every page of the bible and I go to church every Sunday."

Sasha tried to make a run for it. Jonathan leaped and grabbed her by the wrist, pulling her to him. He looked at her with crazy, evil eyes as he ran his hands through her hair and inhaled her perfume.

"My my, Lisa. You sure smell exquisite," he commented. The alcohol was potent in his breath. He closed his eyes and inhaled deeply in admiration.

"Please let me go, sir. You're scaring me," Sasha pleaded, trying to break free of his grip. "I will leave and pretend none of this ever happened."

"Calm down and listen to me, Lisa," he ordered. "If you don't listen to what I have to say, I am going to get upset, and I'm not the nicest person when I am mad."

Sasha stopped trying to escape his bear hug. She sobbed and choked on her breath as she forced herself to stop crying.

"Now, are you familiar with the bible?"

"No."

"In the bible it states that prostitution is an abomination. God never liked whores and faggots."

Jonathan turned Sasha around so she was facing him. He stared in her scared, brown eyes and planted a wet, sloppy kiss on her lips. Sasha tried to move away but his hold on her was to strong. He tried to stick his tongue down her throat, but Sasha made an acclaimed effort in keeping her mouth closed.

Jonathan stepped back and looked at her in awe, still holding her by her shoulders. He pulled her into him and held her in his arms. "For the lips of an immoral woman drip honey, and her mouth is smoother than oil." Jonathans breathing grew heavy. He pulled Sasha's hair so she was looking up at him. "But in the end she is bitter as wormwood, sharp as a two-edged sword. Her feet go down to death. Her steps lay hold of hell."

Jonathan dragged Sasha by the hair through the condo to his bedroom. He threw Sasha on the bed. Sasha jumped out of the bed and tried to make a run to the door, but Jonathan caught her and threw her back. He straddled himself on top of her and held her hands over her head.

"I will stop prostituting myself if you let me go," Sasha cried as she tried to wiggle her way out from underneath him.

"Let you go?" he laughed evilly. "Lisa, I have no intentions of letting you go. No, I must act in the name of the lord. Faggots and prostitutes are the reason why there are no longer any family values. Why men and women cheat on their partners to fulfill their lust."

Jonathan held her hands with one hand and used the other to tug down on Sasha's panty. Sasha tried to wiggle free, but Jonathan had her in a position where she couldn't even turn to her side if she wanted to.

"Please don't do this," Sasha choked on her words. She closed her eyes wishing it was all a dream.

"Are you familiar with S&M?" he asked ignoring her pleas.

"Yes I am, but I do not provide those services."

Sasha was asked numerous times if she offered BDSM services. She never knew what it was at first. Her stomach turned when she searched 'BDSM' on Google and read the results. She couldn't understand how people could find pleasure from pain and torture. Sasha decided then and there it was not her forte.

"So, you prefer vanilla relationships," he smirked.

Sasha wasn't clueless to what he was saying. She

remembered reading about the Dominant being the person who carries out the action and the sub being the person who received it. She didn't like the idea of being gagged, whipped, blindfolded or tied up. To her, it was demeaning and immoral.

"If you so much as flinch," Jonathan warned her.

If Jonathan's green eyes could grow any darker, they would be black. He got up and searched for something under the bed. He didn't take his eyes of Sasha.

"I love these moments," he said as he exhaled slowly. "The suspense of what's going to happen next...Ah here we go!"

Jonathan pulled out a black box from underneath the bed and placed it down beside Sasha. Sasha cringed in fear. She looked at the door hopelessly then back at him.

Jonathan shook his head, reading Sasha's mind. "Don't even think about it."

He took a black bandana out of the box. He straddled over Sasha and looked at her like the inamorata she was. "Hold your hair up."

"Please let me go. You don't have to—"

"I said hold your hair up!"

Sasha quickly leaned up and held her hair up with her shaking hands. "Why is this happening to me?"

"Because you remind me of a sub I once knew. She sleeps with her boss at work. She is also my wife."

Jonathan sat on the edge of the bed. His face softened and there was pain his eyes. It was all coming together. His wife was cheating on him and he was obviously very hurt by it.

"The wage for sin is death. Everyone must pay for their sins. Be accountable for their actions." He murmured.

"So you killed your wife?" Sasha asked not sure if she

was able to handle the ugly truth.

"Fuck no! I would never kill my wife." He looked at Sasha as if she were the crazy one. "What kind of man do you think I am? I have the best divorce lawyer that Toronto has to offer."

"Then why are you doing this? I don't understand."

"Because I need to take it out on someone, Lisa," he slurred on his words. The alcohol was bringing out his pain. Jonathan tied the bandana around Sasha's mouth then reached for the box and pulled out a silk blindfold. "I'm a churchgoing man, and my wife is fucking her boss. I'm feeling really fucked up about my marriage and I blame it on whores. I blame it on you."

Jonathan put the blindfold on Sasha and lay her back down. He lay himself on top of her, and took a deep breath of her scent as he his trailed his hands down her body.

"If you only you knew how long it has been since I touched another woman," he moaned.

Sasha cringed as Jonathan groped her breasts. He wandered his hands down her stomach and past her navel. He put his hands up her dress and pulled her panties to the side. Sasha closed her eyes in disbelief, but the tears still crept its way down her face as he violated her privacy.

Jonathan took a small paddle out of the black box. Sasha's eyes widened with fear. Before she could prepare herself for the blows, Jonathan wacked Sasha on her crotch. She shrieked in pain. He grinned devilishly. He was amused. He wacked Sasha again. She tried to break free.

"I'm going to have to tie up your arms," he said as he reached into the black box again. This time he pulled out two pieces of rope.

He tied Sasha's hands to the two hooks on the headboard. Sasha never noticed them before because they were covered by the pillows on the bed.

Sasha couldn't believe what was happening to her. She felt hopeless with her hands tied to the bed. Thoughts of death cross her mind. Sasha wondered if this was the cost of her selling her body—God taking her life.

Jonathan sat in between Sasha's legs. He ran the wooden paddle up her legs slowly. He hit her hard again with the paddle, this time on her upper thigh. Sasha quailed. Her thigh turned red and started puffing. He ran the paddle up and down her thigh again. Sasha took a deep breath as she tried to prepare herself for the next blow. The blindfold was drenched with tears.

Jonathan hit Sasha with the paddle five more times before he ripped her panties off and rammed two fingers inside of her. Sasha bawled in pain, horror and disgust. Meanwhile Jonathan looked like he was in heaven. He used his other hand to take off his pants and boxers. He straddled himself on top of Sasha. He pulled down her dress exposing her breasts. He stroked himself as he gazed at Sasha with his hungry eyes and reached his hand back into the box. Sasha's heart skipped a beat when she heard him fumbling through it again.

Jonathan slowly rubbed on each of her nipples with his fingers, making them stand tall. Sasha tried to recoil as he palmed her breasts. She shook her head anxiously. Her heart was trying to claw its way out of her chest. Her mind was running wild and was giving her migraine. She wasn't sure if she was more afraid of Jonathan or the black box.

Sasha felt a cold, plastic, narrow object against her nipples. She couldn't make out what it was, but she was sure it wasn't a dildo. Then, suddenly, Sasha felt the same object squeeze her nipple like a clamp. She groaned in discomfort.

"I told you not to scream," he said. His voice was shaky.

The room went silent, forcing Sasha to fall victim to her imagination. She dared to put anything past Jonathan. She squirmed around the bed, but she couldn't find any comfortable way to lay with two clamps on her nipples, a bandana round her mouth, a blindfold covering her eyes and her hands tied to the headboard.

Jonathan hit her with a paddle again, this time on her other thigh, breaking Sasha from her thoughts. She screamed in pain. He hit Sasha blow after blow, taking out his anger on her until she was in so much pain, she almost passed out.

"I think that's enough," he said out of breath.

He dropped the paddle on the floor bedside the bed. Sasha heard foil paper crackling. She knew what was going to come next but she was in too much pain to put up another fight. She just wanted him to hurry and finish.

Jonathan lay himself on top of Sasha and plunged himself inside of her. She groaned in disgust. He pulled Sasha's legs to her chest and ripped the blindfold off, forcing Sasha to look into his sadistic, green eyes. She closed her eyes, wishing she still had the blindfold on.

Jonathan groaned as he found his release. He pulled out of Sasha, tore the condom off, and came all over Sasha's stomach. Sasha quivered in disgust. He got up and walked into the ensuite bathroom. He returned with two small towels. He wiped himself up with one, threw it on floor then finally took off the nipple clamps.

Sasha sighed in relief as Jonathan put the clamps back into the box. Sasha thought it was over finally, but Jonathan took a large, red candle out of the box. He lit the candle with a lighter and placed it on the nightstand.

Jonathan opened the bedroom door. "Are you ready for your drink yet? You look like you could use it."

Soon as he disappeared Sasha tugged and pulled, but the rope were tight and secure around her wrist. Sasha burst into tears again realizing that there was no way in hell she was going to be able to break free. Jonathan returned moments later humming with the bottle of Jack Daniels in his hand.

"Call it what you want to call it," he laughed as he took a chug.

Jonathan picked up the wax filled, red candle. He looked at Sasha with zealous eyes. He pour the wax slowly over her stomach. Sasha tensed up, but quickly relaxed when she realized the pain was bearable. It was better than getting wacked with the wooden peddle or getting her nipples clamped.

"Why are whores so exotic?" he asked as he ran his hands across her breast. "Your skin is so flawless and your eyes are so luring. You remind me of my wife."

Jonathan's face saddened again as he spoke of his cheating wife. He placed the candle back down and picked up the bottle. "You women are all the same. Users. You use us for our money, for our loyalty, and for our love, and what do we get in return?" He took another gulp of the bottle and clumsily put it on the nightstand, almost knocking it over.

Sasha tried desperately to wiggle free. Her wrist burned from rubbing against the rope. She didn't care. She was either going to break free or die trying. She kept her eyes locked on Jonathan's as she tried eagerly to loosen the rope. Jonathan picked the paddle up off the floor.

"Pick a number between three and seven," he

instructed as he trailed the paddle along her body.

"Three."

"Three good blows it is," he smirked.

He hit Sasha just inches away from her crotch. Sasha tried desperately to loosen the knot before he took the second hit.

"Where, oh where will I blow? The thigh or the arm, nobody knows," he sang.

Sasha exhaled slowly preparing herself for the second hit. This time he hit her on the thigh. Sasha squinted. Tears ran down her face, but she didn't lose focus on her mission. She continued to pull and tug on the knot until it was loose enough for her hand to slip through. She closed her eyes and sighed in relief. Jonathan took his last blow on her left thigh. Her legs stung.

When Jonathan turned his back to her, Sasha slipped her hand out of the rope, picked up the Jack Daniel bottle, and smashed it on his head. Jonathan howled as he fell to the floor. Sasha fumbled as she untied her other hand and darted out of the bedroom into the living room. Before Sasha could grab her bag, Jonathan lunged towards her. Luckily for her, he was drunk and clumsy. Sasha punched him in the face then she grabbed his nuts and squeezed them.

"When you let me go I am going to kill you," he threatened.

"I have no intentions of letting you go," Sasha hissed. "I'm going to fix my fucking dress, grab my money and my purse, and get the fuck out of here. If you so much as fucking flinch. So help me fucking god!"

They stared at each other with vengeful eyes before Sasha reached for her clutch. Jonathan pulled his arms around her neck and squeezed. Sasha let Jonathan go in panic as she gagged for air. She punched and slapped his arms but he didn't budge.

"And in all your abominations and your whorings, you did not remember the days of your youth, when you were naked and bare, wallowing in your blood," he recited.

"My mother was a crack head," Sasha choked on her words as she fumbled for her bag.

"And she too will meet her maker," he snapped. "The wage of sin is death. But live a righteous life in God's name and the gift is eternal life."

"I'm not your wife," Sasha choked on her words.

Jonathan squeezed Sasha's neck so hard Sasha couldn't breathe. She fumbled around desperately in her clutch and found a pen. Sasha stabbed Jonathan in his arm as hard as she could without any hesitation. Jonathan cried in pain as he let her neck go. She grabbed her bag and a handful of cash and made a run for it. Sasha was only a couple feet from the front door, but something told her to run into the kitchen first. She grabbed a knife from the knife rack. When Sasha turned around, Jonathan was behind her, towering over her with dark, evil eyes. His arm was bleeding from the stab wound. He lunged towards Sasha and she pierced the knife into his stomach. They looked into each other's eyes as Jonathan fell to the floor on his knees.

Sasha grabbed her clutch off the counter and ran out the front door, not daring to look back. She didn't even take the elevator. She ran to the staircase and quickly fixed her dress. Her panty could barely stay up so she took it off. Sasha ran down twenty four flights of stairs feeling thankful to have gotten away. She ran out of the side door and sighed in relief. The door led to the side street that her car was parked on.

Sasha ran to her car. She fumbled with her keys as she hit the button that opened it and jumped inside. Sasha put her shaking hands on the steering wheel and took a deep breath. She felt sick to her stomach. Her heart was racing. She looked at her hands. Her wrists were red and bruised from the rope. There was blood on her right hand. Jonathan's blood. Sasha pounded the steering wheel as she tried to clear her head. She had to do something and do something quick.

Chapter 22

"911 what's your emergency?" said the female operator.

"I am a victim of a rape, and I just stabbed a man," Sasha sobbed on the phone.

"Are you hurt?"

Sasha looked at herself through the rear-view mirror. One side of her face was red and a bit swollen from when he slapped her. Her body ached and stung all over. She had welts all over legs from being hit with the paddle. "I have a few scratches and bruises."

"Where did this take place? Are you still at the scene?"

"I ran out of the condo and outside before I called you. I'm at 34 Berkins Way."

"What is your name?"

"My name is Sasha Brown."

Sasha had almost forgotten that she had used a fake name when she met Jonathan as she did with all her clients. Not only would she have to explain her fake alias to the police, she would have to explain why she was with him in the first place.

"Where is the man now?"

"I don't know. I stabbed him and I ran. He may still be in the apartment."

Sasha sunk into the driver's seat and looked out the window. Every car that passed made her jump with anxiety. She couldn't keep her eyes off the condo. She kept a watch on all the doors in her view in case Jonathan decided to come after her.

"Can you describe him?"

Sasha quivered as she pictured the old, rich, crazy man tying her up and torturing her. She gave the operator a detailed description of Jonathan. She told the operator truthfully that she had just met him that same day and she wasn't sure if that was his real name.

Sasha could feel a headache surfacing. She shouldn't have gone to see Jonathan by herself. She should have followed her gut instinct and turned him down the second she saw how crazy he looked when she first arrived. Sasha wished she had turned around and went back to her car.

"Hello, Ms Brown?" said the operator, breaking Sasha away from her thoughts.

Sasha shook her head, trying to gain back her concentration. "Yes, sorry."

"The police are on their way. I need you to stay calm until they get there."

Sasha grabbed a jacket from the backseat of the car and slipped it on, hoping to cover the blood on her dress. Then she walked up the street, away from her car, sat on the curb and waited. Five minutes later, she could hear the sound of sirens getting louder and louder until she saw flashing lights coming from both sides of the street towards her. A cop car spotted Sasha sitting on the curb and pulled up beside her.

A white female cop with blonde hair jumped out of the passenger side. "Sasha Brown?"

Sasha got up and nodding her head still trembling and traumatized by the events that had just taken place.

"My name is officer Gordon. Are you ok?"

Sasha nodded.

"What apartment number is Jonathan in?"

"2403" Sasha replied wondering if he was even still there.

Officer Gordon nodded to her male partner who drove into the condo and parked behind the ambulance truck.

Pedestrians on the streets stopped to see what all the commotion was about. Cars slowed down to eyeball Sasha and officer Gordon. Sasha felt like she was in a scene from a movie. A short, Trinidadian, female paramedic introduced herself and checked Sasha for any injuries.

"We will have to bring you to the hospital to perform a rape kit," the paramedic told her.

Sasha sighed. She knew she couldn't refuse especially if she wanted the police to be in her favor. The paramedic looked at the police officer who nodded, giving them the OK to leave.

"I didn't mean to hurt him," Sasha pleaded to the officer. "I was scared, and I thought he was going to kill me. I didn't mean to hurt him. I swear."

Sasha started to cry. She wasn't sure if she felt more afraid to go jail or embarrassed to tell everyone the truth. Nobody was going to take her seriously once they discovered she was a prostitute. Sasha knew the risks of prostitution, but she never once thought she would be a victim of rape and torture.

"We are going to get a full statement from you at the

station to figure out what was going on," Officer Gordon assured her. "But you seem awfully young. How old are you, Sasha?"

"I'm eighteen."

Sasha felt relieved to be the age of majority. That meant the police didn't have to call Theresa to notify her of Sasha's situation. Sasha's stomach tightened at the thought of her mother.

The officer looked at Sasha suspiciously. "So, what was a young girl like you doing in an old man's house?"

"He invited me over," said Sasha, debating if she was going to tell them she was a prostitute.

"Invited you over? I think that's a bit much. It's almost one o'clock in the morning," officer Gordon pushed.

"He was upset about his wife cheating on him, and I went there to offer him some support."

"How well did you know him?" Gordon continued.

"I'm just going to answer all the questions at the station if you don't mind."

Gordon nodded her head but still gazed at Sasha suspiciously. She knew there was more to the story. Sasha shifted from foot to foot nervously. She watched as they carried Jonathan into the ambulance. Sasha was slightly relieved to see that he was still alive but judging by the way the paramedics and officers were rushing, it didn't look good.

Sasha was in the hospital for almost three hours. She didn't want to call Mel until she knew what was going on for sure. Sasha spent the majority of the time alone in a private room with two officers outside her door waiting for a doctor or nurse to see her. When the first nurse came, she smirked when she saw the candle wax and the bruises around Sasha's groin.

"You don't strike me as the bondage type," said the nurse as she placed the chart she was holding on the bed beside Sasha.

Sasha raised an eyebrow. "And you don't strike me as the type that gets any at all."

The nurse made up her face but didn't say anything back. She took swabs from Sasha's mouth, finger nails, vagina and ass. She also ran a comb through Sasha's hair and took a tube of Sasha's blood.

"You have no major injuries, just a few scratches and bruises. There is no need for a prescription. Tylenol and some rest will do the trick. We would also recommend that you take a Plan B pill to eliminate any chances of pregnancy," the nurse explained as she scribbled something on to his note pad.

"Am I free to go?" asked Sasha almost relieved that it was finally over.

"The police would like to have a word with you first."

The nurse left Sasha's room, allowing her to have privacy with officer Gordon and her partner. They told Sasha that she needed to come to the station for questioning. Sasha didn't want to make anything hard on herself so she agreed to go with them.

Sasha rode in the backseat of the cop car to the station. Although she was not handcuffed, she felt like a criminal as people broke their necks to see who was sitting in the backseat. Sasha didn't know what she was more embarrassed about: being a prostitute or riding in the back of the cop car. When they finally arrived at the station, Sasha was told that Jonathan died on the way to the hospital. Sasha nearly vomited in the interrogation room. Although Jonathan raped and tortured Sasha, she didn't want his life taken. All she wanted was to see him get thrown behind bars. Justice would not be served because he was dead and now all Sasha had to rely on was her side of the story.

Once there was word of Jonathan's death, the police came at Sasha with smoking guns. She was no longer being treated like a victim. She was now their primary suspect in a potential homicide. The police gave Sasha a long intensive interrogation on her relation with Jonathan and her connection to prostitution. While searching Jonathan's house, the police found Jonathan's goodie box and other instruments that were affiliated with BDSM. Sasha's confession to stabbing Jonathan, her role as a prostitute and the BDSM box was enough for the police to charge her with manslaughter. Officer Gordon detained Sasha and promised her that she would have a bail hearing the next day. Someone would take down the names and telephone numbers of any friends and/or family who could possibly bail her out before she saw the judge.

They brought Sasha to the female holding cells in the basement of the station and checked her in. She cringed when she saw the cement based holding cell. It had a flat, cement surface for a bed, and it had a water fountain and toilet made out of stainless steel There was a camera pointing directly into the cell, giving Sasha no privacy what so ever.

It was torture for Sasha being there overnight. She had nobody to talk or anyone who could at least listen. All she had was herself and her thoughts. Mel was probably worried sick about her and would be wondering where she was. She wondered if Jahkai would bail her out if she put his name down on the list. Sasha wondered if she would have still gotten arrested had Jonathan lived.

It was just Sasha's luck to come across a customer like

Jonathan. She read a bunch of newspaper articles and seen stories about prostitutes being stabbed, raped and even abducted, but her love of money gave her courage to see past it all. Sasha put money before her safety and as result, she almost died in the process.

Sasha thought about Theresa and how disappointed she would be when she found out Sasha was prostituting. Sasha shook her head at the irony. A year ago, Sasha never cared about what her mother thought about her. Christ, a year ago, Theresa could care less what Sasha was out on the streets doing. Sasha didn't want to look like the loser in their new relationship. Theresa did so much to change her life around while Sasha was still running wild and out of control. For the first time in years, Theresa's opinion and approval mattered. Sasha's heart sunk to her stomach when she thought about how she was going to explain this all to her. Theresa had enough going on her plate—being a former addict and HIV positive. Sasha didn't want to bring more drama to her, but Sasha had no choice. She had to tell her what was going on.

Sitting in the holding cell overnight made Sasha realize how sucked into the game she was. Sasha made thousands of dollars and never had anything to show for it. Sasha was renting a condo and her car was given to her by someone who could afford to give away cars as gifts. If anyone took those two things away from her, she would have nothing. Sasha and Mel had been living on their own for months. They talked about going to school and getting their lives back together all the time, but neither of them had taken the initiative to see it through. A lot of their money went towards shopping sprees, VIP at the club and a shit load of weed. Sasha had some money saved up but the majority of it was already going towards paying for Theresa's Rehab. The rest of it, if not all of it, was going to be used to pay for a lawyer. Truthfully, Sasha hated her job and was thankful that she didn't get caught up on drugs, but her story wasn't going to look good in court.

Despite the fact that Sasha really was raped, the police were calling it BDSM gone bad. They looked at Sasha like a young, naive prostitute. They showed no sympathy for her when their so called evidence came to light. It was like they forgot her side of the story and threw her in a cage.

By the time Sasha was tired enough to fall asleep, she was awaken by a male officer. He handed her a plain bagel with butter and an orange juice from McDonalds. The bagel was tough and cold, but Sasha was extremely famished and ate every crumb. Soon after she was done eating, the officer came back and escorted Sasha out of the cell into a paddy wagon.

Ten minutes later, they arrived at the court house. Sasha was brought to another holding cell in the basement of the courthouse where she was met by another young woman who gave her a pair of loose jeans and a sweater to wear in front of the judge.

"I'm here to get the names and phone numbers of anyone who can possibly bail you out today," said the woman as she eye-balled Sasha.

Sasha gave the lady Mel and Jahkai's telephone number. She had even contemplated on giving them Genesis's number, but she hadn't spoken to her in a long time. She didn't feel it was an appropriate reunion.

After the woman left, Sasha sat in the cell anxiously wondering who would pick up the phone call or get the message in time to come to court. She wondered if Jahkai would bail her out and what he would say to her if he did.

Her heart banged on her chest, making her feel the unwanted pain of a broken heart as she thought about their last conversation. A bail hearing wasn't the best reunion either, but it would have to do. Theresa wasn't an option because she was still in rehab. Mel and Jahkai were all Sasha had.

After a couple of hours, a court officer came for Sasha and three other women. They were brought upstairs and into the stands inside the courtroom. Sasha was relieved when she saw both Mel and Jahkai. She smiled at them, letting them know she was ok.

When Sasha's name was called, she stood up and a tall, skinny Jewish man with grey, wary eyes stood up and came to the front. Sasha looked at Mel and Mel mouthed out "lawyer" back to her. Sasha sighed in relief. She wasn't surprised that Mel had everything on the outside under control. Mel had been such a great friend to Sasha since the first day they met. Sasha was grateful to have her on her side.

The lawyer introduced himself as John Greenburg. Sasha was unsure of what Mel said to him but he seemed to have everything under control. He described Sasha as lost with no real guidance and in need of some support to get on the right track. Greenburg raised the point that Sasha had never been in trouble with the law prior to this and was not a major threat to society, thus, should be released on bail.

The judge didn't see anything wrong with granting Sasha bail. When asked who would be her surety, Jahkai raised his hand. He had no charges or convictions and had a self-owned business that allowed him to show a sort of legal income. The judge granted Sasha bail at five thousand dollars. She was put on curfew and was not to leave her house between the hours of midnight and seven o'clock in the morning.

Sasha waited a hour and a half before she was finally released from the court house. Jahkai sat waiting for her patiently with an emotionless face. Sasha tried her best to avoid eye contact with him as the court administrator explained to them both her bail conditions and her next court date.

They gave Sasha back her jewellery in a property bag and kept her cell phone as evidence. Sasha followed Jahkai and Mel back to the car in silence. Her mind was on overdrive. She was still trying to figure out why she was being charged when she was the victim in the whole situation. Even more so, Sasha wanted to know why Jahkai bailed her out after giving her the cold shoulder all that time.

Sasha's thoughts were interrupted by her stomach growling. Outside of the tough bagel she had in the morning she hadn't eaten since she had left house. She was emotionally and physically tired from everything that happened in the last twenty four hours.

"Are you ok?" asked Jahkai, keeping his eyes on the road. There was worry on his face.

Sasha nodded as she looked out window lost in her thoughts. "I don't know what happened, Jahkai." her voice cracked. "I don't even know how I got away."

A tear ran down Sasha's face as she looked at her wrists. They were red from the rope. She pulled the sweater sleeves down so it would cover them. Mel reached over the passenger seat to rub Sasha on her shoulders.

"I was so worried about you. Why did you go without me?" Mel sounded like she wanted to cry. "I would have been there to protect you."

"There was nothing you or anyone could do," Sasha

admitted. "Once I was upstairs, the only person who I could have counted on was God himself."

"If that trick wasn't dead already," Jahkai fumed. His eyes were dark and dangerous. "I don't want you tricking no more."

"But Jahkai—"

"No more mother fucking tricks. End of fucking story," he growled, scaring both Sasha and Mel.

The rest of the car ride was silent. They stopped at a local food joint so Sasha could eat. She ate a homemade cheeseburger, fries, a salad and drank two large glasses of ice tea. When they left the restaurant, Jahkai had some errands to run. He dropped Sasha and Mel down the street from Jonathan's condo so Mel could drive Sasha's car back home. Jahkai promised to check up on her all day and to pick her up in the evening after he was done taking care of business.

Chapter 23

Sasha woke up with an unpleasant headache. She took a deep breath and rubbed her face. Her mind went straight to the night with Jonathan. Sasha's brain felt like it had not gotten any rest despite of her full nights rest on a real bed. Flashes of him raping her made her cower. She looked at her phone. It was eight in the morning. Surprisingly, Jahkai was fast asleep beside her. Sasha smiled to herself She had no idea what time she fell asleep or when he arrived, but she was so happy that he was there.

Sasha wrapped herself around Jahkai and kissed him on the cheek. He squirmed around before he opened his eyes.

"What time is it?" he asked as he rubbed his eyes and yawned.

"It's eight in the morning."

"How are you feeling?"

"Still in shock, but I guess I will just have to take it one day at a time," she said disappointingly.

Jahkai turned to his side so he was laying down facing

Sasha. He wrapped his arms around her and kissed her on the forehead. "I won't let nothing like that happen to you again. I promise."

Sasha snuggled into his chest, savoring his scent and his words. She believed him reluctantly, but it was satisfying enough to make her smile. They lay in each other's arms in and out of sleep for another hour before Sasha heard noises coming from the kitchen. Sasha crawled out of bed trying her best not to wake Jahkai. Mel was putting away dishes from the dishwasher.

"How are you feeling?" asked Mel as she pulled Sasha to her. She hugged Sasha tightly.

"I'm alive," said Sasha nonchalantly. "I want to thank you for getting me a lawyer yesterday. I don't know if I would have gotten out with duty counsel representing me."

Soon as Mel heard about what had happened, she spent all night and morning searching for a lawyer to represent Sasha. She finally found John Greenburg who agreed to represent Sasha for her bail hearing at a cost of six hundred dollars. Mel had no choice but to see it through, she had called seven lawyers before him who were either unavailable or far too expensive.

Mel poured some water into the kettle. "It was the least I could do. I wanted to bail you out myself, but I had no proof of income. Would you like some tea or Milo?"

"I want a large cup of tea. Orange pekoe please."

Mel made them both a cup of tea and sat at the kitchen island beside Sasha. "So, you have to go see the lawyer today at two o'clock at his office to discuss your case."

Sasha rolled her eyes and sighed. "Fucking cops. Soon as they found out I was tricking, it was like the red lights went off and all of a sudden I was the suspect. They didn't show me any sympathy what so ever."

"I know it's easier said than done, but don't let it sweat you. You are one of the strongest girls I know. And, one of the smartest too. There is no situation you haven't been able to get yourself out of."

"I wish it were so easy. I think hoeing finally caught up to me."

Sasha took a sip of her tea as she thought about all the clients she had seen and all the money she had made in the process. Before the incident with Jonathan, she hadn't put a definite date on when she was going to stop.

"It's called paying homage. Regular people pay taxes, hustlers pay homage. Nobody goes in and out of the game with a clean slate. I've had my share of burns. Not to that extent, but it happens to the best of us." Mel took a sip of her tea. "Shit, I remember I did an outcall this one time. I went to go see some young, Portuguese guy for an hour. You know that mother fucker had the audacity to give me counterfeits? I was so pissed."

Sasha smiled as she reached to hug Mel. "Mel, you are so good to me. I'm so happy to have you as my friend."

Mel made up her face but still managed to pull out a smile as she hugged Sasha. "I will always have your back."

Jahkai walked out of Sasha's room fully clothed with his shoes on and his cell phone in his hand. He finished sending a text before he directed his attention to Sasha. "I have to go on the road right quick. I want you to get dressed. We are going out for lunch."

Sasha got up to walk Jahkai to the door. She hugged him tightly and gave him a long passionate kiss.

"I will pick you up in an hour," he whispered in her ear.

Jahkai kissed her on the cheek and left, leaving Sasha

and Mel alone again.

"That boy really cares for you," said Mel with a slight tone of jealousy.

"And Jason really cares for you too," Sasha reminded her.

"Yeah, but I don't know if Jason would bail me out of jail," Mel joked. "I would have had to call my mama."

"Shit, I don't even know what I am going to tell my mom." Sasha shook her head. "And, she is coming out of rehab in a couple days too. The last thing I need to do is give her the burden of a prostitute daughter with a murder charge."

"Well, you have to tell her. You can't keep this from her. You need all the support you can get right now, especially from your mom. She is the best support you can have."

Sasha didn't want to admit it to herself, but Mel was right. She was going to have to tell Theresa as soon as she got out. With Theresa's new view of life, Sasha knew that Theresa would be highly disappointed and/or even worst would blame herself for everything. Sasha would have to assure Theresa that it was her choice to start prostituting and her choice to see Jonathan. Nobody reflected her decisions but the money.

"So, you are seriously done with tricking?" asked Mel in a serious tone.

Sasha hadn't given it much thought if she was going to continue after everything happened. It was obvious that she had to stop but paying a lawyer was going to take a good chunk of the money she had saved up if not all of it. Plus, their condo was not cheap, Sasha would still have to come up with her half of the rent and money to put towards their home bills. Working a job for minimum wage was not going to cover her expenses.

"I don't know what I am going to do," she admitted to Mel. "I have so much shit going on right now. I don't know what I am going to do about anything."

Sasha went on to tell Mel what happened between her and Jonathan. They cried together as Sasha went into details about Jonathan's brutal attack on her. Mel cussed at Sasha asking her why she went without her. The agreement was that they would go to their outcalls together as security. Sasha shouldn't have went alone, but Mel never answered her cell.

Sasha took another shower and slipped on a pair of fitted jeans, a black tank top and a pair of black booties. Just because she was on a murder charge didn't mean she couldn't look good.

Jahkai picked her up within the hour as promised. They drove to Eaton Centre, and Jahkai bought Sasha a brand new Iphone and SIM card. Sasha was relieved that she had a new phone but upset that she lost all her numbers. Most of them were her regular high paying customers that she didn't want to lose contact with. The others were just important numbers she had collected over time. Once they were out of the store, Sasha called Mel and Greengrass and gave them her new number. Those were the two most important people that she needed to be in constant contact with. Everything and everyone else were secondary. Jahkai took a stroll through Holt Renfrew and picked himself up a new cologne. He also bought Sasha an Ed Hardy perfume and pair of Gucci shades before they left the mall.

"I have to meet my lawyer for one," Sasha reminded Jahkai as she looked at the time on her cell phone. It was minutes to twelve.

Jahkai grinded his teeth together. Sasha fumbled with her fingers. It was obvious that she wasn't the only one affected by her situation. Greenburg's office was also downtown so they went to a restaurant nearby to kill time. Sasha had way too much on her mind to eat even if she was hungry. All she could think about was how her life slowly came crashing down before her. The thoughts of being convicted for murder and being sent to jail for god knows how long made her eyes water.

"Everything is going to be ok," Jahkai assured her.

Sasha rolled her eyes at him. He was only trying to help but Sasha wasn't as optimistic as Jahkai. She sipped on the rum and coke she ordered, hoping that it would serve its purpose before she went to go meet with Greenburg.

"Self-defense. Stick to your story and don't break it. Those mother fuckers are going to try and eat you alive. They are going to try and get you to plea or break a deal with you. Don't do it. It doesn't matter how you ended up there. The point is when you go there, that is what happened. As long as you have a good lawyer who believes in your story you will be ok."

Sasha sat silently, absorbing everything that Jahkai was telling her. Lord knows she needed all the advice she could get. Sasha never had a meeting with a lawyer a day in her life. She had no idea how to tell a good lawyer from a bad one.

"There are two types of lawyers, the players and the bankers. The players see win/lose. They want to win their cases and will go through great measures to do so. The bankers are in it for the money. The more money you spend the more passionate they will be about your case. Make sure Greenburg isn't a banker." Jahkai explained.

"I'm nervous as hell. I don't like the idea of trusting a stranger with my life."

"Someone has to do it. If it were up to me I would

QUEENY

represent you but they would eat us alive."

Sasha laughed but the worry and anticipation was still on her face.

"Just tell the truth," he reminded her as he took her hand into his.

At 12:45 P.M. Jahkai paid for the bill and then walked Sasha to Greenburg's office.

"Do you want me to come inside with you?" he asked once they were at the door.

Sasha thought about it for a moment then shook her head. "I think this is something I need to do alone. Keep your phone close. I will call you if I need you."

Sasha walked in to Greenburg's office nervously. It had hardwood floors, burgundy leather couches, a forty-two inch flat screen, an oak desk, and lots of paintings. There was a picture of what looked like his wife, daughter and dog. Greenburg wore an expensive, beige suit with black, leather, dress shoes.

"Sasha Brown?" he acknowledged in her a stern business tone.

Sasha smiled nervously still standing at the door.

"Take a seat," he said directing his attention to the papers in his hands.

Sasha sat down and watched as he skimmed through the papers in silence. He sighed a couple times and tilted his head as he read through her discloser.

"So, you went to see a john and shit got out of hand?" he asked her bluntly.

Sasha nodded her head. She told Greenburg the truth about what happened. She was careful not to miss any important detail.

He looked at her with apprising eyes. "The police are saying it was BDSM gone bad. There were three boxes under the bed. All three boxes contained BDSM toys."

Sasha looked at Greenburg blankly. She was unaware that there were more boxes under the bed. She wasn't surprised either.

"There were clamps, cuffs, collars, restraints, spreader bars, candles, blindfolds—you name it." Greenburg smirked.

"I provide a safe girlfriend experience. I do not do bondage or any of those services. In my world, we call that a porn star experience. If he had told me that was what he wanted when he called, I would have turned him down."

Sasha could feel her blood rising. She took a deep breath. She felt like she was defending her story rather than expressing it.

"It's apparent that restraint was used on you," he continued, making note of her wrists and her neck. "But unfortunately for you, that is common in BDSM. The court will argue that the bruises were from the restraints used at the time of service."

"He tied me up and raped me!" Sasha snapped. "And when I tried to get away, he tried to kill me. That man was a sick fuck, and I am lucky to be alive telling you this fucking story."

"I'm not saying that your story isn't true. What I am saying is they have a strong case. I think you should let me try and cut a deal so we can cut you less time."

"Less time? How much time are we talking? I admit that I did stab him but I had no intentions of killing him. He was trying to kill me and I was defending myself. I wish he was alive so I could see him rot in jail but it was self-defense, Mr Greenburg. When I left his apartment, he was very much alive. I promise you that."

"Right now it's your word against the evidence, Sasha.

It's not what you know it is what you can prove in courts, and right now they could prove you guilty."

"Are you going to fight for me or am I going to pay you to send me to jail, Mr Greenburg?"

"I'm going to make this a win-win situation," he replied bluntly.

"Fuck you! I pray for your family, Mr Greenburg. I pray nothing like this happens to your daughter. I pray nobody in your family has to feel what I am feeling right now."

Sasha spat on his desk and stormed out furious. She wanted to cry, but she was able to swallow her disappointment and hold in her tears. She called Jahkai, and he was at the front of the office five minutes later. Sasha jumped into his car and slammed the door close.

"He was a fucking banker," she snapped.

"Don't lose your head," he said, rubbing on her thigh. "He is just one of hundreds of criminal lawyers in the city. We will find you a new one in no time."

"You have no idea how cynical I feel about everything right now," Sasha cried. "I can't even get someone to defend me. I am going to spend the rest of my life locked up because of this stupid fuck."

"Sasha, relax," said Jahkai as he drove onto the highway. "You are worrying about the wrong things."
Sasha couldn't help but worry. Her life was at a major breakthrough. She was worried about everything. Sasha was worried about Theresa's reaction, but even more so, Sasha was worried about her money. She still hadn't decided if she was going to stop prostituting for good or not. Her face wasn't in the media, so it was easier for her to pick up where she left off without rising any suspicion with her clients. It was probably a bad idea jumping back in so soon with the police watching her and all, but Sasha

had no time to take breaks. With everything going on, Sasha needed to make money more than ever.

Chapter 24

The cool November breeze snuck its way into Jahkai's car and through Sasha's jacket, making her shiver. She threw her half smoked cigarette out the window and wound it back up. Smoking being prohibited on the rehab property was a rule Sasha was not going to miss.

"I'm going to go in and get her. Wait here," she instructed.

She looked at Jahkai, and he gave her a reassuring smile. She kissed Jahkai and then hopped out the car, greeting the cool breeze once more. She shimmied into her jacket as she walked to the main entrance.

The receptionist smiled once she saw Sasha's familiar face. "How is everything going?" she asked as she printed out some forms.

"Life sure is a challenge."

"Your mother will be out shortly. I just need you to sign this release form." The blond haired receptionist quickly handed Sasha two sheets of paper. "This is explaining that she is going to be released under your supervision, and if for any reason you feel she will relapse within the next sixty days, you can bring her back. The package you chose also includes a sixty day relapse period I'm not sure if you were aware of that.

Sasha nodded as she skimmed through the papers confirming what the receptionist had said. Putting Theresa in rehab was more than what Sasha could afford but it was worth every dollar. She quickly signed and dated the last piece of paper and sat in the waiting area. Fifteen minutes later, Theresa and Megan joined them. Theresa hugged Sasha nervously, trying her hardest not to cry.

Sasha held Theresa tightly. "Are you ok?"

"I'm just scared. This is the first time I will be out this place sober." Theresa admitted timidly.

Sasha rubbed Theresa's back. "You will be fine."

Theresa let go of Sasha and directed her attention to Megan. Theresa hugged Megan tightly. A tear ran down her face. "Thank you for everything," she sobbed. "I don't know what I would do without you."

Megan patted Theresa on the back. She looked like she was on the verge of crying too. "It's been a pleasure having you here. I can't believe how much you have changed since you first stepped into these doors."

Theresa was laughing so hard she had to hold her stomach. "I was your problem child for the first few days. I thought you guys would have kicked me out."

Megan threw her arm around Theresa. "We would have never thrown you out. Nobody said that withdrawal was easy."

"You can say that again!"

They laughed together as Megan recalled some of the memories she had with Theresa while she was there. Theresa fought and screamed with anyone who approached her during her detoxification. When Megan finally sat down and explained her story, Theresa finally began to take the rehab seriously again. Megan was once addicted to heroin. Her daughter was taken away from her when she was nine years old after Megan was caught on the corner strung out trying to turn a trick. When the police arrested her, she explained to them that her nine year daughter was home alone and was expecting her. The cops picked up her daughter and gave her to Children's Aid Society. Megan continued doing heroin for another seven years until one day she was approached by a gorgeous, young teenage girl. It was her daughter who came to tell her that she missed her and to stop taking drugs. A week later, Megan checked into a free clinic and cleaned herself up. She is eight years clean now. Megan's past and experiences touched Theresa and reminded her that she had a daughter herself who was depending on her to get clean. Greengrass surely served its purpose. It changed Theresa's life for the better. She was coming out a whole new woman.

Megan walked them to the main entrance. Theresa and Sasha said goodbye and hugged her once more. Jahkai came out the car to the greet them as they approached him. Theresa smiled at the site of Jahkai.

"How's it going, Miss Brown?" he asked as he reached to hug her.

"Please call me Theresa. I'm not that old," she joked.

They drove to the Rainforest Cafe at Yorkedale Mall. Theresa hadn't been to a restaurant since Silva died. She ate an eight ounce New York steak with mash potatoes. Sasha and Jahkai didn't each much. Sasha was overwhelmed at the site of a clean and happy Theresa sitting across from her at a restaurant. She wondered when the right time would be to tell her the bad news. Theresa was grateful for her meal and took a slice of cheesecake to go, but her mood quickly changed once they were in the parking lot.

"What's wrong mom?" asked Sasha as she put her arm around Theresa.

"I'm scared to go back to the apartment. Everyone who is there is going to be expecting the old me. I didn't tell anyone I was going to rehab. They probably thought I got locked up or something. They are going to be throwing that shit into my face, and I don't know if I can deal with all of that." Theresa jumped into the back seat fumbling her hands nervously. "And don't get me started about my apartment. How am I suppose to walk into the place with all those memories?"

"I got that all covered, Miss Brown," Jahkai intervened.

"Theresa," she corrected him.

"You are right about going back to your old apartment. You can't go back there, especially not alone. That's just asking for a relapse. You need a real fresh start. You need a new apartment."

Sasha tilted her head and looked at Jahkai confusingly. They never discussed anything about getting Theresa a new apartment. There was no doubt that it was the best thing for Theresa, but Sasha couldn't afford to add another expense to her list.

Jahkai looked back at Sasha with protecting, reassuring eyes. "I have an empty apartment in Etobicoke. It's clean, its upscale, and its furnished."

"Is it legit?" asked Theresa sternly.

Sasha folded her arms. Jahkai was only trying to be nice but somehow she still found herself upset about his idea of putting Theresa in a new place. "When did you plan on telling me this? You can't just move my mom like that?"

"Baby, calm down—"

"Don't tell me to calm down!" Sasha yelled. "You can't make these decisions by yourself, Jahkai. Who's going to compensate you for my mother? She ain't got no money and all my money is about to go the lawyer."

The silence in the car was so tense it could be sliced three ways. The words came out of her mouth before she had time to think about what she was saying. She looked at Jahkai. His face was as pale as a ghost.

"Lawyer? What do you need a lawyer for? Are you in some kind of trouble?" Theresa asked practically reading their minds.

Sasha stared out the window thinking about what she was going to say and how she was going to say it. She didn't want to talk about her case two hours after Theresa's release from rehab.

"Sasha Brown, you better answer me," Theresa pressed.

"Let's get you settled into your new place first. Then I will explain to you everything that`s going on."

The apartment was a fifteen minute drive from Yorkdale in an area that was dominated by Indian and black people. There was a plaza nearby with a bank, supermarket, convenience store and dollar store. It was twenty minutes away from Sasha`s house, but both of their places were off the highway.

The apartment was on the fifth floor of a clean, newly renovated apartment building. It had five appliances including a dishwasher, washer and dryer. It had one large bedroom and one and a half bathrooms. There was carpet throughout the place and a solarium with wall to wall windows.

The furniture was brand new, and the cable and internet were already hooked up. Theresa didn`t have much care for a computer while she was using drugs, but when she was in rehab, part of the program included learning basic computer skills. Theresa learned how to type, search the internet and operate the basic functions of Microsoft Office.

Sasha quickly got over her hunch about letting Theresa stay there. She couldn`t stop thanking Jahkai for his generosity. After they took a tour of the place, they headed to the grocery store. Jahkai and Sasha filled the cupboards and fridge so Theresa wouldn't need groceries for the next couple of weeks. Most of the stuff Theresa had back in Jane and Finch was old, broken and full of dark memories. There were some things of sentimental value Theresa didn`t want to leave behind. She wrote them down on a piece of paper and told Sasha where she could find them. Sasha promised to pick them up and bring them back to her within the next couple of days.

Telling Theresa about the case was one of the hardest things that Sasha ever had to do. She explained in detail everything that happened. She started from the day she ran away from home. Sasha didn`t mention anything about Breezy's involvement with her getting into prostitution. Instead, she told Theresa a vague story about staying at a friend's house until she was on her feet before she got a place with Mel.

By the time Sasha was done, she and Theresa were both in tears. It tore Sasha apart to see the hurt and disappointment in Theresa's face. It took all of Sasha's strength to go on about the night she went to see Jonathan.

"I'm sorry about what you are going through. This is all my fault. If I was a better mother, you wouldn't have ended up on these streets." Theresa put her face in her hands. "I was such a horrible mother to you. I abused myself, I abused you, and then you abused yourself too."

A part of Sasha wanted to scream at her mother and agree that it was her fault but Theresa wasn't entirely to blame. Sasha blamed the drugs. The drugs dictated Theresa's life and made all her decisions. Sasha knew all along that Theresa would be fine once she was clean. She knew since she was nine years old.

"Mom, you didn't put me on the streets and tell me to start selling myself. I did."

"But I planted the seed. I should have taught you to be better than that," Theresa's mood quickly changed to a disappointment. "But to be honest with you, I'm surprised you didn't learn from my mistakes. You went through so much shit at home. Why did you run to the streets knowing what it did to me?"

"Because the streets took me in," Sasha retorted. "And if there is anything you taught me it was how to survive."

"Prostitution ain't no joke." Theresa lectured her. "How do you expect to earn a man's respect if you are out here selling your pussy? I bet you couldn't even tell a gentleman if you saw one." Theresa looked at Jahkai and he smiled back at her, letting her no he took no offense to what she just said. "I have been robbed, raped, kidnapped—everything in the book while I was prostituting myself. Nobody has respect for the industry, not even the tricks. Everyone just looks at you like an object."

"She's right," said Jahkai as he looked at Sasha with serious eyes.

"What good is all that money if you don't have a foundation to spend it on?" Theresa continued. "Do you think these 'professionals' are fucking for Gucci and Ralph Lauren? The smart hoes are paying for school. They own their homes. They own their cars. But you know what else? Most of them are single and do you know why?"

"Because nobody wants to turn a hoe into a housewife," Jahkai smirked as he glared at Sasha.

Theresa nodded her head. "Exactly. You are eighteen and you have a grade ten education. I bet you have never worked a day in your life. You better hold on to this young man, because after finding out how fucked up you are, he is still here."

Sasha put her head down and sighed. She closed her eyes and tried to pull herself together. She felt sadder than a tree with no leaves. Theresa's words were tearing her apart, blow by blow.

Theresa rubbed Sasha's back and rocked her from side to side. "You used to be so good in school. I remember when you got your first A in math class."

Sasha was astounded. She remembered that day as if it were yesterday. Theresa didn't even look like she cared. She shooed Sasha off and made her feel like it wasn't enough. No matter how many good grades Sasha brought home it was never enough. Sasha's eyes watered. She wiped her tears with her sleeve.

Theresa looked at Sasha with eyes of a true, concerned parent. "What happened, baby? I may have fucked up, but you learned a long time ago that the only person you could depend is you. You used to have such high expectations for yourself."

"I still do," Sasha intervened.

"No, Sasha you don't. You tried to take the easy way out, and it bit you in the ass, that's what happened." Theresa shook her head. "Life wasn't made to be easy. I may not have been there for you, but you knew what needed to be done in order for you to live right. You should have stayed in school, found yourself a part-time job and went off to college. You didn't need me to tell you that. How many more tricks before enough is enough? What line has to be crossed before you quit? Was this man not an eye-opener? That man may have been crazy, but he was still a living person and he lost his life to *your* hands. Isn't that enough for you to realize it's time to put an end to this prostitution shit?" Theresa began to cry again. "A parent should never have to bury their child. I could have lost you. I already lost you once, I'm not going to lose you again. Especially to some crazy ass trick.

"I may not have been the best example before, but I am trying to set an example for you now. It took me having to lose you and get you back to realize that I was taking life for a joke. I did a full three-sixty with my life for you. Do the same for yourself, Sasha. Start at the beginning. It's not too late, you are still young. Get out before it's too late—before it kills you."

Jahkai nodded at Sasha, indicating that Theresa was right. Sasha didn't want to admit it, but she was addicted to fast cash. She wasn't ready to let it go, despite the damage it was doing to her life. Cash was her high, and she was willing to do anything for it. She was just as bad as her mother.

Sasha spent the next couple of nights at Theresa's. Theresa wasn't ready to be alone and Sasha wasn't ready to get back to her life. They watched movies together including Theresa's favourite *Bonnie and Clyde*. Jahkai gave Sasha one thousand dollars to take Theresa shopping. Sasha took Theresa to Orfus Rd and bought her new clothes, shoes, make-up and accessories. After they were done shopping, Sasha took Theresa to a hair dresser for a wash, treatment and cornrows. Sasha bought her a brown and black lace front, that made Theresa look young and vibrant. They could have passed as sisters. Despite the fact Sasha could possibly be going to jail on a murder charge, she was the happiest she had ever been. She finally got her mom back.

Chapter 25

When Sasha returned home, she went straight onto her computer and cell phone to find a new lawyer. The majority of them were either too expensive or sounded like bankers. The thought of putting her life in someone else's hands made Sasha feel uneasy, but she didn't have a choice. Like Jahkai said, she couldn't stand in front of the judge and represent herself. The prosecutor would eat her alive.

At the end of the day, when Sasha was ready to give up her search, Jahkai came through with a lawyer. Jahkai knew a few hustler chicks and one of them suggested a female lawyer named Nicole Cooper. Jahkai's friend vouched that Cooper was a fighter, a winner and a female advocate. She handled a few cases similar to Sasha's and would know exactly how to go about it. Jahkai trusted the words of his female friends because he didn't have many. He passed the name and number on to Sasha.

Sasha wasted no time to call Coopers office and make an appointment to see her the next day. The appointment went better than she had planned. Cooper had history working in the streets before she became a lawyer and she seemed very knowledgeable about Sasha's type of case. She was empathetic, she wasn't too expensive and she was sexy. Sasha left Coopers office feeling confident. It was still a grip in Sasha's pocket, but her instincts were to trust Cooper. Maybe she was going to be the one to see that she stayed out of jail.

When Sasha got home, she threw her bag on the kitchen counter and flopped herself on the couch. She had only been home for a few minutes and already found herself bored. It had been almost a week since she posted an ad. Sasha was doing a lot more spending then she was making. She hadn't taken any calls since the incident with Jonathan. If it came down to Sasha needing some money, Jahkai would give it to her, but Sasha didn't want to ask him for any money, especially when she was capable of making it herself.

The conversation she had with Theresa kept creeping into her thoughts. *How many more tricks before enough is enough? What line has to be crossed before you quit?* She had every intentions of quitting. She just couldn't quite yet. She had to maintain an income until something else came along.

Sasha sighed and folded her arms as she thought about her money situation. In order for her to post again, she would have to start from the beginning. She never realized how much work she put into gaining and maintaining regular clients and posting ads. For something that was illegal it sure felt like a real job. Sasha had to edit her old pictures and create new ads with her new number. After she posted her ads, Sasha prepared herself a turkey sandwich. Before she could finish it her phone rang. She quickly swallowed the half chewed food in her mouth and answered her phone

"Hello, hi! Is this Lisa?" said an older man with a deep voice.

"Yes this is she."

"I am calling about your ad."

"How can I help you today?"

"Are you available?"

Sasha looked at her sandwich. She didn't want to go anywhere. She didn't want to take any calls, but she needed the money. "What time would you like to book the appointment?"

The man sounded anxious. "For right now if that is possible."

"For how long?"

"How much for the hour?"

"Where are you located, baby?"

"I'm located in Mississauga on Mississauga Road."

Sasha put her sandwich back down "It's going to be three hundred dollars. Please call me back in fifteen minutes to confirm," she instructed as she got up and headed towards her bedroom. "And I didn't catch your name."

"Its Derrick," he smiled over the phone.

Sasha chose a black mini skirt and a see-through black silk shirt to wear. She took out a red, Victoria Secret bra and g-string set and lay it on the bed beside her outfit. She took a quick shower, and shaved herself bare. When Sasha was done showering she checked her phone, but there were no missed calls. As she was putting on her red g-string, her phone rang. As she suspected it was Derrick calling back.

"Hello, Derrick?" she answered as she pulled her G-string over her butt.

"Hey, Lisa, just calling to confirm our appointment," he said confidently.

"Ok, I am just putting on my clothes now. I will be walking out the door in literally two minutes. Are you calling me off of a cell phone?"

"Yes."

"Text me your address. I will call you back when I am close if that's ok."

"Ok, I am texting it now as we speak," Derrick said excitedly. "Yeah, save my number, if this goes well, I may be calling you again."

Sasha quickly finished getting ready. She put on some make-up and a clear, lip-gloss then flew out the door. She stopped at an Esso gas station around the corner from her house and filled her tank up for eighty dollars. Half an hour later, Sasha exited off the highway and called Derrick to let him know she was close by. She pulled in front of Derricks three car garage, stone brick house and was not surprised at how big and beautiful it was. Mississauga road was known for its five bedroom houses and three car garages. Sasha had the luxury of meeting a few clients in the area in the past. The community in itself was rich.

Sasha parked beside Derricks silver, Mercedes-Benz convertible. She turned on the light and touched up her make-up. The time was 9:35 P.M. Sasha checked her purse to make sure she had three condoms in her bag before she hopped out the car and strolled to the door. The cool breeze of the evening air gave her goosed bumps as it blew on her skin.

Sasha rang the bell and heard a high pitch bark come to the door. She kissed her teeth and rolled her eyes as she shifted from foot to foot, trying to stay warm. Sasha hated dogs and hated when her clients never gave her a heads up when they had pets. What if she was allergic? Thankfully, the dog sounded small. Sasha could put up with small dogs and puppies. It was the big ones with the deep barks and heavy growls that made her want to run in the other direction and never look back.

A tall, masculine dark skin man answered the door and gazed at Sasha with brown eyes of approval.

"Hi, I'm Lisa," she smiled seductively.

"Please come inside," he said as he licked his lips and checked her out from head to toe.

Sasha walked in slowly. She could feel his eyes devouring her body as she looked around the well-appointed house. Most of the furniture was handmade into unique shapes and looked expensive. The home smelt like freshly burnt incense, but it did not kill the weed smell that Derrick was trying to hide.

"You're home is amazing," Sasha commented. "But I wish you would have told me you had a dog."

Derrick picked up the small, white dog. "Montana wouldn't hurt a fly. Trust me, he is one of the friendliest dogs you'll meet."

"I'm sure," Sasha muttered.

"I will put him in the laundry room until you leave. How does that sound?"

"Please, do you mind? I'm sorry, I'm just edgy around dogs. I have had more than enough bad experiences."

Derrick disappeared down the corridor with the dog then came back and directed Sasha upstairs to a guest room. A small, brown envelope was on the nightstand. She picked up the envelope and opened it. There were three, brown, hundred dollar bills and two red fifties. Sasha put the money back in the envelope and put the envelope in her purse. She placed her purse on the night table.

Derrick stood by the door and held his erection in his pants. "Do you prefer the lights on or off?"

Sasha made Derrick turn off the lights. The windows were big and allowed the street light from outside to illuminate the bedroom.

Sasha walked over to Derrick. He pulled her into his arms and held her tightly around the waist. Sasha gasped. She stood on her tippy toes and began kissing on his neck as his hands explored her body. Sasha planted her lips on Derricks as she unbuttoned his shirt and exposed his muscular body. Derrick put his hands up her skirt and gripped her ass in the palm of his hands. Without any effort, he lifted Sasha up and wrapped her legs around his waist. He walked over to the bed and lay Sasha on her back She sunk into the duvet. Derrick gazed at Sasha adoringly before he lay on top of her. He kissed Sasha gently on her lips, down to her neck. He pulled Sasha's blouse over her head and ran his hands down her body. He pulled her skirt down, but left her panties on.

Sasha watched as Derrick tore off his shirt. He had an amazing body. The light from the outside slashed him on his stomach and gave Sasha a peak of his washboard abs. Sasha caught herself devouring Derrick with her eyes and looked out at the quiet street as she tried to regain her composure.

Sasha reached for her purse and pulled out a condom. She sat on her knees in front of Derrick and kissed along his waist as she unbuttoned his pants. She pulled them down to his ankles and pulled out his stiff penis. She put the condom on with her mouth. Derrick moaned as he took her hair into his hands and tilted his head back. Sasha moaned as she sucked him. When Derrick was as hard a rock, Sasha lay on the bed with her legs wide and Derrick took her by the waist and slid himself inside of her.

"Can I have something to drink?" she asked as she curled up into the bed.

"Do you drink white wine?"

"Yes, thank you."

Derrick left the room naked. Sasha listened as he made his way downstairs. She grabbed her phone out of her bag. She had six missed calls and nine new text messages. She went through the text messages but did not open any. They were all potential clients, none of them were from Mel or Jahkai. She texted Mel, letting her know she was almost done then threw her phone back on the nightstand.

"Damn, you are one fine woman," said Derrick as he walked into the room. "I'm sure you have men all over the city chasing you down."

"Not anymore than your typical fine woman," Sasha joked as she took her glass.

As they sipped their wine, Derrick told Sasha a bit about himself. He was a business management consultant and had a wife and two kids. They were all away at his sister-in-law's house for the weekend in London.

Derrick was a gentlemen when Sasha was ready to leave. He thanked her for coming over and promised that he would be calling back in the future to make another appointment. Sasha went straight home and into the shower. She washed off Derricks sweat, scent and sex. When she was done, she threw one a pair of black, Brazilian panties and climbed into bed. Sasha turned on her IPod and hooked it up to the speakers on her nightstand. She picked up *The Coldest Winter Ever* where she had left off. Before Sasha shut her eyes for the night, she called Mel. The phone rang out and Sasha was about to hang up when Mel answered out of breath.

"Hold on girl, I'm just jumping in the taxi." Mel

scrambled into the taxi and gave the driver their address. "I just did a call. This trick just paid me four hundred dollars for me to piss in his mouth."

Sasha made up her face in disgust. "I can't believe how nasty some people are. But then again, all you have to do is log on to your favorite porn site."

"It's true! Anyway, how did that meeting go with that lawyer chick?" Mel's attitude quickly changed as she spoke to Sasha about Cooper. "I hope she isn't a douche bag like that other guy."

"Actually she was great. She is going to represent me. Hopefully everything goes smoothly and it doesn't go to trial. If it does I am going to have to pay her more money."

"Well how much do you have pay her right now?"

Sasha sighed. "Too much."

"Yeah. I hear you. Well who knows. Let's hope that this lawyer chick actually does her job and you can eventually move on with your life and put that shit behind you. What did you do today?"

"Nothing. I went to see the lawyer then I did a call. I just got back not too long ago."

Sasha grinned as she replayed her episode with Derrick in her head. He was a fine, dark skin man but if there was one thing she never asked from tricks it was love. She was perfectly fine with Jahkai and couldn't ask for a better man.

"Don't worry Sash, everything will work out for the best. My phone is dying. I will talk to you more about this when I get home."

"Ok. I might fall asleep before you get here. Love you."

Mel smiled through the phone. "Love you too, super woman."

Chapter 26

It was a Friday, December 8th, 2006. Sasha had finished eating the peppery, curry chicken Theresa cooked for her. She insisted that Jahkai pick some up and drop it off over to Sasha. There was too much pepper and it burned Sasha's mouth, but every bite was worth it. Sasha couldn't recall any memories of Theresa putting in any effort when she cooked. It was Deedee who always brought the half decent food.

Sasha had the day to herself, something she hadn't had in a while. Jahkai was on the road making moves, Theresa went to the rehab centre to do her one week check up and Mel was on the road with Jason. Sasha didn't want to stay in the house, but she didn't want to be seen driving around Toronto because she still didn't have a license.

Sasha called for a taxi and put on her long, burgundy, leather jacket that matched the four inch, burgundy, Guess booties she was wearing. She found herself at Yorkdale Mall to do some therapeutic shopping. Sasha was trying her hardest to forget about the trial, and for a while it was actually working. With every purchase, a genuine smile would slowly sneak its way on to Sasha's face. She even picked up a pair of black, thigh-high boots for Mel, a couple pair of jeans for Theresa and a pair of Jordans to add to Jahkai's sneaker collection. Her gifts ended up running her a few hundred, especially for the boots and the Jordans, but she didn't care. It had been a while since Sasha treated herself. All her money was going towards everything but what she really wanted. It gave her a warm feeling inside that she was lacking. Sasha made her way through the mall, struggling to find an entrance with her hands full of shopping bags out. As she was walking, she made out a familiar face in the distance. Her heart nearly skipped a beat when she realized it was Breezy. Sasha turned into a jewelry store hoping he didn't see her. Her heart was racing through her chest like it was trying to run for its own life. Sasha rubbed the back of her neck and took a deep breath. She walked around the store as if she was a customer. She tried to focus her attention on the precious diamonds before her eyes.

Breezy managed to sneak up on Sasha from behind. He pressed himself onto her and whispered into her ear. "You know I saw you long before you saw me."

Sasha jumped, but she didn't turn around nor did she budge. After everything that happened with Jonathan, it would take a lot more than Breezy to scare her.

"What do you want Breezy?" she snapped in a low voice.

Breezy stepped back and took a good look at Sasha. "I see you been doing well for yourself. You got a Guess bag in your hand. Footlocker and shit. You are balling now!"

"I don't have time for this. I have to go," muttered Sasha.

She tried to walk around Breezy, but he grabbed her

by the wrist. Sasha jerked away.

"Don't ever put your fucking hands on me again," she hissed.

Breezy tilted his head to the side. He was stunned at Sasha's reaction. "What the fuck? Did you grow some balls too since you been gone?" He stepped into Sasha's face. "I don't appreciate the way you cut without saying goodbye. I put that shit behind me a long time ago, but shorty, you owe me money."

"I don't owe you shit. Now if you excuse me, I have to go." Sasha retorted as she tried to walk around him.

He grabbed her wrist again and pulled her to him. "I don't know which trick got you thinking that you are superwoman, but you need to cut that shit out," he hissed.

A saleswoman who was watching the confrontation intervened. "Is everything ok?" she looked at Breezy suspiciously.

Sasha freed herself from his hold and gave the sales woman a fake smile without taking her eyes off Breezy. "Everything is fine. We were just leaving."

Breezy smiled slyly and took some of the bags out of Sasha's hand. "Let me walk you to your ride."

They strolled through the mall in silence. Sasha's heart was racing. A million thoughts were pouring through her head. Was it a coincidence seeing him or had he been following her the whole time? Sasha looked at her phone as she thought about Mel. She hoped that Breezy hadn't found her first.

"So how you been making all this money?" Breezy asked breaking the ice.

"How do you think?"

They strolled through the food court. The smell of fresh Cinnabuns was dominating. It made Sasha's belly talk to her as if she hadn't eaten all day.

"You working for another nigga now?" he pressed.

"I don't have a pimp. I work for myself. I learned from the best," she smirked.

Breezy nodded his head in agreement. "So I can see. Well, let me teach you another lesson about the hoeing industry."

"I think I have had my share of lessons from you."

"When you working with a team you don't just ditch your team like that, especially without paying out. You don't pay out, you are still mine. You and that dumb hoe, Mel."

Sasha stopped walking. Her heart grew heavy in her chest. She looked around for the closest mall entrance. "Let's get one thing straight. This is the 21st century. I'm not your slave. I don't owe you shit, and neither does Mel."

Breezy stepped towards Sasha. She didn't budge. She looked at him with challenging eyes.

"You and that bitch owe me money," he grunted. "Pay out of pocket or through your ass, I don't give a fuck. I want my money. I want five grand. That's twenty-five hundred each."

Sasha nearly died of laughter. Breezy had to be out of his mind if he thought that Sasha and Mel were going to hand over five grand to him. Sasha cocked her head to the side and raised her eye brows.

"We don't owe you shit," she snapped.

"I'm only going to say this once, Sasha," Breezy's eyes were burning with rage, but he kept his composure because they were in the middle of the mall. "I want my fucking money. Next time I see you, you better have some money for me."

"I'm not the same girl that jumped out a taxi with no

place to go, Breezy,"

"No, Sasha. You are exactly the same bitch that jumped out of a taxi with no place to go. You're still young, dumb and fucked up. We will be seeing each other again. I promise you that."

"Fuck you."

Sasha grabbed her bags from Breezy and stormed towards the mall entrance. Her blood was boiling with anger. With everything else going on in her life, the last thing she needed was Breezy up her ass for money. Sasha flagged down a taxi to take her home.

Sasha walked into a full house. Mel, Jason and Jahkai were in the living room smoking a blunt together. There was a bottle of Hennessy and a bottle of St. Remy in the kitchen. Sasha sighed in relief. She was hoping to catch Mel alone, but she was happy to know that she was safe and sound. Sasha faked a smile and said hello to everyone. She walked over to Jahkai and bent over to give him a hug and a kiss. His eyes were red and low from smoking.

"What's wrong?" he whispered in to her ears as he kissed her on the cheek.

"I don't know. Maybe my period is coming," she lied.

Jahkai nodded his head and took the blunt from Jason. Mel looked at Sasha suspiciously. She knew it was more than just Sasha's period.

"Mel, I picked up a pair of boots for you at the mall. I know how much you wanted a pair of knee-high boots," said Sasha as she searched through her bags for Mel's shoes.

Mel jumped up and lunged towards Sasha. She gave her a sloppy kiss on the cheek and hugged her. "Girl, you are too good to me. Thank you so much. Let's go in your room so I can check out the rest of the stuff you got."

As soon they were in Sasha's room. Mel closed the door and got serious. She folded her arms and stood by the door. "Now are you going to tell me what has you all hot and bothered? I know your period don't have you feeling like that."

Sasha turned on some music so Jahkai and Jason couldn't hear what she was saying. In a low voice she told Mel about bumping into Breezy.

"Did he put his hands on you?" asked Mel angrily.

"He grabbed me by my wrist, but that's it. We were in the mall. What was he going to do? Beat me down with everyone watching?"

Mel shrugged her shoulders. "When it comes to his stupid ass you never know. We aren't going to pay him are we?"

Sasha jumped up at Mel's audacity. "Are you high? I ain't paying that nigga shit. If you want to pay him twenty five hundred dollars out of our hard, earned money then be my guess, but he isn't getting another dollar from me."

"I don't want to pay him but if it insures that I will never have to deal with that punk nigga again, I am considering it."

"Fuck that shit! Breezy isn't going to do shit to us," Sasha boasted. "And if he does, trust me, I will go out of my way to make sure he regrets it, because at this point I don't give a fuck anymore. We can all go to fucking jail!"

Sasha had enough bills to deal with already. She still had to pay off the rehab centre, pay her lawyer, and she was taking care of what welfare didn't take care of for Theresa. There was no way she was going to add Breezy to her list of expenses. If she had to walk with pepper spray everywhere she went, she didn't care. She wasn't going to let Breezy dictate her.

Sasha showed Mel all the stuff she got from the mall.

In no time they were smiling and laughing again. They made their way back into the living room to greet their men. Sasha rolled another blunt for her and Jahkai and they all watched *Set It Off* together. Sasha couldn't concentrate on the movie. All she could think about was seeing Breezy again. Hearing his voice made her stomach turn. It was as if the devil had found her again. When the movie was done Jahkai and Sasha excused themselves and headed into Sasha's bedroom.

"Are you sure you are ok?" Jahkai asked once they were alone.

Sasha stood in front of Jahkai. She slipped her hands up his shirt and ran them along his back. "I'm good, baby."

Jahkai gazed into her eyes. He grinned at her and kissed her on her forehead. Sasha scratched on his back lightly and he groaned. Jahkai lifted Sasha up and lay her on the bed. He took off her clothes with one hand as he kissed her intensely on the lips. Sasha moaned as his hands explored her naked body. They trailed over her lips, down her neck, around her breasts, and to her navel. They were followed by a trail of kisses down to her crotch. Sasha closed her eyes as he kissed in between her legs. She moved her waist to his rhythm. He worked his tongue on her clit and fingered her at the same time.

"Fuck, baby! Yes!" she moaned as her body tensed.

When Sasha came, Jahkai pulled his pants down, and in one motion he lay himself on top of Sasha and plunged himself inside of her. Sasha grabbed the sheets with one hand and held him close with the other. Jahkai lift her legs onto his shoulders and pounded Sasha, causing the bed to bang on the wall. When they were done, he lay down beside her and they fell asleep instantly in each other's arms.

Chapter 27

Sasha woke up feeling replenished. She checked the time on her phone. It was a quarter after nine in the morning. Jahkai was already gone. Sasha kissed her teeth. She hated when he left without saying goodbye. She jumped out of the bed and stretched. The cool air was unwelcoming. Sasha threw on a t-shirt and a pair of sweat pants. She went into the living room to make herself a cup of tea. Mel was already awake. She was sitting alone in the living room watching cartoons.

"Where is Jason?" asked Sasha as she filled the kettle with water.

"He left with Jahkai at like six in the morning. You know those two live on the road." Mel rolled her eyes. It was obvious she shared the same frustration as Sasha. "I locked the doors behind them."

"Well at least Jason said bye to you. I woke up and Jahkai was gone. Would you like some tea?"

"Milo please."

Sasha made the tea and hot chocolate, turned the heat on and plopped herself on the couch beside Mel.

"What are your plans for the day?" she asked as she took a sip of her tea.

"Nothing really. I may post an ad and see if I can get any calls, but to be honest with you, I am feeling lazy today."

Sasha shrugged. A payment for the rehab clinic was due at the end of the week, rent was due the following week and she had to make a payment to her lawyer. "I have to go see my lawyer today to go over some stuff. I am going to post when I leave. I can't slack even if I wanted to. I got too much shit to pay out in the next couple of weeks and I don't want to ask Jahkai for any money."

Mel shook her head at Sasha. "It's ok to ask for help you know. You don't' have to do everything alone."

"I know that. I just don't want to burden him with my finances."

"The man put your mother in a fucking condo. How much more of a burden can you be?"

Sasha fiddled with her hands. What Mel was saying made sense, but Sasha was never one to ask anyone for anything. The last person she asked for help ended up pimping her. Jahkai would never do that to Sasha, but she still didn't feel right asking for more. He was already doing a lot for her and her mother.

Sasha finished her tea in silence. She thought about her life as a prostitute. It had been over two years since she saw her first client. She felt like she was in the same position she was in when she left Theresa's house but with a lot more expenses. Too many expenses to quit prostitution for good. She had no choice but to ride it out until her case was over.

Sasha didn't bother making herself breakfast. She took a long hot shower, shaved her legs and washed her hair.

When Sasha was done she got Mel to cornrow her hair straight back. Sasha threw on an eighteen inch straight, blonde lace front, a new pair of black pants she bought at Guess and a grey sweater.

When she was ready to leave, Mel was still wrapped up in a comforter on the couch watching cartoons. Sasha envied how peaceful Mel looked. She wished she could stay home and watch cartoons all day, but it was coming like every day had a series of new events for her. If it wasn't the lawyer, it was her mother. If wasn't her mother it was Jahkai, and now she had Breezy to deal with.

When Mel looked up at Sasha she could see the irritation in Sasha's face. She got up and walked over to her. She rested Sasha's head on her shoulders and rubbed her back. "Don't worry, ma. Everything is going to be ok."

Sasha's chest hurt. She fought the tears from coming. "I just want everything to go back to normal. I'm so fucking tired of this shit."

Mel looked at Sasha with an empathetic smile. She knew what it was like to want more. The only difference was Mel gave up on herself a long time ago. But Mel knew that Sasha was strong. Sasha had it in her to do better in life. "And it will," she told her. "Hang in there. One day at a time. Everything will come together."

Sasha stepped back from Mel. "Yeah, but what if it doesn't? What if they don't believe me? I will be thrown in jail for murder."

"Burn that bridge when you get there." Mel opened the front door. "Right now, just focus on going to see your lawyer and finding out what is going on with your case."

Sasha gave Mel a hug. Mel held Sasha tightly and stole a kiss on Sasha's cheek. Sasha pushed her away playfully.

"Girl, if you weren't my best friend I would swear you were crushing on me."

Mel gave Sasha a devilish grin. "Do you want me to drive you to see your lawyer? I have nothing else better to do."

Sasha stepped back inside the house. "Can You? Any dollar I can save right now helps. I shouldn't even be taking a taxi."

Sasha waited five minutes for Mel to throw on something warm to wear. She grabbed the cars keys and her pack of cigarettes and they headed out the door. There was traffic on the highway due to an accident and Sasha ended up being late by ten minutes. Jahkai called her just as she was jumping out the car. Sasha clicked the ignore button, ran inside the office building and squeezed herself into the full elevator.

Thankfully, Cooper didn't have any other appointments after Sasha's so her tardiness wasn't that big of an issue. Cooper went through some notes then directed her attention to Sasha who sat nervously in the chair in front of her. "So how are things going with you?"

Sasha sighed. "Well things could always be better. My mom is out of rehab. She is doing great."

"Did you tell her about the case yet?"

"Yes, I told her the day that she came out."

Cooper nodded and scribbled something into her notes. "Now I have good news and I have bad news. What would you like to hear first?"

Sasha didn't like the idea of hearing bad news. Her stomach turned at thoughts of what the bad news could be. Was Cooper going to tell her to plead guilty? Was her case weak?

"Give the good news first."

"Well, the good news is that one of my private

investigators was able to set up a meeting with Kelly Hall."

"Who is that?"

"Michael Hall's wife."

Cooper paused and Sasha shifted in her seat. Sasha wondered what his wife would think when she found that he was sleeping with a prostitute. She couldn't understand how talking to his wife was good on her behalf. Her cell phone started vibrating again. It was Jahkai calling back. She clicked ignore again.

"Would you like to take that call?" asked Cooper.

Sasha shook her head. "It's my boyfriend. I will call him when I get out of here."

"After a detailed interview about their relationship, we were able to determine that Michael was in fact a strong lover of BDSM," Cooper explained. "She was his sub for two years before he asked her to marry him."

"Did she tell you that she cheated on him?"

Cooper nodded her head. "She admitted that she was having an affair with her boss. Not only that, after they got married, she and Michael stopped fucking around with BDSM. They kept a few toys to keep their sex life spicy, but they took it down a notch. Michal wasn't as keen about letting old habits go as did Kelly. He had a drinking problem, and when he drank he would become violent with her. She described him as being dark with no sense of morals. He would force her to have sex with him as if she was still his sub. That is why she started having an affair in the first place."

Sasha exhaled in relief. She couldn't have heard better news. She didn't know much about the court system, but she did know that witnesses made cases stronger. She sat straight and placed her steeple hands on her lap. "What is the bad news?"

Coopers demeanor quickly changed. "Your story. You say he raped you in the bedroom and you ran away?"

Sasha nodded her head in confusion.

"Why didn't you run out the door? Why did you stop and grab your bag?"

"Because I needed my bag. My wallet was in there. It had my keys, my cell phone, and my money." Sasha was confused why Cooper was asking her the same question again. She already explained the story to both Cooper and the police.

"But then you got your wallet and you ran into the kitchen. Why didn't you run out the front door?"

Sasha burst out into tears. "I don't know why I ran into the kitchen. It was my survival instinct to get protection from myself. That man raped me! He would have killed me to if he had the chance."

"So you killed him first?"

Sasha jumped out her seat out. "I didn't mean to kill him, Nicole, I swear. I was just trying to protect myself. When I turned around he was in front of me. He leaped towards me and I stabbed him and ran out the door. I didn't even know he was dead until the police told me."

Sasha placed her hands on her head and began pacing the office back and forth. Jahkai called back. She ignored the call again and put her phone on silent.

"I can't go to jail, Nicole. I am only eighteen. I haven't even gotten a chance to live yet. I didn't mean to kill him. It was self-defense."

Nicole felt sorry for Sasha. She had similar cases before and the court was no joke. It was like the frontline for lawyers to slaughter each other in front of a small audience. There were was no room for error. It was a game of facts and persuasion. "Sasha, I need you to sit down and calm down."

Sasha wiped the tears from her face. She took a Kleenex from the desk and sat down. Her eyes burned and her head was starting to hurt her.

"We still have a very good chance of winning this case," Nicole assured her. "I am going to do everything I can to make sure you don't go to jail. I just need you to be honest with me at all times."

Cooper went over some more minor details with Sasha in regards to the case. Having Kelly testify on their behalf was good, but it wasn't enough. Cooper would need more to prove that Sasha was in fact, innocent. Sasha gave Cooper Mel, Jahkai and her mother's cell phone numbers so Cooper could interview them and determine whether or not they would be suitable to be put on the stand if needed. Sasha wasn't worried about Jahkai and Mel, but she didn't know how Theresa would handle that sort of pressure. Court sounded like a real good reason to relapse.

Sasha left Coopers office feeling more confident than she did when she arrived. She trusted Cooper reluctantly. Cooper sounded like she knew what she was doing, but Sasha had a lot at stake. She still felt uncomfortable trusting a stranger with her life, but if it wasn't Cooper it would have to be someone else.

Mel was waiting in the car in the front of the building. Sasha zipped up her jacket and sprinted to the car. She jumped inside and rubbed her hands together. Sasha turned to say something to Mel but was distracted by Mel's tense body language.

Sasha raised her eyebrow. "Is everything ok?"

"Did you talk to Jahkai?"

Sasha took her phone out of her pocket. She had ten missed calls from him. "Holy shit! He's been ringing down my phone. I couldn't take the call because I was in a serious conversation with the lawyer."

"You're mom is in the hospital. She had a heart attack this morning."

Chapter 28

Mel dropped Sasha off at the front of the hospital, and she parked the car. Sasha's heart felt like it was weighing her down as she raced into the hospital. Jahkai was already there waiting for her. When Sasha saw him she burst into tears again and ran into his arms.

"Where is she? Where is my mom?" she whimpered.

Jahkai looked distraught. "She is in emergency. I never went in. I was waiting for you."

Sasha shoved Jahkai out of her way as she darted towards the emergency room. She stopped a short, white nurse walking through the corridors. "Excuse me, I am looking for Theresa Brown. My mother. Do you know where I could find her?"

The nurse led Sasha passed the registration section to the patients waiting area. Sasha and Jahkai sat down. "What happened?" she asked.

"I'm not sure. I got a call from the hospital saying that your mom had a major heart attack. They called your phone and couldn't get through so they called me." Jahkai's eyes were glossy. He pulled Sasha to him and

283

held her tightly.

A young male doctor walked into the waiting area. He called Sasha's name. Sasha squeezed Jahkai before she let him go and wiped her teary face. She got up to meet the doctor.

"Are you Sasha Brown?" he asked as he glanced at Jahkai.

Sasha rolled her eyes. "Yes, and that's my boyfriend."

Jahkai took the hint. "I'm going to go to Tim Hortons. Do you want anything?"

Sasha shook her head. "You stay right here. What's wrong with my mom?"

"My name is Doctor Peterson. I've been assigned to your mother, Theresa Brown." The doctors face saddened. He looked through his charts. "The years of heavy drug abuse has taken a toll on her body. Your mother had a severe heart attack. It caused damage to the brain leaving her brain dead for about thirty minutes."

"What are you trying to say?" Sasha asked pushing for him to get the point. All the small talk was making her sick. "When can I take my mom home?"

Doctor Peterson gave Sasha a moment to absorb what he was saying before he continued. "Sasha, your mother had another heart attack ten minutes ago. I'm sorry, but she never made it."

Sasha's legs grew weak. She collapsed into Jahkai's arms. "She can't be dead. I was just with her. She looked so healthy. Where is my mom. I want to see my mom!"

Mel had just found her way to the waiting area. She looked at Jahkai. Jahkai wiped a tear from his face and shook his head. Mel burst into tears and ran to hug Sasha.

The doctor lead them to the room Theresa was in. Jahkai and Mel excused themselves from the cubical so that Sasha could be alone with her mother. Theresa was wearing a gas mask and there was an IV running through her hand. She didn't look like she was dead. She didn't look like she had experienced a fatal heart attack. Theresa looked like she was in a deep sleep.

Sasha's head was spinning. Her eyes were puffy and she felt light headed. Sasha pulled a chair up to the bed. She took her mother's lifeless hands into hers.

Memories of Sasha's eerie childhood flooded her mind. She tried to remember her father, but she was only two years old when he died. Her childhood was tainted with unwanted memories of sexual abuse, neglect and drugs. She recalled her exaggerated attempts to get Theresa to stop smoking crack. She remembered the beatings she took when she used to throw out Theresa's pipe or flush her crack down the toilet. Anything it took to keep her mom sober for even a couple of hours.

Sasha waited eighteen years to have a relationship with her mother, and just like that it was gone. Sasha needed Theresa more than ever, especially with the case going on. Although their relationship was still fresh, Sasha savored every moment she had with Theresa. Sasha earned for her approval. She wanted Theresa to be proud of her. There was nothing Sasha wanted more.

You used to have such high expectations for yourself.

Sasha genuinely thought she did, but she realized she was no different from Theresa. Money and materialist things were her high. It was her drug and she was willing to do anything for it. Sasha set her financial standards higher but lowed her personal standards and lost her self-respect in the process.

How many more tricks before enough is enough?
Get out before it's too late. Before it kills you!

Sasha shook her head in disappointment. How could she be so naïve? She was tired of tricking a long time ago.

Why hadn't she stopped when she and Mel ran away from Breezy? They could have gotten on welfare, and that would have been enough to at least pay for an apartment for them. They didn't need to live in a brand new condo downtown. Sasha wanted to live the luxurious life and was willing to try and cut corners to do it. Sasha never really had a concrete out plan. She came up with every reason why she needed to stay in the game.

Life wasn't made to be easy.

Theresa was right about Sasha learning that at a tender young age. Sasha knew that school was her ticket to a normal life. Sasha got so caught up with getting money, at one point, she forgot about life. Why did she give up on herself?

Sasha squeezed Theresa's hand. "I'm sorry, mom. I should have been stronger for the both of us. I was young and ignorant. But you didn't make it any easier for me. I became a woman too quickly. I was tired of being so responsible so young. I had to take care of me. I had to take care of you. I was tired of being hungry, tired of being broke and I was tired of watching you and Deedee get high." Sasha wiped her wet face. "I just wanted something normal. I wanted something better. I forgive you, mom." Sasha busted into tears. "I forgive you."

Sasha sat staring at Theresa until the doctor came back and told her it was time for her to leave. Sasha kissed Theresa on the forehead. She met Jahkai and Mel in the emergency waiting room.

Sasha wanted to go home and lay down but Jahkai managed to talk her into spending the night with him. He wanted to be there for Sasha. Mel took Sasha's car and Sasha rode with Jahkai in silence and in deep thought straight to his house. Jahkai ran Sasha a hot bath. He bathed her and dressed her in one of his large white tshirts.

Jahkai took a call in the living room while Sasha lay in his bed. She could feel herself falling into a state of depression. She mourned and longed for Theresa. All Sasha ever wanted was her mother and now she was gone forever. She closed her eyes to keep the tears from falling. When Jahkai was finished with the call he came back in the bedroom with a tall glass.

He handed the glass to Sasha. "It's more rum than coke. There nothing more soothing than a blunt and a drink."

Sasha took the drink and shot down a mouthful of the rum and coke. It burned her chest. She exhaled slowly, took another sip and placed the glass down. "Thank you."

"Do you want to talk about it?" Jahkai asked as he lay in the bedside her. He pulled Sasha into his body and she snuggled into his chest.

"I don't want to talk about it. I just want this day to be over. I want this whole fucking month to be over. It has been nothing but crosses for me," Sasha whined as she stared off into space.

Jahkai pulled Sasha's face by the chin so that she was looking up at him. "I know what it's like to lose your mom. I was only a year younger than you when mine died. I remember my nosy neighbor, Suzette running through the hood, looking for me, screaming 'They shot Brenda! Where is Kaikai? They shot Brenda!" Jahkai took a deep breath. He looked lost in his thoughts. "My mother was literally my back bone. She never bothered me about being in the streets. She taught me how to be a gentlemen and respect women. If it wasn't for her, I would be out here fucking these hoes and not giving a shit." Jahkai looked at Sasha with serious eyes. "I think you should consider what you're mom said to you about going legit."

Sasha made up her face. She didn't want to talk about her mother nor about tricking. All she wanted to do was sleep.

"I know you got this whole independent thing going on, but you are my girl now," Jahkai continued. "We haven't been together that long but I have seen you go through hell and back. You are strong, you are smart and you are beautiful. You have the ability to do anything you want."

"You sound like my mother." said Sasha in a brittle voice.

"I'm not your mother but I listened to the way your mom talked about your childhood. You don't need to be caught up in this bullshit. I don't want my wife caught up in this bullshit."

Sasha leaned up more. "So what am I suppose to do? I don't have a job. I don't even know how to look for one. I'm eighteen with no concrete education. I have never worked a day in my life."

"See that's your problem. You are worried about all the small stuff. I am here to help you, Sasha. When are you going to get it?"

"I don't need you to care of me."

"You need to me to care of you." Jahkai told her as a matter of fact. "You are still young and naïve. You need someone that will keep you on track. You need someone that will help you get back on your feet because you obviously can't do it alone. You need someone to hold you at night and tell you that everything is going to be ok. You need to grow the fuck up, and I want to be there when it happens."

Jahkai reached into the top drawer of the nightstand. He pulled out a narrow, grey, velvet box. He looked at

Sasha nervously before handing it to her.

Sasha looked at Jahkai with shuttered eyes as she opened the box. Inside there was a silver, three-ring, interlocking pendant on a thin, silver chain. Sasha touched the pendant on her neck. For a long while, she forgot that Dessy was the one who bought it for her and that Dessy was Breezy's cousin. Dessy knew all along that Breezy was a pimp, and he sent Sasha to him knowing that she would get sucked right into his web of lies. Her necklace suddenly felt cold and stung her neck like a hot, branding iron. It was redolent of Breezy, memories that were etched in her mind. She stared at the silver necklace in the box with mixed emotions. "Jahkai, this is beautiful. I don't know what to say."

Jahkai gazed at Sasha with his dreamy, brown eyes. "I'm sorry all this shit is happening to you. If there was way that I could fix it all I would." He took Sasha's hands into his. "Say that you are mine and you will let me take care of you. I want you to move in with me."

Sasha nearly choked on her breath as she looked at Jahkai slack-jawed and wide-eyed. She wasn't sure how she felt about moving again, especially with Jahkai. Sasha was still claiming her independency. "Don't you think it's too soon for us to be moving in with each other?" she asked honestly.

"What do you have to lose?" he challenged. "You would rather stress about paying rent than living here and focus on you?"

Jahkai raised a good argument. She still had to finish paying off Greengrass and her lawyer. "What about Mel? Mel can't afford that place on her own."

"Jason is trying to lock down Mel. If she moves in with him, it works out in both your favors." he smirked. "And I am dealing with your lawyer for you and I will continue making the monthly payments to the rehab centre."

Sasha grinned. Jahkai had it all figured it out. He truly was her knight in shining armor. "And breaking the lease?"

Jahkai made up his face. "What lease? Come on, Sasha. I know you guys cut corners to get that place. Cut corners to get out. I wouldn't be surprised if your landlord was a trick. But you have to stop tricking and go back to school. That is my one rule," he said sternly.

Sasha sighed. She had downcast eyes and looked reluctant. She wasn't sure how she felt about being financially depending on Jahkai. "I will find a part-time job."

"Do what you have to do," he retorted. "But tricking isn't an option anymore. I want you legit. If a part-time job will make you sleep better at night, get one. But I want you to focus on finishing school." Jahkai took the velvet box from Sasha. "Now come here and let me put this necklace on you."

Sasha turned over so her back was facing Jahkai. She pulled her hair up off her neck. Jahkai took her necklace off and placed it on the bed beside her. He put the new necklace on her and the silver felt cold on her hot skin. It bounced radiantly to the beat of her heart on her chest. Sasha held the pendant in her hand. She closed her eyes and exhaled. It was the start of her new life.

Chapter 29

The sun shined bright into Sasha's face. She wiggled under the blanket before she opened her eyes. Jahkai was fast asleep on his stomach beside. Sasha smiled and climbed out the bed. She washed her face and brushed her teeth then she headed to the kitchen to make herself a cup of tea.

As she sat at the table sipping on her orange pekoe tea, she thought about everything that had happened the night before. Theresa was dead and Jahkai wanted her to move in with him. Sasha touched the pendant on her neck. Theresa was right about Sasha being lucky to have a man like Jahkai—someone who genuinely cared for her wellbeing and wanted to see her do well in life.

Sasha's cell phone rang from the bedroom. She hurried to her room to answer it before it woke up Jahkai. She looked at the caller ID and it was her lawyer calling.

"Hello, Sasha. How are you doing?"

"Not too well. My mom died yesterday."

"I'm sorry to hear. What happened?"

Sasha's heart grew heavy. "She had a heart attack."

There was silence over the phone. Sasha could hear the wind blowing and cars passing in the background.

"You know what? I am going to give you a call tomorrow. You have enough on your plate as it is. '

Sasha sighed. She could really use a day to herself, but knowing her, it would probably be spent in her bed crying as she thought about how much her life sucked. "No, it's fine. I need to get this dealt with. What's up?"

"I need to see your friend, Mel, to interview her. The sooner the better. I have some questions I want to ask her."

Sasha looked at the time on her phone. It was minutes after nine. She had nothing to do for the day and as far as she knew Mel had an open schedule too.

"I can bring her in for eleven."

"That's perfect. I will see you guys then. I am sorry for your loss."

Sasha squeezed her eyes together. "Thank you," she squeaked and hung up the phone.

Sasha took her time to finish her tea then she went into the bedroom to wake up Jahkai. She lay down on top of him and kissed the back of his neck.

He moaned and spoke with his eyes closed. "What time is it?"

"It's just a little bit past nine," Sasha replied between kisses.

Jahkai flipped over so he was laying on his back. "You sound a lot better."

"I've been through a lot of shit in my life, Jahkai. I will get over it. The show must go on." Sasha smiled at Jahkai with brooding eyes. It was taking every piece of life she had in her to be strong.

"Who was that calling, Mel?"

"No, it was the lawyer. She wants to ask Mel a few

questions. She thinks we can use her for the case."

Jahkai sat up and propped behind him. "That's good, baby. It sounds like you are making progress."

Sasha gave Jahkai a faint smile. Mel's potential testimonial was definitely good news. Between Mel and Kelly's testimonial, Sasha was starting to believe she had a chance in beating her case.

Sasha called Mel and told her to get ready. They were pressed on time because it was already after nine. Mel was at the condo hung over and feeling sick, but she agreed to go with Sasha because it was important. They picked up Mel and bought breakfast at Tim Horton's on the way.

"Are you nervous?" Sasha asked Mel once they were in the elevator.

Mel shrugged her shoulders. "No not really. Nothing I say can be used against me."

"But it could be used against me. If you go on the stand, my lawyer won't be the only one interrogating you."

"But if I am telling the truth, we have nothing to worry about, right?"

Sasha nodded in agreement, but she felt unmoved. Mel had her back but she had no idea what Cooper was going to ask her. Sasha wasn't comfortable with Mel being asked personal questions about her but it was a process that had to be done if it meant freedom.

They waited for five minutes before the receptionist escorted them into Coopers office. Mel looked around the room as she followed Sasha inside.

"Nicole, this is my best friend, Mel," said Sasha as she took a seat.

Mel shook her hand and took a seat in the chair beside Sasha. Cooper sat back down and crossed her legs. She directed her attention back to Sasha. "Before we begin. I want to remind you that you have a court date on Thursday. You don't have to go in. I will go in for you."

Sasha nodded. She was relieved she didn't have to go. The courts scared her.

Cooper turned to Mel. "So basically I am going to interview you on Sasha. I want to know how you feel about her and the case. Nothing that is said in court will be held against you. Do you understand?"

Mel looked at Sasha and nodded.

Cooper picked up a pen and her notepad. "What is your full name for the record?"

"My name is Melanie Stewart."

"How long have you known Sasha?"

"Two years. I've known her since she was sixteen."

"And how did you guys meet?"

Mel looked at Sasha with a worried face. Sasha never told Nicole about Breezy and Mel wasn't sure what to say. "A mutual friend hooked us up," she replied.

Nicole eyed Mel as she jotted down some more notes. "Describe the type of work you do."

Mel coiled in her seat with downcast eyes.

"What kind of work do you do, Mel?" asked Cooper sternly.

"I'm an escort. I offer companionship to males."

"What kind of services do you provide?"

"I provide a safe girlfriend experience."

"And what about Sasha?"

Mel looked at Sasha and back at Cooper feeling more confident in her answers. "She provides the same services. We don't do anything extreme. We don't offer porn star experiences or BDSM."

"How do you know that Sasha doesn't provide these services?"

"Because we live together and work out of our condo.

I hear when she answers her calls and the discussions that follow."

Sasha sat silently and expressionlessly, listening to Cooper interrogate Mel.

"Have you guys ever slept together or performed any duo services?" asked Cooper.

"What difference does it make if we are sleeping together?" Mel retorted.

"Because they are going to want to know what kind of relationship you have with Sasha. How close you guys are," Cooper explained. "Answer the question."

Mel looked at Sasha reluctantly. Sasha was just as puzzled as she was. Sasha wasn't gay and she didn't want to be viewed as gay either.

"When you guys slept together did you guys ever use toys?" Cooper pushed.

"Is this really necessary?" Mel asked. She was starting to look uncomfortable.

Sasha gave Mel a reassuring smile. "Just answer the question, Mel. I trust her."

"We have used toys occasionally," Mel answered flatly.

Cooper looked at Mel and Sasha. She raised her eyebrow as she jotted something down.

Mel stood to her feet. "I have never tied her up or done anything thing that would hurt her."

"But you have slapped her ass before haven't you?"

"Yeah, but it was all consensual. I wasn't trying to hurt her."

"One of the main rules in BDSM is everything being consensual. What difference does it make if you are being slapped on the thigh or the ass? A slap is a slap, isn't it? Even if its consensual."

"Yes—"

Cooper stood up and leaned over her desk. She

slapped her hands on her desk. "Then how do you know that the bruises and welts left on Sasha's body weren't consensual? It's not normal for girls to go around asking to get slapped while they are having sex," she challenged.

"Nicole, slapping someone's ass with your hand and hitting them with a paddle are two completely different things."

"Are they?"

Sasha leaned back into her seat. "I'm going to jail," she sighed.

Cooper sat down and looked at Sasha with reassuring eyes. "You are not going to jail, Sasha. I promise you that."

Cooper asked Mel another series of questions that made Mel and Sasha coil in their seats. It was an uncertain experience, but Sasha had no choice but to trust Cooper because her life depended on it. Cooper assured Sasha that Mel's testimony was sufficient and she would put Mel on the stand if needed.

Sasha put on a pair of black, mesh stockings. It complimented the black, Victoria Secret lace bra and g-string set she was wearing. She didn't want to take any more calls but she was home alone bored with nothing to do. Mel was gone out with Jason and Sasha had no idea when she would be home. Sasha hadn't posted an ad since her talk with Jahkai about moving in with him. Every time her phone rang, she looked at it bitterly and put her phone on ignore. It was hard for Sasha to take a call knowing that Theresa had died three days ago and her ghost was out there watching for her to do the one thing she asked Sasha to stop doing. After thinking it over, Sasha figured she should have as much money saved up incase Jahkai ever changed his mind about her. She refused to start over again—she did it once after running away from home and again when she ran away from Breezy. Sasha promised herself she would never post again and would see clients, if she was in the mood, if they still called. The only reason why Sasha took the call was because Christophe, her client, was a regular and she felt she owed her regulars a notice of resignation.

When Christophe came, Sasha opened the door and gave him an emotionless hug. Right then and there he knew something was up.

"What's wrong?" he asked her as he walked into the condo. He placed a hundred dollars in twenties on the kitchen counter.

"Nothing's wrong baby. I just have something to tell you," Sasha told him as she looked at the money on the table.

"Do you want to tell me now or when we are done?"

"It's up to you."

"I would rather you tell me after because you look sexy and I want to get my hands on you," he told her honestly. "But you can tell me now if you want."

Sasha sat by the kitchen island. She took a deep breath and looked at Christophe nervously. "I have decided not to be an escort anymore."

Christophe raised an eyebrow. "Are you taking a break or is this for good?"

"No, this is for good," Sasha retorted. "This is going to be the last time you see me, babe?"

Christophe looked at Sasha with eyes of disappointment. He had been seeing Sasha biweekly for the past two months and was entrenched with her company. He sat down on the stool beside her. "Well that definitely kill's the mood."

"I didn't mean to spoil our appointment," Sasha

apologized. She smiled faintly at Christophe and placed her hand on his leg. "It doesn't mean I can't please you one last time."

"I don't know. It seems kind of weird now," he told her honestly. He got up and looked at the time on his cell phone. "I think I am going to just go."

Sasha got up and took Christophe's hand. "I'm sorry. You can have your money back if you want."

Christophe picked up the money off the kitchen counter. He took forty dollars and left Sasha with the remaining the sixty. "Keep this. I will feel like I help towards a righteous cause," he chuckled.

Sasha hugged Christophe tightly and he held onto her ass trying to savour his last touch. After he left, she went into her room into the small, Coach travel bag that she kept all her money in. She counted out $5855 and smiled in approval. She took $855 and put the rest of the money in her bag. Five thousand dollars was more than enough money for a rainy day if Jahkai ever decided to leave her or vice versa. The only thing that was left was to tell Mel everything that was going on. Mel wasn't going to be happy about Sasha's plans to move, but Sasha knew that if Mel really wanted to she could afford the twelve hundred dollars for rent herself. They were used to making a thousand dollars in less than week. She wouldn't have considered moving if she felt Mel was going to end up screwed over, or even worse back in another pimp's pockets. And, if Mel didn't want to keep the condo she also had the option of downsizing or moving in Jason.

Mel came home shortly after. It was just after ten o'clock in the evening. She walked into the house radiantly and gave Sasha a warm, friendly hug. Sasha had a pre-rolled blunt and a bottle of wine waiting in the living room.

Mel sat beside Sasha on the couch and sparked the blunt she looked at Sasha and smiled. "I'm so happy things are slowly starting to turn around for you."

Sasha folded her legs together in the couch. "You and me both. I just want this shit to be over. But I need to talk to about something."

Mel inhaled the blunt and eyed Sasha suspiciously. "I don't like the way you sound right now. Is it good new or bad?"

"It depends on how you take what I have to say," Sasha told her honestly.

Mel sat up straight and flicked the blunt on the corner of the table. Sasha took a deep breath and took the blunt from Mel as she tried to figure out the easiest way to share her news.

"Well, there isn't an easy way to say this," Sasha started. "Things have been going good with me and Jahkai," Sasha smiled as she zoned out into her own world. "Really good actually," she chirped. "He is one of the best things that has happened to me since I befriended you."

Mel gave Sasha a faint smile but didn't say anything. She looked at Sasha with anticipation.

"After my mom's funeral, when I was at Jahkai's house he gave me this necklace," Sasha lifted the pendant off her neck to show Mel. "And he asked me to move in with him."

"Sasha I need you. I can't do this by myself. Who is going to have my back?" Mel squeaked. Her eyes were glossy.

"I'm always going to have your back, Mel, and I am always going to be a call away." Sasha assured her. She pulled Mel to hug her. Mel rested her head on Sasha's shoulder.

"What am I going to do without you?" asked Mel melancholy.

"You are going to do you and keep doing Jason in the process." Sasha laughed as she rubbed Mel's back.

"I'm not ready to be alone. You have always been the brains. I just know how to get shit done."

Sasha looked Mel in the eyes. "Mel, you are never going to be alone. You have me, you have Jahkai and you have Jason. That boy loves you to death. He wants you to move in with him."

Mel rolled her eyes and sighed. 'I know. I don't think I am ready to live with a man right now. I went through a lot of shit with Breezy."

"He's not just any man. He is your man," Sasha reminded her. "Maybe now is the time you should consider focusing on doing something for yourself and working on your relationship with your man."

"But it doesn't mean I have to live with him," Mel argued. She wiped a tear from her face.

"Then get you own place. You don't have to live here alone if you don't want to. Look at all those one bedroom apartments we saw when we were looking for a place. You can find somewhere a lot cheaper and save. Remember when I first told you I was running away from Breezy?"

Mel sniffled as she nodded her head.

"Do you remember what I said I wanted to do when we left?"

"You said you wanted to go back to school and get your life together."

Sasha took another hit off the blunt as she put her legs on the floor and sat up straight. "I still want to do that and Jahkai is giving me that opportunity."

"You can go to school and get your life together here,

Sasha. You don't understand. I'm not strong like you. I need you."

Sasha tried her hardest to convince Mel that moving on was the best thing for the both of them when they were interrupted by a loud knock on the door. They looked at each other in confusion.

"Are you expecting someone?" asked Mel in a low voice.

Sasha shook her head. The person knocked on the door again. This time knocked harder. Sasha's heart beat hard and her stomach turned. Something didn't feel right. Sasha texted Jahkai that someone was at the condo and she was scared before she went to answer the door.

A young, blonde girl was standing nervously on the other side. When Sasha opened the door Breezy jumped out of nowhere.

"I told you we would be seeing each other again," he groaned.

Sasha tried to slam the door shut but Breezy pushed his way through and knocked Sasha to the ground. He closed the door behind him and locked it leaving the young, blonde girl in the hall.

"You were talking a lot of shit at the mall the other day," he growled as he lifted Sasha up to her feet by the hair. Sasha shrieked in pain. She tried to punch and kick Breezy but he wouldn't budge. He backhanded her in the face and she fell the floor. Sasha burst into tears. She crawled away from him but Breezy towered over her like a cloud on fire apoplectic with rage. He looked down at Sasha with fierce eyes before crouching down. He grabbed her by the shirt and slapped her in the face again. Sasha coiled as she held the side of her face. It stung with pain and hurt much she felt like she was going to pass out. Breezy continued to beat on Sasha like a drunken

301

father would beat his son. He cursed at her and called her names. He told her she was worthless and just another hoe looking for a dollar. When he was finished with Sasha he stood over her panting with bloodshot eyes. He looked around the condo. "And I know that bitch, Mel, is up in here somewhere," he yelled. "I'm disappointed in you, Mel. I'm going to find you and I'm going to beat that ass because you should know better than to fuck with me."

Breezy found Mel crouched in the closet in her bedroom. Sasha listed as he dragged Mel out of the closet. Mel shrieked in pain after every hit and begged Breezy to stop but he wouldn't listen. He continued to beat her and told her that she was his property and she was coming home with him. Sasha's head was pounding and she felt dizzy, but she couldn't lay there on the kitchen floor while her friend was being beaten to death. Sasha struggled to her two feet. She placed her hands on the counter and took a deep breath, trying to pull herself together. As Sasha was grabbing a kitchen knife out of the drawer she heard a set of keys going through the front door. Jahkai and Jason walked in. Sasha tried to run to Jahkai and stumbled to the floor. He dropped everything to catch Sash in his arms.

"He's here!" Sasha cried. "He has Mel in the bedroom."

"Who has Mel?" asked Jason in confusion. He fell into a blind rage like fire was running as he pulled a gun from his waist.

"Our old pimp. He was the guy who put us on. We ran away from him and got this place here."

Jahkai's eyes grew dark and his face tightened. His chest bounced up and down as he as he looked at Jahkai with eyes a of a man about to commit a crime of passion.

"Stay here and don't fucking move," Jahkai ordered Sasha as he pushed her gently aside.

Jahkai and Jason kicked down the bedroom door. Mel came running out her bedroom with half her clothes on and in tears. She stumbled into Sasha's arms. Sasha squeezed her tight and ran her hands through Mel's hair. Mel sobbed in Sasha's arms. She was trembling.

"Don't make him take me, Sasha," Mel pleaded as she snuggled into Sasha's arms.

Breezy walked out of the room holding his pants up in his hands. Jahkai and Jason were close behind him. The each were holding a gun to his back.

"Yo, Jahkai I didn't know that was your girl," Breezy pleaded. He fumbled to pull his pants up. "You know I got mad respect for your pops. I wouldn't try to disrespect him."

Jahkai made up his face. "We aren't little kids any more, Brendon."

Sasha and Mel looked at each other in confusion. Sasha had no idea that Jahkai knew Breezy. It was hard to believe considering they were in two different sides of the game. Jahkai didn't know seem like he associated himself with pimps after declaring that he was such a gentlemen—then again, he didn't look too pleased to see Breezy.

"Jahkai, come on man. Don't do me like that, bro." Breezy pleaded as he fixed his pants. "Me and you go back to Jamestown days when our pops used to run the streets together. We are practically brothers."

"No nigga we used to be like brothers. You went you're way and I went mine. I told you this pimping shit was going to catch up to you. You lay your hands on my woman." Jahkai rubbed his finger on the trigger.

Sasha's heart nearly skipped a beat as she grabbed

Jahkai by the arm. "No, Jahkai please don't."

Jahkai kept his burning, hazel eyes on Breezy. He leaned into Breezy until their faces were an inch away. Breezy was so nervous his hands were shaking and his face was drenched in sweat.

"Didn't your mother ever teach you how to respect a woman?" asked Jahkai angrily.

"My mama was a hoe, you know that," Breezy retorted.

"So that gives you the excuse to do the same thing to these girls? If our fathers could see you now."

Breezy cut his eyes at Jahkai and flared his nose. "Whatever, nigga. Don't try to come at me like your shit don't stink. I may have pimping bitches, but you are out there selling drugs. The same shit that got Sasha's mom all fucked up. The same shit that brought her to me in the first place."

Jason hit Breezy with the back of his gun and Breezy fell to the floor. When he looked up his face was bleeding. He looked at Sasha and she smirked.

Jason pulled Breezy up by his collar and pressed his gun into Breezy's throat. "If I see you putting your hands on another woman again, I swear to God on my dead mother's grave, I will kill you. Now apologize."

Breezy kissed his teeth and rolled his eyes. "I ain't apologizing to these bitches, they knew what they were getting themselves into."

Jahkai hit Breezy in the back of head with his gun. "I know you're not deaf, mother fucker! He said apologize!"

Breezy looked at Sasha and Mel with rage and embarrassment. "I'm sorry for any trouble I put you ladies through but it couldn't have been that bad because ya'll still doing the same shit."

"And we aren't giving you five grand either," Mel

huffed. She rolled her eyes and folded her arms.

"Five thousand dollars?" Jason couldn't believe his ears. He kicked Breezy in the back. "Get the fuck out of here before I shoot you."

Breezy gave Sasha and Mel a cold gaze before he walked out the door. Sasha slammed the door and locked it behind him. She leaned on the door, put her hand on her chest and sighed in relief. Breezy was out of her life for good. She thanked God in her mind for saving her yet again.

By the time they calmed down from the drama with Breezy, Sasha's face was swollen on the left side and her lip was cut. She had a massive headache and she was physically and emotionally exhausted from all the drama. Sasha took a long, hot shower and threw on a pair of sweats. Jahkai was in her room smoking a blunt and listening to the music. Sasha closed the door behind her.

"So are you going to tell me how you know Breezy?" she questioned as she sat down beside him on her bed.

"Our pops use to roll together back in the day." Jahkai took a hard pull off the blunt. "We were never really friends, but we were always around each other because our pops took use everywhere with them. When my pops got deported, I didn't fuck with him anymore. Especially because he was into the pimping shit. I hated that."

Sasha took the blunt from Jahkai. "So you guys were never really friends?"

Jahkai shook his head. He pulled Sasha so that she was sitting on his lap. "Nah. I don't fuck with that lame."

Sasha kissed Jahkai on the lips. He obliged with a dancing tongue. They fell into a deep kiss. Sasha positioned herself to straddle Jahkai. She gazed into his eyes. "I love you, Jahkai."

Jahkai smiled and kissed Sasha on her neck. He rubbed

his nose under her chin. "I love you too, Sasha Brown."

Sasha's heart fluttered. She took Jahkai's face into her hands and stared into his eyes. "One day I am going to be your wife."

"You already are," he whispered softly into her ears.

Chapter 30

On December 14th 2006 a funeral was held for Theresa at a small funeral home, downtown Toronto. Jahkai offered to take care of everything. At first, Sasha thought the idea of a funeral was pointless. She didn't know who to invite or how to contact them. Jahkai hired a private investigator to track down Genesis, Rebecca, Deedee and Sasha's grandparents if they were still alive. Even if it was just Sasha, Jahkai, Mel and Jason there, Theresa deserved even a small wake. Jahkai also coughed up some money for a decent casket and flowers. Sasha thought he was doing more than he needed to and insisted that he kept it simple and cheap, but Jahkai knew what it was like to lose a parent. He wouldn't see it any other way.

Sasha drove to the funeral with Jahkai, Mel and Jason. It was a house-shaped, split-level building with a big, green sign on the grass that read "Smith's Funeral Home". Sasha wore an over-the-knee, black dress and knee-high, leather, stiletto boots. She switched her hair to a long, bone-straight, black lace front with bangs. She was also sure to wear water-resilient eyeliner and mascara for all the crying she planned on doing during the service. Jahkai let Sasha and Mel out at the front so he could park the car and talk to Jason about something. Sasha looked at the double wooden doors and sighed.

Mel took Sasha's hand into hers and squeezed it. "Everything is ok. Me, Jahkai and Jason are right here. Don't worry," Mel assured as they walked inside.

Inside the funeral home it was carpeted, cavernous and divided into five rooms. Theresa's wake was in the room closest to the front lobby. Sasha felt like she walked into a reunion. Rebecca, Genesis and Deedee were standing by the window in the far end of the room talking. It saddened Sasha to see Deedee was still on drugs. Deedee was able to wear all black, but her clothes were informal, dirty, wrinkly and torn. Her hair was in a messy bun and she wasn't wearing any make up. Seeing Deedee made Sasha remember the old Theresa—the mean, bitter drug addict that didn't give a fuck about anything but her drugs.

When they finally saw Sasha at the room entrance, Deedee smiled wanly and approached her. She fidgeted with her hands and looked at the floor.

"Wild Flower, you look so beautiful. I'm so sorry about Theresa." Deedee wiped her wet face with a napkin. Her eyes were puffy from crying. "You know as fucked up as she was that woman cared for you. The dope really had a hold on her."

Sasha gave Deedee a disappointing glaze and Deedee looked at her feet. She had no right talking about how the drugs had Theresa when she was still using. "I am so happy she was able to kick the habit before she died," Sasha retorted.

"Dope is the devil," Deedee admitted. She looked at Sasha and grinned. "And when it takes you, it takes you.

But enough of all this dope talk. How are things with you? You still live in that condo downtown?"

"Yes, I do actually. That's my roommate, my boyfriend and his brother over there."

Sasha pointed to her clique. They were sitting down and keeping to themselves. They waved shyly at Deedee. Deedee smiled and waved back at them and then looked at Sasha as she began fidgeting again.

"I know this isn't the right place to ask you but I spent my last twenty dollars buying flowers and taking the bus to get here," Deedee explained.

Sasha's blood boiled but she wasn't surprised Deedee was asking for money. Drugs had no manners or consideration for the dead or the mourning. She took a deep breath and then reached into her purse. She pulled out a twenty dollar bill and gave it to Deedee. Deedee quickly tried to take the money but Sasha never let go.

"It's never too late to change, Deedee. My mother taught me that." Sasha let go of the money and left Deedee to join Genesis.

Genesis was the only friend that Sasha had that wasn't caught up in any bullshit. Genesis was currently attending college for human resource management and basketball, and she was seeing some dude who went to the same school as her. Even Rebecca kicked her cocaine habit and was glowing.

Sasha searched around for her grandparents but they were nowhere to be found. She wondered if the purposely never showed or if they were dead. Sasha never had a care for them until Theresa died. She thought maybe should would have a chance to finally meet them. She wanted to know she still had some sort of family out there.

The service was beautiful. Deedee was first to get on

the stand and make a speech. She fidgeted her way to the front of the stage and took the microphone in her hand. She stared at her small audience and took a gulp of air. "Theresa was my best friend for almost twenty years. I remember when her and Sasha first moved to Jane and Finch. Sasha was only two then." Deedee smiled at Sasha. "It's no secret that Theresa had a drug problem. I'm not going to lie. I still do. She was my partner in crime. There was nothing we wouldn't do for the rock." Deedee chuckled to herself as she recalled her memories with her dear friend. "There was only thing Theresa loved more than the rock and that was her daughter. She loved Sasha with all her heart but the drugs never allowed her to show it the way she wanted to. I never knew the sober Theresa but I can only imagine that she would have been a smart, sassy woman. I'm going to miss my dear friend." Deedee turned around so that she was facing the coffin. "I'm going to miss you, T. See you soon." Deedee wiped her face with a tissue as she stepped off the stage.

Sasha got up next. She looked at her mother sleeping lifelessly in the coffin. Sasha leaned into the coffin and kissed Theresa on the cheek. "I love you, mom," she whispered before finally taking the microphone. "I've never done a speech before. I never thought my first speech would be at my mother's funeral. My mother put me through so much shit growing up. At one point I think I actually hated her. The house was always messy. There was never any food in the house. Thank god for Deedee or I would have starved to death. My mom never had to worry about me taking drugs because seeing her on them was good enough for me. I hated the drugs for making her the way she was. The first time I hid my mom's pipe I was nine years old. She beat the shit out of me and every time after that. "Sasha leaned into the podium. She looked at Deedee, Genesis and Rebecca. They all looked back at her in tears. "The point that I am trying to make is that I could write a book about all the bad memories I have of my mother. She wasn't the nicest or most honest person when she was on drugs but despite how much she used and how long she did it for, she stopped and she stopped for me. She showed me that people can make a change for themselves. It was never too late to right yourself. For the first time in my life my mother was disappointed in me. She taught me self-respect and how to love myself. She taught me not to accept and it's ok to want more out of life. She taught me there was a right way and a wrong way to do everything. She taught me how to grow up. She did all of that in the few weeks she was clean. I am grateful for those few weeks I spent with her. I am so upset that she had to go so soon, especially because we just started building a bond. But you know what? At least I can say my mom died a clean woman. I love you, mom. You will be missed and you will always be in my heart."

Sasha walked to her seat in tears. She sat beside Jahkai and he wrapped his arms around her. The pastor said a few more words before they buried Theresa in the small cemetery out back. When the funeral was over Sasha exchanged numbers with Genesis and promised to keep in touch with her. She wanted to keep in touch with Deedee but decided not to. Sasha appreciated everything Deedee did for her as a child, but she didn't want to associate herself with Deedee if she was still using. There was nothing Sasha could do for her at this point but pray that she would clean herself up before God closed her eyes for good.

At the end of December, Mel and Sasha cleared their condo and moved in separately with Jason and Jahkai.

Marcello tried his hardest to talk them out of moving—for his own selfish reasons but it didn't take long for him to give into the pressure of the two, beautiful ladies. Marcello allowed them to break the lease and even gave them back their last month's rent as a sign of good faith.

Sasha missed the all-around company of her best friend but she had no problems adjusting to her new living arrangements. In a matter of days she was able to brush off her doubts and feel right at home. Jahkai re-organized the walk-in closet and bought a large wardrobe for Sasha's clothing. She put all the furniture from the condo in storage until she and Mel were able to sell it online. They gave the items they couldn't sell to Salvation Army and other charities. Once she was settled in, Sasha made the first step and registered herself to an alternative program to get her high school diploma in February 2007. It was a program designed through a compact learning system to get high school credits quicker via independent learning booklets. Sasha still had over fifteen credits to get in order to get her diploma. The program promised to have her finished within three semesters at four to five credits per semester.

Genesis offered to get Sasha a job at the clothing store she was working at but Sasha kindly declined. With the house bills being covered and over five thousand dollars saved, the only thing Sasha wanted to think about was school. Jahkai told Sasha to call Genesis back and take the job. Even though Sasha wanted to focus on school, she still needed the relative work experience along with the education to get a decent job, especially now that she was turning nineteen.

Sasha's preliminary hearing was in March 2007. The night before the preliminary hearing, Sasha barely slept.

The hearing would determine whether or not her case would go to trial. Cooper told Sasha that the crown had a weak case but at the end of the day it was up to the judge to decide whether they would proceed. Trial wasn't necessarily a bad thing. Sasha had a good case and a good lawyer. Trial only meant that it would take longer for the case to close. Cooper promised Sasha it was very unlikely that Sasha would be convicted. Her story was legit and all the facts checked out. Kelly Hall testifying on their behalf made their case even more stronger than it was before. Jonathan was clearly sick. He liked drinking and beating woman for sexual pleasure. There was no dispute in that.

Jahkai and Mel went with Sasha for support. When they arrived, Cooper was already there in a peach, pantsuit. She was sitting on of the seats outside of the court doors flipping through some papers. Cooper got up when she saw Sasha to shake her hand.

"How are you feeling today?" she asked.

Sasha smiled radiantly. "I'm doing great. Things have really turned around since the year had started."

"Well hopefully today, we can put an end to this for good and you can get on your with your life."

Sasha smiled reluctantly. The odds were in her favor but she didn't want to get her hopes up. Cooper shook hands with Mel and Jahkai then directed her attention back to the files she had in her hand.

"So, what's going to happen is we are going to see a judge. There is no jury or anything of that nature. This is just to see whether or not the case should go to trial, which you already know."

Sasha nodded her head in agreement.

"I spoke with Kelly before you guys got here. She should be here any minute."

"Who is Kelly?"

"Jonathan's wife."

Chills ran through Sasha's body. She nodded her head and tried her best to smile. Sasha was grateful that Kelly would be testifying on her behalf but she didn't like the thought that she would eventually have to meet her. Sasha was in no way prepared to meet the wife of her rapist.

"Everything will be ok," Cooper assured her. "Kelly has no hard feelings against you. If anything she sympathizes with you."

"And I surely hope you sympathized with me too," said a females voice from behind.

A tall, slim, black woman wearing a burgundy skirt suit joined then. She looked at Sasha thoroughly and Sasha smiled nervously.

"I'm Kelly Hall. You must be Sasha," she said as she looked into Sasha's eyes.

Sasha was lost at words. She wiped her sweaty hands on her pants and shook Kelly's right hand.

"I'm truly sorry for everything you are going through," Kelly continued. She placed her left hand on top of Sasha's. "My husband was a lying, cheating, drunk bastard. Although I wish he was rotting in jail, rotting in hell is a lot better in my books." Kelly checked Sasha out once more and grinned. "You sure are pretty little thing. I can't argue with that."

Sasha smiled still unsure of what to say. She introduced Kelly to Mel and Jahkai and then Kelly left them to take a phone call. They sat in the hall and waited for two hours before Sasha's name was finally called.

The judge was an old, blonde, white woman. She looked stern in the face and ready for business. The crown presented their evidence. They had Sasha's cell phone log and they didn't hesitate to point out that Sasha had been prostituting since before she turned eighteen. The transcript between her and Jonathan only showed one phone call that lasted just over two minutes, a text from Jonathan with his address and a text from Sasha stating she was on her way. They also had Jonathan's two boxes that contained his BDSM toys and the pen and the knife that Sasha stabbed him with. They told the judge that Sasha was young and money hungry. She was a prostitute and her mother, a dead crack whore was the girlfriend of the dead kingpin, Silva. They argued that Sasha knew exactly what she was doing and she killed Jonathan so she could get the money. It made her look money hungry, and cold-blooded. She knew they weren't going to let her go so easily but regardless of how they could portray Sasha, they still didn't have enough evidence to prove that the violent sex was consensual.

When it was Coopers turn to speak. She argued that they lacked any real evidence to charge Sasha. The fact was Jonathan was a sick sadist who used pain to get off. Kelly Hall sat before the court and told about her relationship with Jonathan. Kelly Hall and Jonathan had met at a swingers club in Pickering in the summer of 2003. They used to have sex in the Red Room. The Red Room was BDSM themed and they used to meet in there every other Saturday at 1:00 A.M for three months until they went on a real date and she became him sub. After two years, they finally got married and their sex game slowed down dramatically. Kelly thought it was for the better, although she enjoyed engaging in BDSM to a certain degree, she felt it was time to put it behind her and slow it down a notch. Jonathan had no intentions of changing their sex life and would often get drunk and force her to have sex with him. It became hard for Kelly to stay in love with Jonathan and she began cheating on him with her boss at work. Kelly worked for a marketing firm and her boss was a handsome, French man who adored her. When Jonathan found out, he went to the office and beat up her manager, who didn't press charges. After all, he was fucking Jonathan's wife. Jonathan packed a bag and left for the condo where he met Sasha. He had been staying there for three days before he called her.

Evidence proved the Jonathan was indeed drunk when he met Sasha. He drank over two thirds of the bottle of whisky before Sasha smashed it on his head. Sasha didn't know this at the time, but Jonathan was also high on cocaine. There was no dispute that Sasha was there on a call. Had there been no paddles, candle wax, ropes and blindfolds, it might have been consensual but things got out of hand and Sasha was forced to fend for her life. It wasn't about the money at that point, it was about her safety. Sasha did take the money when she was leaving, but it was luckily beside her bag. She wouldn't have taken it if she had to go out of her way to find. Her life was far more important than that.

Carrying the case to trial was a waste of money and time on everyone's count. Cooper argued that if they case went to trial, it could possibly hit the media and people would lose faith in the court system for not defending battered woman whether it's domestic or prostitution. Sasha never had a easy life and got sucked into a life she thought would be better. Sasha had no prior charges or involvement with the police. She was currently enrolled in school and had a part-time job at a clothing store in the mall. She was no longer involved in prostitution.

The preliminary was lengthy but after all was said and done, the judge ruled that the crown didn't have a strong enough case and lacked evidence to proceed to trial and dropped Sasha's charges. Sasha was a victim of rape and was lucky to be alive to speak about it. The judge sympathized for Sasha and recommended that she seek counseling to help deal with her traumatic experiences.

Sasha walked out of the courtroom with her chest held high. She felt like she was closing a chapter in her life for good. A huge weight was lifted off her shoulders. It was hard for her to really let go of everything in her past with the case dragging into her future. Now that it was finally over, Sasha could put all her focus into school and work. As Sasha walked toward Jahkai she looked up into the sky. It was a shame Theresa wasn't there in the flesh to see how much Sasha had transformed. She would have been so proud.

Stay connected with Queeny!

Instagram: queeny_empress
Twitter: Queenywrites
Facebook: Queeny Writes

To book speaking events and all other business related
inquires please email: info@queenywrites.com

SASHA'S TRUTH

www.ingramcontent.com/pod-product-compliance
Lightning Source LLC
Chambersburg PA
CBHW050554260626
47157CB00002B/553